Loco-Thology
Tales of Fantasy and Science Fiction

Loconeal Publishing
Amherst

Loco-Thology
Tales of Fantasy and Science Fiction

Loco-Thology Copyright © 2011 Benjamin Abbott, James O. Barnes, Karl Beecher, Tracy Chowdhury, Catherine A. Callaghan, Sara Camarata, Sarah Drew, Terry W. Ervin, II, Robert Lowell Russell, Joshua M. Young.

Edited by Barbara Taft Verducci, and special thanks to Faith Van Horne and Gary Wedlund

Loconeal books may be ordered through booksellers or by contacting:
www.loconeal.com
216-772-8380

Loconeal Publishing can bring authors to your live event. Contact Loconeal Publishing at 216-772-8380.

Published by Loconeal Publishing, LLC
Printed in the United States of America

First Loconeal Publishing edition: August, 2011

Visit our website: www.loconeal.com

ISBN: 978-0-9825653-9-1 (Trade Paperback)

Table of Contents

Golden Curls
by Sarah Drew

The speaker at the podium is giving me that look.

It's the same look I get every time someone hears my name, puts together who I am, who I resemble. I meet the woman's stare from across the room. I can see the gratitude in her eyes, the love. But the gratitude isn't for me.

"It's been six years since the passing of our colleague, Dr. Clara Scott," the woman at the podium says. "And on this day, the anniversary of Dr. Scott's great act of bravery, we're naming this building the Clara M. Scott Observatory in her honor, so that our students can watch the skies in constant vigilance, and never forget what Dr. Scott did for the world."

The professor sitting next to me sighs and shuffles in his seat.

"Although Dr. Scott is no longer with us, I'm very pleased to welcome her daughter Emma Scott as we dedicate this building. Ms. Scott has recently arrived at this university and hopes to follow in her mother's footsteps to pursue a Ph.D. in evolutionary biology."

I stand up. The professor next to me looks stunned as it dawns on him who he's been sharing his table with. I get that a lot. It always makes me feel small, as if I should apologize to the people around me for the inconvenience. Thankfully, it's much easier to be anonymous now. When I was a little girl, I went to school with two dour Secret Service agents in tow.

On my way to the front of the room, I try to ignore the

stares of the professors and administrators at the tables around me. We're holding this ceremony in a large classroom. The telescope's off in another area, pointed up at the dark, fearful skies.

When I reach the podium, I watch as the sea of faces before me shift, the blank stares warming into grins of affection. I feel small again.

"My mother was at her heart a biologist. Life, and its endless forms, fascinated her more than anything else the world had to offer, which is why she continued to teach at this university even after she became famous, and all through her cancer treatments, until the very end. So I know she'd be flattered to have this beautiful observatory named in her honor."

The woman at the podium claps, and the room bursts into applause. I make my way back to my seat, focusing on the concrete floor of the classroom. It seems out of place against the linen-covered tables and guests in fancy dress. Back at my table, the Professor is watching me soberly. Before I have a chance to sit down, he grabs my hand.

"I was there." His eyes are glassy and distant. "I was there when your mother faced the aliens. When the golden curls appeared in the sky."

The curls materialized one morning over the city of Oslo, blending with the rosy hues of dawn. My mother was attending a conference in the city, one of the many international biology seminars she visited each year. Like many others, she made her way onto the streets to watch the spectacle but, unlike the others, when the curls spiraled to the ground, she did not run away. The golden tips made no sound when they struck earth, and the ground did not quake despite their enormity. The few people left outside fled when something emerged from the nearest curl, leaving my mother alone. Instead of running, she spoke to the thing. The discourse lasted a full twelve hours, plenty of time for television crews to set up and record the event. They were still recording when the golden curls thrust back into the sky, to be lost among the purple of dusk.

In the resulting confusion, my mother slipped back to her hotel, where she fell asleep until the next afternoon. When she awoke, she was greeted with the news that the curls had been bristling with weapons, fission bombs shaped like jagged, broken teeth, which were only spotted later under video analysis. She was hailed as an international hero. I was eight-years-old at the time.

"Were you actually in the city of Oslo?" I say.

"Well. Not exactly," the Professor says, frowning. "I was vacationing in the Norwegian countryside with my wife and son. We watched the whole thing on television."

He's squeezing my hand so hard I have to politely, but firmly, pull my arm away. I've heard this story before, people who were there, but not quite. These stories have become the defining moment of their lives, the tale they pass down to their grandchildren.

The Professor studies my face intensely. I know he wants me to say something profound, something my mother would say. But I have nothing for him.

"I have to go," I say.

I need to lift my violin in my hands, to hold the thin wood. Sometimes I feel as if I could break it with a twist of my wrists. As I leave the observatory, people turn and stare. No one says anything. I'm not outside long before the Professor appears again, following me across the grass to the sidewalk. I stop so he can catch up.

"I want to apologize for my behavior," he says. "I always get emotional when I talk about the aliens. My son wouldn't stop crying when they appeared on the news. He was six-years-old at the time and was so sure they were going to kill us."

"I understand," I say.

"I'm Edward Bell." He shakes my hand. His palms are wet with sweat. "I teach contemporary history. So, where are you headed?"

"I'm going home. It's not far away," I say.

"It's pretty late now. Do you have anyone who can escort you?"

I try hard not to laugh, but it comes out as a thin smile.

"No, but I'd love to have you along. I haven't had a security detail in a long time."

"Oh?"

"When mom became famous, she was assigned bodyguards. Secret Service agents. Mom was a national treasure, and they didn't want her being assassinated. Dad and I got the same security. Most of the agents were distant, except for one I had in middle school. He had me call him Agent Frank, and he gave me colored pencils."

"Who'd try to kill your mother? Everybody loved her. She saved the world."

I'd watched my mother stand on the front porch, opening a large envelope that'd just arrived in the mail. She dropped it to the ground when she saw its contents. White powder spilled from its folds and spread across the grass. It'd been sent by UFO nuts, people who believed she'd sold the human race out to aliens. This time they'd only sent us laundry detergent, but the Secret Service started handling our mail after that.

"The bodyguards went away when mom died. But the government still keeps an eye on me and dad. I know all the signs: a spotless green car following me around town, men with military haircuts lingering outside a restaurant where I'm eating, and the ease my father and I have passing through airport security."

The Professor and I talk until my apartment complex looms ahead. Every window in the building seems to be lighted except mine. I can picture the couples in the other apartments laughing and smiling, and settling down for an evening in each other's arms.

"Would you like to come up?" I ask.

The Professor's face lights up, like a child in a candy store.

"Sure. I'd love to."

We settle on cups of coffee, and Prof. Bell takes a seat near the window while I play. My violin is old; I've owned it since I was a child. The maple neck has become an extension of my fingers.

"That was wonderful," Prof. Bell complimented when I finished. "And I'm not saying that to be polite. That was professional quality."

"I almost applied to the music education program at this university. I'd have to start over again because a Masters in biology would be useless, but it'd be possible to change if I had the nerve."

"Why don't you?"

I open the case that covers the keys of my piano and run my fingers over their cool smoothness.

"It'd be a disappointment to everyone. The great Clara Scott's only child sitting in a middle school, teaching children music scales."

"Being a music teacher is still a great accomplishment."

"It's not enough."

I begin to play, feeling the weight behind each key of the piano. The Professor's starting to sound like my father. It's comforting in a way; I haven't seen him in a long time.

The last time I spoke to my father he was on his way to a conference in Berlin. Now that mother's gone, he's always traveling, as if he can't stand the feeling of ground beneath his feet. He spends most of his time giving speeches about her.

People have built a philosophy around my mother. In her lifetime she wrote nearly a dozen books, all on evolution. They're really treatises on how humankind is one giant family, and, when we go to war, we're really killing ourselves. She's become a symbol of peace, of world-wide unity. He believes in the symbol she's become, but I think he's forgotten what she was like.

It wasn't uncommon for her to forget to eat, and every morning was a crisis; she either couldn't find her papers or her keys. In the right company, she could talk about the most fascinating subjects for hours, but, when it came to remembering where she'd parked her car, she was helpless. My father was a math professor—the kind of man that made lists, especially ones with numbers. When mother was home, it was as if he were taking care of two children.

A few years after the incident in Oslo, the money from my mother's books started coming in. My father quit his job and focused on raising me. That's when I started taking music lessons, straining to play the violin with my small, tender hands. He loved to listen to me just as much as I loved playing for him. My mother never had time to listen; she was always off speaking or working. The golden curls had driven a wedge between her and me, just as they'd separated her from the rest of the world.

I finish playing. Prof. Bell stands and places his hand against the square of my back. Normally I'd shrink from a stranger's touch, but his palm is warm.

"When my son was a teenager, he told me he wanted to join the army, to become part of the force that was building up to defend us from the golden curls, if they ever came again. He'd felt so frightened and helpless when they first appeared that he wanted to make sure he'd never have to feel that way again."

"What'd you say to him?"

"I told him no. I wanted him to be a doctor. I thought joining the army would be a waste of his intelligence. When he turned 22, he went to a recruiting office and signed up anyway. I didn't find out about it until the day he shipped out for basic training. I said some nasty things to him on that day, things I'd rather not remember. We didn't talk for years, but we did slowly start communicating. He's a Captain now, and I'm so proud of him, of the man he's become. I know now that, if he'd done what I wanted and become a doctor, he would've been miserable. I'm grateful that he didn't listen to me."

"Things aren't that simple for me."

My mother's face comes to me, the way she looked the first time I saw her after that visit to Oslo. She was so pale, haggard, and her hair hadn't been combed in days. I'd never seen her so disheveled; it seemed as if the world was falling apart. The government took her somewhere before letting her return to us. She never talked about it, but, whenever the subject came up, I could see the fear reflected in the back of her eyes. But she was never afraid to tell me about what came out of the golden curls.

I look up from the piano bench.

"Do you know what my mom said to the aliens?"

"She justified mankind. Persuaded them not to kill us," Prof. Bell says.

"That's what people were told, but that's not what happened. She was going to be a guest speaker at a biology conference, so she recited her speech for them. It was about the evolutionary changes in bones. After about three hours she ran out of material, so she just kept talking. She told them everything she could think of: the fine wingspan of a bird, the hollow, delicate bones that taper into feathers, the whales with their useless, atavistic leg bones that told of their earlier lives as land-dwellers, and the humans, the strangest of all— mammals with hip bones that let them walk constantly upright, the only animal on Earth capable of doing so." I pause for a moment.

"It was all just an accident. She had no idea what she was doing, and she was just as surprised as everyone else that they left without hurting anyone."

Prof. Bell shrugs his shoulders.

"What your mother did may have been an accident, but she still did the right thing. That's what makes her a hero."

I pull the cover down over my piano's keys. The exhaustion of the long night settles on me. I'm going to ask Prof. Bell if he'd like me to call him a cab, and maybe make him one last cup of coffee before sending him off.

His hand is shaking; I can feel it against my back. He's looking at something outside the window. I walk to the edge of the room and draw the curtains back. The golden curls are there. They're luminous, bigger than the tallest buildings. There is no need for bravery; their tips are already on the streets. Not a single building, street lamp or cobblestone was harmed by their landing.

My mother explained this to me once, why the streets of Oslo hadn't been damaged by the golden curls falling to Earth. She reasoned that they were extra-dimensional objects with more than three dimensions. As they move through our three-dimensional world, they seem to pass through solid matter, like the stories of people being abducted by aliens, how the little grey beings could pass through walls. And when the aliens really do come, it is exactly like that. They are not here. Then they are. They surround Prof. Bell and me.

The Professor makes a choking noise and collapses back onto his seat near the window. He tucks his feet underneath himself for good measure, as if touching the aliens will contaminate him.

The aliens are yellow and vaguely round, and sometimes large enough to brush the ceiling. I can't tell how many there are because their forms shift as they drift around the room, the result of their bodies passing through our three-dimensional world. They may look entirely different, or they may look like people, but, since I'm stuck in so few dimensions, I lack the ability to see them whole.

The keys of my piano are rattling. I'm gripping the keyboard cover, and my hands are shaking so hard I have no idea how to stop them. The aliens don't seem to notice the sound. They shift as they brush the furniture of the room. They're the bright yellow of a dandelion, then the dusty gold of a lion's pelt. It's the anniversary of their first appearance, and a quick glance at the clock confirms it's near dawn. They must be looking for my mother. I pull one of her books off the shelf, crack it open, and look for a good place to read aloud. The creatures become the color of a caution sign. They circle me like anxious children.

I know that half of an offspring's genes come from their

mother. I'm an only child, and my mother had no siblings. The aliens aren't looking for my mother; they think I'm her. They're probably giving me those same looks, the ones I always get for her, the gratitude that's never for me. This time I can't swallow my irritation down.

"I'm not her." I toss the book at the nearest thing.

It passes through the yellow shape and hits the table, knocking Prof. Bell's cup to the floor. The coffee splatters in an arc, and the mug splits into three pieces. They're ugly and jagged, like the fission bombs that line the golden curls.

"What are you doing?" the Professor hisses from his place near the window. His face is drained white, and his eyes are wide. He's fixed on me with a pleading look.

I sit down at the piano, flip open the keyboard cover, and begin to play. The music's terrible as I'm too nervous to keep proper time, but I manage to finish the piece. The things in the room sway clockwise. They are the color of a freshly-cut apple. When I play again, the music's better; I go faster to compensate for my clumsy fingers.

My violin is sitting on the other side of the room. I ease my way towards it, as if I'm moving over an old, rotting dock. On the way, I pass through one of the things. It smells like the burning edge of a migraine, and, although I feel nothing, the thought of it moving through my insides – heart, lungs, and intestines– makes me shudder.

I settle the violin under my chin and start to play. The panic fades, as if I'm being comforted by an old friend. The whole world is nothing but music; it fills the air, completes it. I play some Vivaldi and "Twinkle, Twinkle, Little Star", which I memorized in childhood. The sound is so sweet I have to close my eyes against it.

When the chemotherapy made mother sick and she lost her

hair, she asked me to play for her. Every weekend I drove hours to get to her house, where she'd sit on the couch and listen to me until evening fell. Eventually, she got too sick to sit up, so I played for her while she lay in bed. Near the end, when she was in the hospital, I hid my violin in a bag and performed for her in her room. After each session, no matter how sick she was, she always told me I'd made her feel better.

I open my eyes and see that the things are the color of the sun when it peeks through the clouds. They are sweeping the room in a circle, sometimes falling out of the walls, the floor. I play until I can think of nothing else, and then I improvise. Surely there can be no greater joy than this, to teach this pleasure to others.

The aliens return to their golden curls at dusk, twisting back into the sky. I place my violin on the floor when they go. The tips of my fingers leave bloodstains on the carpet. Somehow, I'm sitting in front of the piano again, although I have no memory of walking there. Prof. Bell comes to my side; it's the first time he's moved in hours. He's saying something, but the words don't fit together. The Professor nearly carries me outside. There are reporters, military and bystanders spread across the lawn, a compact circus of humanity. We make our way to the nearest ambulance.

It takes me two days to recover and even longer to find a way around the crushing media surrounding the hospital. The first thing I do is return to the university. I drop my classes and sign up for the music education program.

When I was in the hospital, Prof. Bell asked me what I thought about the aliens, why they left this time. I told him they were looking for passion, joy—signs of humanity. How I conveyed these things didn't matter; it was just the fact that I did. Perhaps they'll be back again in my lifetime, or maybe they'll come to my children. I don't know. My only hope is that they get what they ask for.

Sarah A. Drew, graduated from Edinboro University with a bachelor's degree in Writing and attended DePaul University in North Chicago. She currently works for Ohio State University and resides in Columbus, OH. Her time with the North Columbus Fantasy/SciFi writers group and Ohio Writers group has been invaluable to her.

Illustration © by Celia Yost.

A Simple Twist of Fate
by Tracy Chowdhury

Evening was approaching, and the forest had become eerily quiet. Sydonnia's breath plumed into the chilly air as he turned in place, his faelin eyes straining to see into the trees surrounding him. The ragged sound of his breathing was harsh to his ears, and his heart seemed intent upon beating out of his chest. He could no longer hear the sounds of the battle he left behind, a battle that had not the noises one would customarily hear: the hiss of metal sliding out of scabbard, the twang of arrows leaving the bow, the ring of sword upon armor, and the shouts of men fighting one another. Instead he heard only the sickening sound of claw upon flesh, the thud of body against ground or tree, the pop of breaking bone, and the tormented screams of men fighting a terror they had never known before.

With the sleeve of his studded leather tunic, Sydonnia wiped at the sweat threatening to run into his eyes. He held his longsword before him, an uncharacteristic weapon for a hinterlean ranger, and one for which Servial teased him mercilessly. But Sydonnia was no ordinary hinterlean, so why should he carry an ordinary blade? And who was Servial to be the ultimate knowledge upon which weapon a ranger should or should not make his primary?

Sydonnia couldn't help but feel resentment. Before their assignment, he had confronted his brother about Lilandria during the latter part of a journey they were making together. Servial downplayed the accusation. In the ensuing argument, his brother had made Sy out to be the fool, a lovesick pup who couldn't understand the depth of feeling that had arisen between Servial and the lady. And then Servial had asked Sydonnia how he ever could imagine Lily feeling anything but pity for a man who had delusions of reality.

It wasn't the first time Servial had taken interest in a woman to whom Sydonnia felt an attraction. With her long fiery red hair and golden complexion, Lilandria of Kleyshes was quite a lovely woman. However, Sydonnia didn't just find her to be attractive in the physical sense. She was witty and humorous, yet quiet and gentle. Everything about her was perfect. He had come to realize that he was in love with her, and to see her with Servial was heart-wrenching. Sydonnia had rather hoped she would begin to have romantic feelings for him, but it was painfully easy to see that she had fallen for the charms of his philandering brother.

As children the brothers had always been close, and they grew into adulthood as boon companions. Still, in spite of their kinship, Servial felt the urge to compete, for it was simply in his nature. Most likely, Servial probably didn't even realize it, and Sy knew his brother well. As soon as Servial was certain he had her affections, the handsome ranger would leave Lilandria behind, just as he had the multitudes of other women in which he found temporary interest.

Once hearing what his brother had to say when Sy made his accusation, the depth of anger he felt had never before been achieved within his lifetime. He struggled to keep from smashing his fist into Servial's face, for he was sure he would have broken it. The strength it took for him to simply turn and walk away was extraordinary, and he knew he would never be able to achieve the same feat again. The remainder of their journey was intensely strained, and it was a good thing the end was near. Sydonnia had only to suffer the presence of his brother for two more days before they reached the silvery forest realm of Elvandahar, and then each man took his own path back home.

Once reaching the tree-top village of Merithyn, Sydonnia immediately became aware of something amiss. The rangers had all been called to meet at the home daladin of the Hamzin of Filopar, and the king's regent, prince Thalios, was in attendance along with the Hamzin of Kleyshes. Sy went to his own daladin to briefly unload his travel pack and extra equipment before rushing to the gathering. Many of the men had brought their families, most of whom would await them in the courtyard for the duration. His chest ached when he caught a glimpse of Lilandria, as he had a very sinking feeling for whom she would be waiting when the meeting was adjourned.

The next morning, the rangers of the domains of Filopar and Kleyshes left the sanctuary of their families and daladins to answer the call of protective duty to the realm of Elvandahar. The information they had been given in regards to the menace was paltry to say the least. When they met the enemy at the Terrestra River at the border of their domains, the rangers were woefully unprepared.

They were monsters. Standing at least seven or eight feet tall, they bore a strange resemblance to three of the most potentially dangerous animals in the forest: alothere, wemic, and kyrrean. Armed with tooth and claw, they were unnaturally strong and agile, with an ability to withstand ordinary weaponry that was phenomenal. It was painfully obvious they had once been faelin, and that somehow they had become twisted, despicable beings that seemed to harbor no regret with murdering those who had once been their brethren.

Once more, Sydonnia's breath took shape in the chilly air. He stood alone among the trees, the crackle of dried leaves beneath his boots intermingling with the sound of his harsh breaths. It wasn't his intention to abandon his comrades, but he had felt oddly compelled to make his way deeper into the wood. Strangely, in the fore of his mind was the anger he felt towards Servial. The intensity of his emotions swept over him, and Sydonnia heard a voice emanating from the trees behind him. It was deep, and spoke in barely a whisper.

"I can feel your anger."

Sydonnia swung around, brandishing his blade before him. From out of the forest stepped a figure cloaked entirely within the folds of a dark robe. Even the face was hidden within a deep hood.

"I can feel your hate. *"*

Sydonnia swallowed heavily and stepped backward as the figure advanced towards him. A chuckle emerged from within the hood, and the voice spoke with a strange sibilant quality. "I chossse you, Sssydonnia Timberlyn. You are everything I want, everything I *need* to complete what I ssset out to accomplish."

Sydonnia shook his head and pulled his brows into a frown, somehow finding the courage to make a reply. "Who the Hells are you? How do you know my name?" he asked petulantly.

The figure stopped. Sydonnia could sense that the face hidden within the depths of the hood was smiling. "I am Gaknar, the Mehta of the Daemundai. Already you have met sssome of my petsss. But *they* are nothing compared to what *you* will be."

Sydonnia swallowed past the sudden lump in his throat. He

shook his head again, keeping his increasing trepidation under control. "I want nothing from you. Go find somebody else, someone who might actually give a damn."

He spoke with forced bravado in the hopes it would be a deterrent. Once again, he heard a faint chuckle from within the folds of the dark hood. "I think not. I know you, Sssydonnia. Whether you want it or not, I am your dessstiny."

Sydonnia nervously tightened his grip on the hilt of his sword. His hand was sweaty inside the leather glove he wore, and he was glad he had donned it that morning, for the weapon would surely have slipped from his palm by now. Once more the figure began to slowly advance. Sydonnia held his ground, keeping his sword between them. From within the voluminous folds of the cloak, a misshapen hand with wickedly curved claws appeared. Sydonnia felt his eyes widen, but when he tried to retreat, he found himself held in place by some unseen force. He fought to control a surge of fear, knowing that if he allowed it to overwhelm him, the enemy would certainly persevere.

"Even now I can feel it," he hissed. "Your anger isss consssuming you. Give in to your hate, for it can show you a new path."

Sydonnia stoically watched the cloaked figure approach, a yellowish fluid dripping from the claws. Strangely, he felt the anger within him stirring. He wondered about it for a moment, for it should be the last thing on his mind in his present situation. But it seemed as though the cloaked man was bringing it out in him. And until now, Sydonnia had never really realized there was a part of him that actually *hated* his brother. The question was: would he ever consider acting upon that hate?

Suddenly the robed figure was before him. Sydonnia had

no time to react as the claws swept towards him. He caught a glimpse of the visage within the depths of the hood as they met his vulnerable throat. If he had the inclination, he would have recognized the hideousness of it. Instead, Sydonnia grasped at the deep wounds at his neck, struggling to keep his life's blood from soaking the front of his tunic. Time seemed to slow down for a moment as he felt himself fall heavily to his knees. Shifting and wavering around him, the world had a strange quality to it. *So this is what it is like to die.*

He slumped onto his side, his eyes staring vaguely into the space before him. The blood flowed heavily from between his gloved fingers to moisten the ground beneath. All of a sudden, Sydonnia felt something sweep through him, something strangely invigorating. Then the pain came, and he screamed...

1 Decaren CY544

Sydonnia swept through the trees towards the scent of his brother. More than seven moon cycles had passed since Servial, and the other surviving rangers had conducted their agonizingly brief search for him the morning after the massacre. Hidden among the forest brush, Sydonnia had looked on as Servial cut the search short, claiming that he had seen Sydonnia being dragged into the forest by one of the attacking monstrosities. It was a lie, for Sydonnia had walked calmly into the forest of his own accord. Servial had then staged the impression that he was extremely upset over Sydonnia's loss, and that they should return to the capitol city of Alcrostat as quickly as possible in order to report to the king.

Sydonnia knew he could have chosen that moment to enter

the scene. Maybe he should have. He thought more of the idea now simply because, at the time, he had very little understanding of what had befallen him. Standing there within the shadows, he had been afraid of what happened and bore very little understanding of what he had become. Not only had he felt betrayed by his brother, but he felt feel himself an outcast. He had changed in more ways than just the physical. It was mental as well.

Sydonnia had abandoned his comrades, much as they abandoned him. At first he remained in denial. He was loathe to face the monster he had turned into, but the intense satisfaction he derived from the chase as he brought down his victims was something that he could not disavow. And then there was the pleasure he felt in the killing, and the fact that he looked forward to the day his prey would be more than just a simple animal.

Sydonnia remained obscure within the depths offered by the silver wood. He encountered other men, and the first was torn into bits within barely the space of several moments. The next time he was somewhat more restrained. After a while he came to the realization that if he allowed a man to live after delivering his bite, a strange thing happened. The person became fevered and tormented. He writhed about in his unconscious state until a transformation overtook him. When the man awakened, he was no longer the simple faelin he once was. Sydonnia had forged into being a new monstrosity, *fathered* him. And the newly changed man was his *family*.

It wasn't long before Sydonnia and his pack had begun to wreak havoc wherever they went. Their hunger was insatiable. The small villages became their feeding grounds, and Sydonnia saw that not everyone transformed after sustaining his bite. These rare people suffered through the fever and sickness through to the next day, upon which they awakened and began to recover from their ordeal, unchanged. He couldn't understand why they were able to withstand the transformation, but it bothered him very little. Many of these he simply killed once he realized they would not change.

And such was the way it went until the need to see Lilandria struck him, followed closely by his desire to exact revenge upon his brother for the wrongs Sy felt had been done. First Servial had taken Lilandria away from him, and then made him feel the fool when Sydonnia confronted him. Then Servial had lied about Sydonnia being taken into the forest. Finally, his brother had abandoned him to an enemy that had destroyed an entire contingent of rangers within the short space of time it took Shandahar's second moon to join her sister in the evening sky. Why? Was it all because of Lilandria? Or was it that Servial simply couldn't accept that Sydonnia might be able to accomplish something that he could not?

Sydonnia had easily found his brother. It wasn't difficult, for he had trained his senses to hone wholly upon Servial. He had been waiting quite a while for this moment to arrive, biding his time until he felt it was right. All the while he kept Lilandria in his thoughts, remembering the wonderful friendship they had once shared, and the love he knew that lay somewhere deep within her.

Love she felt for him.

Sydonnia stopped a farlo or two from his brother. The area was open, almost devoid of the silver oak trees that comprised the majority in Elvandahar. As of yet, Servial had not sensed him, and Sydonnia smiled in anticipation. Stupid fool. Servial thought himself so lofty that he ceased to extend his senses outward, one of the first things one learned in order to become a good ranger. Sy's grin widened. Obviously Servial was not a good ranger.

Sydonnia stepped out from the concealment of the trees. Servial was instantly aware, finally sensing the predator in his midst. When his gaze settled upon Sydonnia, his eyes widened with shock. Adjusting quickly, Servial schooled his face into an expression of joy.

"Sydonnia, where in the Hells have you been? We thought you were dead!" Servial rushed over to him. He stopped when he was but an arms-length away. "We searched and searched to no avail. Brother, where were you?"

Servial's expression had turned from one of astonishment and joy, to confusion and a small degree of dismay. Sydonnia remained impassive despite the temptation to fall into Servial's trap. His brother hoped to use his charming manner and show of caring in order to draw him in. Sydonnia refused to allow it.

"Did you?" Sydonnia spoke in a deep monotone. It was one of the many things about him that changed since the transformation. His voice had always been rather deep, but now... "Did you really search for me, *Brother?*" He emphasized the last word, spoke it as though it was an expletive. He watched as his Servial's eyes became shuttered and his lips pulled taut. Servial quickly surmised that Sydonnia somehow knew full well the events that had taken place.

"Of course, *Brother.* Why wouldn't I?" Servial's voice had an edge to it as well, and his eyes narrowed slightly.

Sydonnia shrugged his broad shoulders. "I don't know. Why don't you *enlighten* me?"

Servial's eyes narrowed even further. Sydonnia could see the interplay within Servial's mind in spite of his attempts to conceal it. He wasn't accustomed to the Sydonnia who stood before him now, the one who used fancy words and sported a voice as deep as the darkest Silverwood. He wasn't used to the Sydonnia who would stand up to him in defiance as he did now.

"You are a deserter. You could be tried by the hinterlean crown and determined a traitor. You could be banished, and even worse, killed. I doubt you want that, Sydonnia."

Sydonnia smiled widely, baring his sharp canines. "Ah, Brother, you think you know me so well. You even think they could capture me." He laughed then, a full throated one that seemed to reverberate off the trees that circled the clearing. "They have no chance."

Grim understanding seemed to dawn upon Servial then. His body stiffened almost imperceptibly, and the pupils of his eyes widened in response to an instinctual reaction that was suddenly brought to the fore. It was the sensation associated with the presence of a predator and the instinct that danger was near.

Servial swallowed convulsively. "You don't frighten me, Sydonnia. I know what you are, and I know why you have come. You will not have her. Lilandria is mine, and always will be." Servial lowered his voice into a hiss. "You are a fool to have come here."

Sydonnia growled deep in his throat. "You forget how well I know you. You will use Lily just as you do all the women in your acquaintance. After a while you will tire of her and cast her aside just like all the others." Sydonnia cocked his head. "As I recall, one of them even bore you a child. You refused to acknowledge her as your bastard, claiming the mother slept with another man. You have a daughter that you have never seen. I wonder what she must think of you."

Servial shook his head slowly and grinned. "What are you going to do about it, big brother? Are you going to be her champion? As I recall it, Lilandria chose me over you."

"Yes, but she didn't know the dung-eaten calotebas that you really are, and that you left your own brother to die in the forest." Sydonnia grinned in return. "And yes, I am going to be her champion ..."

Sydonnia's sentence was cut short as Servial chose that moment to rush at him. The extra long blade of the hinterlean-style dagger reflected briefly before it was plunged into Sydonnia's unprotected abdomen. It sunk in deep, and with a savage twist, Servial drove it deeper. Damn, it was disheartening to know that one's own brother would so easily attempt to murder him. Of course, Sydonnia had thought to do the same. But Servial had acted first, and he wasn't even the monster.

Sydonnia felt it begin almost instantly. It was the change that took him from a man into something in between, half man and half beast. It was where he could use the best of both worlds, and in this hybrid form, he was also the most powerful. As his fingernails lengthened into claws, he gripped Servial by the front of his vest and pulled the man up off the ground. With his increasing strength, he then threw Servial into the nearest tree. He was gratified to hear the impact of flesh upon wood. As Servial struggled to rise, Sydonnia strode towards him, picked him up once more, and then called out. Just like before, it emerged as a howl, one that told the others of his pack that the hunt was over and the prey taken down.

Sydonnia felt Servial shudder beneath his grip and smiled malevolently. He was so tempted to bite his brother and then leave him to the same fate he now endured. But he knew the impulse was a foolhardy one. Once in possession of the same strengths that Sydonnia now possessed, Servial would surely thwart him. The two would always be at odds with one another, and Sydonnia would see no end until the other man was dead. Yet, despite the darkness that he knew had overtaken his soul, he didn't have the heart to kill his brother. He couldn't help recalling the games they had played together as boys, their plans to raise their families together as one, and the promises they had made to always stand by one another.

Sydonnia angrily cast his brother from him. Servial hit the ground with a resounding thud and Sydonnia barely glanced at his still form before turning away. Servial was right about one thing. Sydonnia was indeed a fool to have come. He should have gone immediately to Lilandria, for he may have had more luck with her. He completed his transformation and swiftly left the area. He could hardly wait to see her.

Seven moon-cycles after the massacre
2 Decaren CY544

Lilandria turned to look behind her for the third time since arriving at the path that would take her to the heated springs. The pools were a boon to the people of Alcrostat and Merithyn, for none like them existed elsewhere within the realm. Usually she had no problem with the walk it took in order to reach them. But today she couldn't shake the feeling that she was being followed, and she was beginning to feel nervous.

Several moon cycles had passed since Servial and a small contingent of surviving rangers returned from the banks of the Terrestra River. She had been distraught to find that Sydonnia was not with them. He was proclaimed missing, for his body had never been found. She lamented the loss of her friend, for they had become quite close during the months leading up to that fateful mission. The details were kept from her and the others who awaited the return of their loved ones. Three fourths of those people never returned. It was a historical moment for all of Elvandahar, and the mourning was long and sorrowful.

But at least Servial had returned from the ill-fated assignment. He had yet to say much about his brother, but she knew that it was only a matter of time before he would confide in her. In spite of her own feelings of loss, she knew that Servial's were so much greater, and she vowed to be his bastion of support when he finally broke down. She was initially taken aback by his lack of emotion concerning Sydonnia, but in the end realized it was simply his way of coping with the loss. She respected that, and she would be there for Servial when he finally came around.

Finally Lilandria reached the springs. Within the center of each of the four heated pools, water bubbled up from within the ground, and mist rose into the air. It was the perfect place for people to get together and mingle whilst they bathed. More often, women visited in the mornings while men did so in the evenings after a long day. Even though she had arrived closer towards mid-day, she was surprised to find herself alone. It was an uncommon occurrence, and it took her slightly aback. This day would have been a good one to have companionship.

Lilandria slowly set her pack upon the ground next to one of the flat rocks situated around the pools. She had always wondered if they were placed there by natural whimsy or faelin inspiration. She hesitated to begin removing the gown she customarily wore to the springs and then admonished herself. By the gods, she was being so silly. What had gotten into her? She would have known if someone were indeed following her. And why would anyone do such a thing anyways? It simply wasn't civilized.

It was only a moment later that her skin began to prickle, and Lilandria immediately felt the unmistakable presence of another person. She would have loved to believe it was someone who had come to bathe, someone much like herself who had a late start to their day. But she instinctively knew it wasn't the truth, for her body reacted as though imperiled. She sensed *danger* emanating from the presence behind her.

Lilandria slowly turned in place. She fought her inclination to close her eyes, an immature reaction to stress. If it can't be seen, it must not really be there. Then she saw him standing at the tree-line, a man she had thought deceased. *Sydonnia.*

She mouthed his name without speaking, her eyes widening with disbelief. She then put a hand to her chest in a subconscious attempt to stop her racing heart. Lilandria thought she must surely be dreaming, but her physical response to his presence was definitely not imaginary. He then stepped towards her with hands outstretched, and she rushed to him without considering her body's earlier warning of danger.

"By the gods, is it really you?" She breathlessly spoke the words so low they were almost a whisper. The feel of his arms around her was not like she remembered, the embrace seeming stronger somehow, more powerful. Yet, the scent of him was familiar in spite of the musky undertone.

"Did you miss me?"

His deep voice carried a bantering quality, and she thought the question a strange one, especially from one who had been considered lost in battle. She pulled back, and through the tears in her eyes, Lilandria took in the ruggedly handsome face. It was much the same as it had always been: the cut of jaw, the shape of his lips, and the arch of his thick brows. But something was different, something she couldn't quite place.

"Sydonnia, where have you been? They went out looking for you, but..."

He placed a forefinger to her lips, and she stopped. Lilandria felt a slight shift in his demeanor, and once more her skin prickled. "Sssh. It doesn't matter. I am here now," he said solemnly.

His voice was so deep, deeper than she recalled it to be. Her breath caught in her throat; *what was happening?* He had disregarded her inquiry without a shred of care or thought. She shook her head. "It *does* matter! I thought you were dead!"

He grinned disarmingly. "Well now you know that I'm not."

Lilandria frowned and took a step back, struggling to discern the slight changes she noticed had taken place. "Sydonnia, that's not good enough. I need to know what happened." She paused and then continued. "Does Servial know you are here?"

Lilandria sensed it immediately. It was a shift in the very air surrounding them. His brown eyes focused piercingly upon her, eyes that seemed almost feral. She thought it strange that particular word popped to mind, and she slowly began to feel a pervading sensation of peril.

Sydonnia regarded her with a frown. "I suppose the two of you have become rather close in my absence. I guess I can't blame you since you thought me deceased," he said gruffly.

Lilandria shook her head and drew her brows together. "Sy, what's gotten into you? Servial and I... what... *how* does our relationship bear any consequence to your whereabouts for all of this time?" she stuttered.

"It has everything to do with it!" he growled. "You think you know my brother." Sydonnia shook his head. "You know nothing! He knew I loved you, but he focused his attentions upon you anyways." Sydonnia paused and then continued. "Don't look so surprised, my dear. You had to have known my attraction to you, an attraction I continue to harbor. And somewhere deep inside, I know you have a similar feeling for me. Only now, Servial's charm has blinded you to it."

Lilandria shook her head once more. "Sydonnia, what are you talking about? This attraction... what has it to do with where you have been? I don't understand!"

Sydonnia closed the gap between them and grabbed her by the arms. "Don't you see? He knew that your attraction was more than just simple friendship. That is why he stopped the search. *Servial never wanted me to be found!*"

Lilandria instinctively tried to pull back from his grip. "By the gods, Sydonnia. Listen to yourself! Do you honestly believe what you are saying? Servial loves you. He would never have left the river knowing you were still there. Hells, he thought you were dead!"

Sydonnia shook his head vehemently. "No! He knew how I felt about you and feared I would take you away from him, much as he had taken you away from me. Before the assignment we had a fight. It was about you. We never reconciled! He left me, Lily! I was there, hiding in the trees, when he stopped the other rangers from continuing the search for me!"

Lilandria regarded him incredulously. "By the gods, this is craziness! This attraction you keep talking about ... Sy, it was never there for me, not the way you think!" Lilandria paused and then continued. "You are wrong to believe Servial purposefully left you at the river! He would never have done that! He had nothing to fear because I was never in love with you!"

Sydonnia suddenly became still. She winced as he tightened his grip upon her arms, and her senses screamed to her of imminent danger. It seemed that he then began to change before her very eyes. His canines began to elongate, the hair around his face thickened, and his stature broadened. Fear swept through her like a scythe, and despite the discomfort she redoubled her efforts to escape his grip.

"My brother has poisoned your mind," he hissed savagely. "Just look deep within, and you will find I speak the truth. I felt it between us, still feel it, a connection that can't be denied," he continued. "Come away with me, Lilandria. I can give you everything you have ever wanted. Before I was weak, but now I have strength I never could have imagined!"

"Sydonnia, please. Let me go." She struggled to keep her voice from wavering. "I don't want any of this."

Sydonnia pulled her close to him, placing his lips near her ear. "You don't know what you are saying. I know that you want me; you have only to look past the shroud my brother has placed over your mind."

The fear became overwhelming, and Lilandria was suddenly aware of what he had become. He was one of those whom everyone spoke so much about, one of the monsters that wreaked havoc upon the outlying villages and towns all across Kleyshes and Filopar. A lycanthrope. By the gods, the innocent people that had been killed already. And the children...

Her breathing accelerated, but she somehow found it difficult to get air. Her heart felt as though it might beat from her chest at any moment. Lilandria felt herself becoming faint, but she resisted it. She looked up at Sydonnia, into the face that she had once found so comforting. All she saw now was a terrible beast. Lilandria began to struggle against him. "I don't want anything to do with you. Get away from me!" she shouted.

The impact of Sydonnia's hand across her face was enough to make her head snap around on her neck. Tears sprang to her eyes, and as her consciousness began to waver, Lilandria felt herself being forced to the ground. Struggling feebly, she vaguely felt her clothing being torn away. Then a sudden penetrating pain overwhelmed her senses, and her world shifted to dark.

Almost 28 years after the massacre...
29 Jicaren CY571

The shadows lengthened as the sun set upon the darkening horizon. Sirion looked down at the length of the young corubis curled around him, light from the nearby fire reflecting off of the dappled tawny fur. The animal was a gift, one bestowed upon him by his father several moon cycles ago. They had waited for the litter to be born, and then they waited even longer until the pups were old enough to be weaned from their mother's milk. It was the day that Sirion was allowed to meet the pups for the very first time, to see if any of the weanlings would single him out from any of the other young faelin men and women who were also present for the auspicious occasion. It was always a special day when a corubis litter was ready for *imprinting*. And Sirion had been one of the lucky ones chosen.

His name was Dramati. Sirion had chosen it from a long

list of hinterlean words that were no longer in use by the general populace. It meant "loyal, steadfast companion" in the ancient texts, and Sirion knew the animal would be just that. It would be good to have Dramati for his next run, one that his father told him would be rather long and arduous. Sirion would be developing even more of the hand-to-hand combat techniques he had at his behest, as well as some additional skill with the blade he would develop from an elite swordsman his father had met many years ago. It didn't feel like much time had elapsed since he left his mother and sister behind in Merithyn, but the passage of the moon cycles was testimony to that. Not to mention, the accomplishments he had made under the tutelage of some of the most renowned masters upon all of western Ansalar.

Sirion glanced up at the fire that his father had built for the evening. Within the pot hanging precipitously over the flames, a stew of ptarmigan and leeks was slowly cooking. They would eat well this night, and Sirion was proud of the contribution he had made to the stew-pot. The game had been difficult to spot within the thick foliage, but he had persevered thanks to the help of Dramati. The long-legged canine was a good hunter despite his young age. His father started to smile at him from the other side of the fire, but stopped when they suddenly heard a resounding howl emanate from the trees around them.

Servial was suddenly at the alert. He stood from his position at the fire as he drew his hinterlean dagger from its sheath strapped to the belt around his waist. Sirion could sense the tension emanating from his father and knew that something was seriously amiss. It was then that he smelled it, a musky odor often associated with a predator. Dramati stirred in his lap, and Sirion knew that he sensed it too. Sirion heard a faint sound coming from the wood, the light trod of a hunter stalking his prey. And it was coming straight towards them.

Sirion froze in place, suddenly recognizing the presence of danger. Dramati sensed it as well, and Sirion felt a low growl begin to emanate from deep within the corubis' body as Dramati took a more defensive position. They both startled when a man walked out of the shadows of the surrounding wood and into the light offered by the fire. He was quite large for a faelin, standing a few hands higher than Servial, and at least two or three hands broader. He walked nonchalantly into their encampment, almost as though he belonged there, and he wore a wide smile on his stubbly face.

"Well, well, well. Who have I come across this time?" he drawled. "Oh, it's my faithful brother, mayhap coming to give me a visit as he passes through the Sheldomar Forest." His thick brows suddenly pulled down into a frown. "Hells, but he never bothered to before." He then cupped a hand beneath his chin in mock thoughtfulness. "Hmm, I suppose I need to remind him of the importance of *family*."

Sirion remained still. He had heard the stories of his father's brother, a man who had died in the fight against the lycanthrope menace almost two decades ago. He had no recollection of another brother. Silence reigned for a moment before his father spoke. "What do you want, Sydonnia?"

Sirion's thoughts began to race when he heard the name, and he gripped at the thick fur circling Dramati's neck. *Sydonnia was the name of his father's dead brother.*

Sydonnia simply shrugged his wide shoulders. "It's been so long, but I vividly recall when last we met. I stood as victor at the end of our little skirmish." He paused for a moment and then continued. "Oh, and so sorry about the leg, Brother. Sometimes I don't know my own strength."

Sydonnia smiled again, his canines shining brightly white in the firelight. Sirion swallowed heavily as feral eyes came to rest upon him in spite of efforts to be invisible. The gaze was coldly calculating, and it almost seemed as though Sydonnia touched the outer fringes of his soul with the intensity of his stare.

"I see you have brought your whelp," he said in a monotone. "It surprises me that you would place him at risk knowing that me and mine are loose within these forests. You are a fool, Servial." Sydonnia growled the last, swinging his gaze back towards his father.

Servial shook his head and curled his lips. "You are only jealous because Lilandria bore my son and not yours," he sneered. "Your life is pathetic, Sydonnia. You have accomplished nothing, and no one cares about you. I *almost* feel sorry for you."

Sirion felt it immediately, a sudden change in the surrounding air. Sydonnia's stature increased, and his voice deepened. "No. You are the pathetic one, Servial. You left her, just as I knew you would. One day, your son will discover the truth about you, and he will come to despise you. Unfortunately, you won't be there." Sydonnia paused and then continued. "You asked me what I wanted, and now I will tell you. I have come to kill you, Brother, much as you left me to die all those many years ago at the Terrestra River."

Servial had barely enough time to raise his dagger before Sydonnia was upon him. The man was monstrous to behold, standing at least two hands higher than he did when first entering the encampment. His body was now covered with hair, and his face strangely elongated. The most terrifying changes were the wickedly clawed hands and sharp canines protruding from the upper jaw. Sirion could only hunker there in abject fear, terrified to the very core of his being.

With unnatural grace and power, Sydonnia leaped at Servial. As their two bodies collided, Sydonnia wrapped his arms around his brother and sunk his sharp claws deep into Servial's back. At such close range, the studded leather offered only minimal resistance. Sydonnia raked them around to the sides and then savagely thrust Servial away from him.

Servial landed upon the ground with a heavy thud. Blood had already begun to stain the tan vest, surrounding the huge tears at the sides and back. Sirion finally found the courage to rush to his feet. He drew his own dagger and without thinking, he sprung towards the enemy with Dramati following beside. With the greatest of ease, Sydonnia blocked the attack. With one hand he took Sirion by the throat, and with the other he swept at Dramati. The corubis flew through the air. Sirion heard a heavy thud followed by a sharp yelp as the animal landed about a farlo away.

Sirion scraped at the hand closed around his throat, desperate to free himself. He looked into the chaotic gaze of his uncle, saw the madness brimming just below the surface. Suddenly remembering he still had the dagger in his hand, Sirion plunged it into Sydonnia's unprotected abdomen. The man gave a vicious growl and then retaliated. Sirion felt the wicked claws slice across him, starting at his shoulder and ending just above his navel. He then felt the crushing power of the hand around his throat, squeezing ... squeezing ... until he began to see a smattering of bright pin-points in the periphery of his vision. Sirion abruptly found himself airborne for a moment, but then his face was scraping against the debris of the forest floor as he suffered a brutal landing.

Unable to move, Sirion slowly opened one of his eyes to a narrow crack. The terrible scene he witnessed would be burned into his memory forever. Servial stood in the middle of the encampment, his blood-drenched tunic and vest hanging in shreds around him. He wore an expression of deep sadness, almost as though remembering something he had once lost. A huge white wemic entered Sirion's line of vision. He knew that the animal was the completely altered form of Sydonnia, *and that all vestiges of reason were gone.*

The wemic attacked Servial where he stood. The man offered no resistance, for he knew it would be futile. The massive jaws closed around Servial's neck and then Sydonnia savagely shook the limp body back and forth. Sirion could hear the sickening sound of cracking bone; blood spraying onto the thick pale fur of Sydonnia's neck. The wemic flung the broken form away from him and then followed to the place where it fell. Sydonnia then proceeded to ravage the lifeless body of his brother until it was barely discernible.

Sydonnia stood over the bloody remains for a moment. He then curled his stained lips into a snarl and slowly turned in Sirion's direction. He could do nothing as the animal padded noiselessly towards him. The feral eyes bore into him, eyes that Sirion could only vaguely sense contained the soul of a man. His heart felt as though it would beat out of his chest, and just as his father had done, Sirion gave himself up to Sydonnia. He knew there was nothing he could do to stop the inevitable. From the massive wounds across his chest, he could feel his life's blood seeping through the fabric of his tunic and into the ground beneath. His vision wavered. The horrific visage of his uncle appeared before him, crimson red lips baring long white teeth. Yet, there was an eerie beauty about the beast.

Sirion had never heard of a white wemic...

51 years after the massacre...
7 Decaren CY594

Adrianna had heard the story. It was told to her in bits and
pieces over the course of time she was getting to know Sirion.
Parts of it were related to her as the Wildrunners journeyed
back to Elvandahar after their battle against the deathmage,
Aasarak. Yet, most of it had been told much earlier than that:
before she and her sister defeated Lord Thane in the Ratik
Mountain Pass, before she went into training within Master
Tallachienan's citadel, and before she met her dragon bond-
mate. Sydonnia had allowed Sirion his life that evening so
long ago in the Sheldomar Forest. Inasmuch, Adria thought it
such a tragedy that someone could be driven to murder his
own brother, and that the brother's son would, in turn, be
fated to return the favor many years later. Such was the basic
premise of the story of Servial and Sydonnia Timberlyn, two
men who once would have laid down his life for the other.

Adrianna glanced about her as the group rode astride the
lloryk and larian that had carried them so far. The silver
canopy of Elvandahar's forest loomed overhead, so thick it
blocked out most of the sunlight that sought to venture
through. It hadn't really been that long since the Wildrunners
last saw the beauty belonging to the realm of the hinterlean
faelin. Yet, that visit had ended with the tragedy of
Sydonnia's death at the hands of his nephew. She was certain
Sirion still suffered the aftershock.

Adrianna sighed and swept a hand through the strands of
pale blond hair that escaped from its customary plait. The
strain of the knowledge she carried weighed heavily upon her,
and she fervently wished she could divulge all of it to Sirion.
Truth be told, she had already returned to Elvandahar within

the interim of this visit and the last. Her visit was one that made quite an interesting tale, one that matched the one she heard told about Servial and Sydonnia before. It was a continuation of it, actually, one which she had the opportunity to experience first-hand.

It had happened as an accident one day whilst in training. She had been worn down by the intensity of her studies, and her misery was perpetuated by an overbearing master. Adria had sought only to escape the confines of Tallachienan and his dark citadel for a time, to visit the place she knew as her childhood home: the city of Sangrilak. She had succeeded in sending herself to a place vastly different from what she remembered.

Adrianna had been shocked when she met Sydonnia outside the limits of a much smaller Sangrilak. Accompanying him was another man, one she had never met. When she noticed the similarity to Sirion, and then discovered that his name was Servial Timberlyn, she made the difficult realization that she existed in a different Time. Hells, how could she have known that the master had taken her into the past in order to meet her training requirements in the present? Knowing she was trapped until Master Tallachienan came to retrieve her, Adrianna found herself in a situation she could not escape without bringing too much attention to herself. Forced into proximity with Sirion's father and uncle, she was given the opportunity to see the story first hand, for she had suddenly become a part of it.

Adrianna found herself pulled away from her thoughts when she felt her larian slowing to a halt. Glancing towards the head of the procession, she saw Sirion standing there, looking into the trees before him. It was then that she noticed it, a familiar musky odor tinged with a predatory undertone.

The hairs at the back of her neck immediately began to rise in response to the danger, and by the look of his stance, she knew that Sirion felt it too. However, instead of reaching for his weapon as he ordinarily would, Sirion stepped forward with his hands at his sides, saying something she couldn't quite decipher despite her excellent faelin hearing. And then, when she saw the individual who stepped out to greet him, her heart almost stopped in her chest. The man had died several moon cycles ago at Sirion's hand. It was Sydonnia Timberlyn.

In shock, Adrianna almost slipped from the back of her larian. The breath caught in her chest and her heart seemed to become still for a moment. No. This wasn't possible. Hells, what was happening? Had she somehow traveled through Time yet again? Or was this some type of terrible dream from which she had a difficult time awakening? She thought back on all of the conversations she and Sirion had shared since her return to the group after her training, and with a blow she realized that not once did Sirion mention the death of his uncle. She hadn't noticed it because there was no reason to state the obvious. The man was dead, so why say it aloud? It was for that reason Adria had forbore to mention it as well.

By the gods, what had she done?

In the past, Adrianna had developed camaraderie with the man she would later know as a monster. Within the time she spent in his company, Sydonnia had become more than just Sirion's deranged uncle; he was a good friend and fierce protector. She had balked at the course of events that would eventually take place, and even more that she could do nothing to stop it. Right from the start, she knew that any changes made in the past would affect the future as she remembered it. She had realized she couldn't take the risk of those changes affecting her relationship with Sirion, for it was their union that most likely influenced the joining of the original Wildrunners with the younger individuals who would one day carry their name. Not to mention that without the merger, Aasarak may never have been defeated.

And the world would still be repeating itself.

A few days after the massacre at the Terrestra River
3 Chanteren CY543

Sydonnia slowly opened his eyes, immediately aware of the chill in the air. Where he lay upon his back, he could see the silvery canopy above, interrupted by widening swaths of blue sky beyond. He moved one leg, and then the other, cringing with the pain the movement caused. The memories of what he endured returned in bits and pieces, and by the time he made it to his feet, it had all come back to him.

He remembered the hideous dark-robed priest, the wickedly curved claws, the feeling of himself beginning to die, and then the terrible pain. The torment had swept over him in an agonizing wave, taking away thought and reason until barely anything was left. His body had writhed upon the ground, muscle tearing and bones snapping until everything had rearranged itself to fit the description of something other than faelin. He had become something more, something much, much more. He just didn't know exactly what that was.

He then began to feel it. It was overpowering in its intensity, a sensation of hunger he had never experienced before. Overcome by the demands of his transformed body, Sydonnia hunted under the pale light of the moons. The urge to kill was strong, and he satisfied it with the life of a young leschera. Sydonnia was surprised with the ease it took for him to bring down the deer-like animal, especially by himself. The pleasure he derived by sinking his elongated canines into the throat of the beast was astounding, and when he felt the heart cease beating, he had already begun to feed. Imagining what the animal might be feeling those last few moments of life was invigorating, and as the leschera died beneath his hands, Sydonnia lifted his head and cried out with ecstasy. The sound that emerged from his throat was a howl, a sound he had often heard from the wemic packs that set their territories along the ground beneath his home village of Merithyn. It was then that his full awareness began to return, and he became truly cognizant of the creature he had become.

And then he remembered his brother and the contingent of rangers whom he had accompanied to the Terrestra River.

As the moons began to wane, Sydonnia made his way back to the banks of the Terrestra. The carnage he passed was gut wrenching, for each of the bodies he passed was someone he knew: childhood friends, comrades in arms, respected citizens of the domains of Kleyshes and Filopar. All of them unceremoniously ripped to shreds, torn apart by beasts such as the one he had become. Then, as the sun began to crest the horizon, he found the survivors. It was easy, for his sense of smell had become so keen. He stood hidden within the trees as they searched for him, afraid to come out lest they see that something was changed about him and mayhap realize what he had become. He struggled to work up the courage to step forward. Yet, he found he hadn't the time. The sun had barely begun its rise into the sky when they were gone. At the behest of his own brother, the rangers cut their search short and abandoned Sydonnia to whatever grisly fate awaited him.

And now he was alone, with nothing but his memories and his lust to kill...

Sydonnia let the anger come, let it envelop him like a shroud. His thoughts returned to a time several moon cycles before ago, when he had first begun to notice the attention Servial was starting to pay Lilandria, a woman whom Sydonnia had begun to develop deep affection. Servial had a propensity for always getting his way with the female population, no matter who might stand in his way. Obviously that included Sydonnia as well. He had every intention of confronting his brother about the situation on their return trip from a journey they were making to the town of Sangrilak on business. But as fate would have it, they came across a lone woman just outside the town limits.

Keilah Laremion was an enigma to them. She was quite attractive, and it was so uncommon to see a faelin of her coloration and appearance in that part of Ansalar. She refused to divulge much about herself, and at first seemed somewhat disoriented. All she would tell them was that her brother would be coming for her. Nevertheless, they took her under their protective wing, unable to simply leave her without a proper escort. A lone female out in the middle of nowhere was unheard of. On the way back to Elvandahar, Sydonnia found a strong rapport with her that turned into friendship. The discussion he wanted to have with Servial about Lilandria was pushed to the background, for somehow Keilah's presence had affected the two brothers and they had started to rediscover the intense bond they had shared since childhood.

Yet, when they had arrived in Merithyn, all of that began to change. Servial started to bestow upon Keilah the type of attention he had shown Lilandria before their business in Sangrilak. All of the negative emotions came rushing back to Sydonnia, but with the added realization that Lily would be hurt when she saw Servial giving his affections to another woman. Interestingly, Keilah seemed virtually immune to Servial's charm, and it served to increase Sydonnia's respect for her.

Just as Keilah began to get settled into life in Elvandahar, the brothers had received a summons for a call to arms. It was agreed that in two days, the rangers of the domains of Filopar and Kleyshes would leave the sanctuary of their families and daladins to answer the call of protective duty to the realm. The information they had been given in regards to the menace was only that the situation was dire, and that people were dying. As the two domains prepared to face the threat, the brother that Keilah had always claimed would come for her finally arrived. Bravin and Keilah stayed the night and early the next morning, Sydonnia felt his heart ache as she embraced him for the last time. He could see a similar ache also reflecting in her eyes before she finally stepped back. As he watched her walk away, he couldn't help but feel that something momentous had happened, and that it would not be the last time he saw her.

Later the same morning, the rangers had met in the city of Alcrostat. There were well over two score, and many of them had corubis companions in accompaniment. Sydonnia was disgusted to see Lilandria in Servial's arms once more, despite what she had seen of his pursuit of Keilah. He must have downplayed it, making her believe that what she saw was nothing but simple friendship and that he had feelings only for her. It wasn't long after that they were leaving the city, and that evening when camp was set, Sydonnia finally confronted his brother.

Of course Servial had trivialized the accusation, and then made Sy out to be a besotted fool. An argument ensued, but before he became too angry to think rationally, Sydonnia walked away. It was one of the most difficult things had had ever done, for all he wanted to do was smash his fist into Servial's sneering face. Subsequently, the remainder of their journey to the Terrestra River was intensely strained. Fortunately, Sydonnia found himself preoccupied with the coming battle and the mysterious threat. But when the group of rangers met the enemy, they were woefully unprepared. A massacre ensued. Sydonnia was lured into the wood.

And now he was a monster.

Yet, in spite of the wrong his brother had committed against him, there was a part of Sydonnia that wanted to return home. Perhaps he would go to see one of the hinterlean wise-men. The nivorlan would know what to do to help Sydonnia, and he would once more be an ordinary man. He would go to Lilandria, make her realize the scoundrel that Servial really was. Sydonnia would tell her.

Sydonnia suddenly took a deep breath, flaring his nostrils He could smell it so clearly, a leschera that slowly approached in the wood beside him. He realized he hadn't eaten for a couple of days now, and he was hungry for the kill.

Seven moon-cycles after the massacre
2 Decaren CY544

Sydonnia watched as the young woman slowly set her pack down upon one of the flat rocks situated around the thermal pools. Even after all that had happened, he still thought her to be the most beautiful woman in the world. While Servial's desertion of him after their failed mission at the Terrestra made him feel as though he died a second death, thoughts of Lilandria had brought Sydonnia back to life. Now, after the passage of almost seven moon-cycles, he made the decision to return to Merithyn, not only to have closure with his brother, but to see her again.

Abandoned, and fueled by anger and betrayal, Sydonnia had turned away from the civilized world, immersing himself in a journey of self-discovery. Instead of remaining in denial, he embraced what he had become. With his venomous bite, he gave others the terrible disease people began to call lycanthropy. With those he transformed, Sydonnia once more had a family. And as the pack grew, so did their insatiable hunger.

The beasts had wreaked havoc upon the nearest villages. They killed the men, ravaged the women, and even began to torment the children. Some people Sydonnia gave the opportunity for transformation, others he did not. Only a rare few of those he transformed carried the 'ability' to transform others. And strangely, not everyone who suffered the bite went through the change. Sydonnia had very little understanding of this, but he really didn't care. All that mattered was the pack he had fathered

Every once in a while he would have dreams of the home he had left behind, the friends he had once known. Many of them had met their demise at the Terrestra River. Then he would think of Keilah. And Lilandria.

Once deciding to return to Merithyn, he had gone to see his brother first. Visions of revenge were prominent in his mind. Yet there was a part of him, albeit a small one, that hoped Servial would prove him wrong, and that he had never meant to desert Sydonnia in the enemy-infested forest. But just as he thought it would be, the meeting was a vast disappointment. He only confirmed that he was right to believe his brother was a traitor. The meeting ended in a fight, but Sydonnia derived very little pleasure from walking away the victor. In a way, he would have much preferred for his brother to finish the job he began by abandoning him at the Terrestra. But then he wouldn't have been able to see Lilandria...

Now, Sydonnia couldn't help but smile when he noticed her hesitation to begin removing her gown. He knew it was because she sensed his presence. Lily had always been very intelligent and perceptive, and those abilities had drawn him to her right away. Deciding to make his identity known, Sydonnia stepped from out of the shadows of the trees. Lilandria slowly turned in place, and when she saw him standing there at the tree-line, her eyes widened with disbelief. Then she mouthed his name without speaking... *Sydonnia.*

He stepped towards her as she rushed to him. "By the gods, is it really you?" She spoke the words so low they were almost a whisper. The feel of her within his arms was just as he remembered, and he reveled in the scent of her after so long.

"Did you miss me?"

The words slipped out before he could stop them. He gave his voice a bantering quality, his way of diffusing the intensity of the inquiry, of arming himself should he receive the answer he feared. But he immediately realized how strange the question sounded, and barely a moment later her tear dampened eyes reflected the same sentiment.

Pulling back, she regarded him in near astonishment. "Sydonnia, where have you been? They went out looking for you, but..."

He placed his fingertips at her lips and she stopped. "Sssh. It doesn't matter. I am here now," he said solemnly.

She shook her head. "It *does* matter! I thought you were dead!"

Sydonnia regarded her solemnly, felt the intensity of her emotion. She was right; it *did* matter where he had been. While certain other things probably didn't matter, some of those were details he felt strongly tempted to tell her. Yet he refrained, somehow knowing that they would be more burden than enlightenment. Unfortunately, the answer would deserve an explanation...

He grinned disarmingly. "Well now you know that I'm not."

Lilandria frowned and took a step back from him. "Sydonnia, that's not good enough. I need to know what happened." She paused and then continued. "Does Servial know you are here?"

Sydonnia inhaled sharply and felt his hackles rise. He could see that she felt it immediately, a shift in the very air surrounding them. He focused his eyes piercingly upon her, felt the animal within him beginning to emerge. She had unwittingly brought forth thoughts of his brother he would sooner have left alone. He hated to be a prisoner to them, and one day he hoped to break free. But not this day.

Calming himself, Sydonnia bit back a caustic retort and shook his head. "No. And it might very well be better this way," he said in a low voice.

Lilandria shook her head and drew her brows together into a slight frown. "Sy, what's wrong with you? Servial is your brother and deserves to know! He has missed you so much these past..."

Sydonnia interrupted her. "No. My presence here is only between you and me." Sydonnia shook his head. "You *must* promise me, Lily."

Lilandria stood still before him. Sydonnia regarded her intently and awaited her response. The air crackled between them, testimony to the energy lying there. He had suddenly become so attuned to her, knew it when she came to the realization that he would be long gone before she had any opportunity to tell Servial of his presence. And he knew when she simply accepted his presence there as a gift...

Sydonnia closed the gap between them and took her by the arms. "Don't you see? It doesn't matter where I've been, only that I am here now." He paused and then continued softly, "I am not the same man I was when I left."

Lilandria nodded slowly, her head lowered. "I know. By the gods, Sydonnia, I can feel it," she said in a near whisper.

"But I still want you the same as I always have. My feelings for you have never subsided."

Lilandria looked up at him, her brows pulling together into a frown. "What are you saying? I never knew..."

Sydonnia placed his fingertips at her lips, once again interrupting her. "You *did* know. You just didn't recognize it. But now I'm *telling* you. Don't be afraid to accept the truth, Lilandria."

She was suddenly still for a moment. He held his breath and waited. He knew that she needed to make the connection on her own. Any pushing on his part would simply make her run away. He remembered a conversation he had once shared with Keilah. Many things were said, but there was one line in particular that came to his mind. He hadn't really understood was she was saying then, but now... *"Sometimes you simply have to let something go so that it can make the decision to come back to you."*

Sydonnia felt it when Lily's barriers finally came crashing down. He could feel that she wanted him, wanted him with the same passion and intensity he felt for her. Sydonnia kissed her for the first time, tasted a sweetness of which he had before only dreamed. Her scent overwhelmed him as he gently lay her down upon the mossy ground, a scent that beckoned to him of what was to come. And he would not have been able to resist it, even had he wanted to.

Eleven moon-cycles after the massacre
15 Cisceren CY544

Ending his patrol for the evening, Servial did one last check before heading back into Alcrostat. Another ranger would meet him on the way, the one who would be replacing him for the night. Sensing nothing amiss, Servial increased his pace to an easy jog. It wasn't long before his leg began to ache, the one that was broken when Sydonnia came to him that day more than four moon-cycles ago. Servial had been rendered unconscious in their struggle, but when he finally came to, he found that his brother had left the area without a trace.

Or should he say, the *monster* that had once been his brother.

Despite the discomfort, Servial kept the pace. Lilandria was waiting for him at her daladin, and he was looking forward to spending the evening with her. His interest in her had become revitalized when, just a few days ago, she had confided her pregnancy. He had always wanted children, and Lilandria would make a good mother. Of course, he had one child already. He had never realized that Sydonnia knew about the girl.

Servial decided to slow down to a walk. Now that his thoughts were centered upon Sydonnia, he suddenly wasn't in such a hurry to get home. It had been a shock to see the image of his brother step out of the trees that day, and even more, that Sydonnia fully realized the crime Servial had committed against him. There was a part of Servial that felt regret for the transgression against his brother, but an even larger part that cared only to serve himself. And it was just as well, for Sydonnia was now nothing but a monster. Servial refused to believe he had any part in making Sydonnia into such a hideous beast.

And then there was Lilandria. She didn't know that Sydonnia still lived and that he had come to the city in search of his brother. It was better that way, for she wouldn't think to yearn for him. And now that she was pregnant, he wouldn't want to burden her with information that might upset her. Sydonnia was a lycanthrope, a threat against hinterlean society. One day, the disease would spread beyond Elvandahar to infect other realms. Servial knew it was his destiny to prevent this from happening. He would one day rid Shandahar of the menace and kill Sydonnia. It was only a matter of time.

Almost 50 years after the massacre
18 Brinaren CY593

Lilandria looked upon her son for the first time in so many years. At one point, she had feared him dead, murdered at the hands of his own father. Once discovering Sirion still lived from his ordeal, she only found herself devastated again several years later when she heard he had been killed in battle against the dreaded Daemundai. To see him standing before her now was nothing short of miraculous.

Despite her best efforts, Lilandria couldn't stop the tears. By the gods, he looked so much like Servial. It was the more subtle features that he inherited from Sydonnia. Sirion quickly crossed the room, and within moments she was ensconced within her son's embrace. "Mother, I have come to tell you I am well. I know that Anya has been here to tell you otherwise, but she does not yet know that I survived," he said softly.

Lilandria felt herself begin to tremble. She would never forget the day, several moons ago, when her daughter came to tell her that Sirion had died. For the second time, Anya had lost a brother, and she a son. Then, only two days ago, when the scouts came to tell her that Sirion still lived, she felt her heart almost leap from her chest. The memories came rushing back to her, memories of his childhood, his birth, and then his conception.

That long ago tryst at the heated pool was the last time she saw Sydonnia. Not much later, Lilandria knew she was pregnant. Counting back the days, she knew the precise time that the child was conceived. She never told Servial about Sydonnia's visit, even when she made the realization that Sydonnia had been to see his brother before he came to her. Servial had suffered a plethora of wounds from their meeting, including one that never properly healed. With time, she came to recognize it as yet another reason for Servial to hate his brother. And she slowly began to wonder exactly what had happed on that failed mission to the Terrestra River.

However, Servial never had a reason to believe Sirion was not his son. And when the boy came of age, Servial took Sirion away from her and never returned. It was the first time she thought Sirion was dead when she discovered that Servial had met his demise at the hand of the same perpetrator. After all Servial's years of tracking down the beast, it was Sydonnia who found Servial. And then Sydonnia killed him. Yet, for some reason he had left young Sirion alive. Lilandria liked to believe it was because something deep within Sydonnia realized the boy was his own flesh and blood.

Lilandria spoke into the silence, finally recovering enough to take control of her voice. "When the scouts came to me two days ago, bearing the tale that you lived, I refused to let myself believe them, afraid that I would get my hopes up for nothing. But here you are, holding me in your arms like I dreamed you would."

Lilandria felt his arms tighten around her. "I will never leave you again," he whispered.

She felt a wave of joy sweep through her. "I believe you." Lilandria wrapped her arms around his neck and kissed his cheek. Finally they stepped apart.

Sirion continued to hold her hands, somehow knowing his mother didn't want him to let her go. "I am also here to serve the realm," he said solemnly. "I am here to aid in the removal of the lycanthrope threat."

Lilandria looked up at him, deep into his eyes. "My son, you *are* the realm."

51 years after the massacre
7 Decaren CY594

Sydonnia's gaze swept over the procession standing behind his nephew. Over the years, the younger man had made a name for himself, and he had proven himself a leader. Hells, Sydonnia couldn't be prouder had Sirion been his own son. But it was then he saw her. She stood among those who made up the small band of people who called themselves the Wildrunners. He could tell she recognized him, the expression upon her beautiful face was adequate testimony. In spite of her disbelief, Keilah Laremion stepped away from the group and slowly began to make her way towards him. Equally astonished, Sydonnia watched his old friend walk out from the confines of his past and into his present.

Adrianna had known the moment he recognized her. His eyes flashed, and his body became still. By the gods, this man was the friend she had left behind no more than several fortnights ago; the friend who would attest more than fifty years had passed since seeing her last. He was the friend who she thought had died by Sirion's hand, the one whom she still cared for very much.

Adrianna didn't stop until she stood before Sydonnia. He was large, his frame carrying much more mass than the man she met in the past. She remembered those arms around her, gentle arms that protected her. Yet, they were the same arms that hurt her when Sydonnia captured her as a way of getting to Sirion.

However, that scenario had obviously not taken place. It was plainly obvious this was the first time Sydonnia had seen her since she left Merithyn all those years ago. In spite of her efforts to be careful, something must have happened during her time spent in the past, some simple twist of fate that had brought into play a new reality.

Adrianna's mind warred with the complexity of the concepts thrust upon her. Her mind was a vortex of mixed emotions, both negative and positive. But the positive ones came to the fore because she found herself holding back a tentative smile. She knew that Sydonnia was not the same being she once knew in the past. He was a monster who had wreaked havoc throughout Elvandahar for decades. But he was still *Sydonnia*, and she couldn't believe that not even a small part of the man she remembered still resided within.

Sydonnia regarded her intently as she approached. By the

gods, she hadn't aged a day since he saw her last. She was still just as beautiful as the day she had left. He vaguely registered the surprise written upon his nephew's face as she passed by him, and Sydonnia wondered what might be between them. Considering it for a moment, he thought the match would be a good one.

"I always knew I would see you again," he said solemnly.

Silence rang throughout the area for a moment before she made her reply. "I thought you were dead."

Once more there was silence. Then, "This isn't the first time you have been erroneously informed."

He saw the corners of her mouth curve slightly upward. "Yes, I think you are right. It's about time I sent my advisor away. Besides, for someone who doesn't know very much, *he is so expensive!*"

She gave him a smile, one he knew was meant solely for him. Suddenly, it didn't matter where she was from and what he had become, only that they were both there now, standing before one another after so long. Sydonnia didn't understand it, but all those years ago she had changed him in ways he would never know. Within the short span of time they spent within one another's company, they had shared experiences that would last a lifetime. But that was another story.

Sydonnia closed the short distance between them, took her gently in his embrace and whispered in her ear. *"I have missed you my friend..."*

Tracy Chowdhury, one of the authors of the Chronicles of Shandahar, graduated from college with a bachelor's degree in Zoology. Since then she has worked for the University of Cincinnati as a scientist in cancer research, gotten married, had four children, and written the first few books in her fantasy/adventure series. When she is not writing and taking care of kids, she is helping her husband run their small real estate business. Tracy currently lives in Cincinnati, Ohio and you can check out her website at www.worldofshandahar.com

Riding with Alan Turing
by Benjamin Abbott

"You've been drinking, haven't you?" Billy asked the car. "Come on, fess up."

It was a sleek 2036 Lexus LS. Glossy black with tinted windows. Billy tapped his cigar, guessing the vehicle cost more than he made in a year. It didn't seem to know how to respond to him. Cars never did.

"Excuse me, sir," it hummed, "but I don't understand your question."

"Don't play dumb with me, you son of a bitch." Moonlight reflected off Billy's badge as he spoke. Bullfrogs croaked loudly in a nearby ditch. "I can smell it. Your breath reeks of booze."

"My sensors tell me that I'm functioning flawlessly, sir. I can send you a full reading."

"None of that shit!" Billy sprayed a few drops of saliva on the driver's side door. "No transmissions. Just talk."

"I still do not understand why you pulled me over, sir. I believe I was observing all traffic regulations. If this is not the case, I am unfit to drive. If it's a software problem, headquarters can repair it remotely. If it's a hardware problem, I'll have to be towed to a service station."

Billy took the cigar from his mouth and rested it between

stout fingers. "Listen to you," he said. "You're drunker than a skunk, rambling on and on about nonsense. I'm going to have to take you down to the county jail and let you sleep it off." He returned the cigar to his lips and blew smoke.

"I don't understand. I am not programmed for full comprehension of English. With your permission, I will send headquarters and let them take over."

"You don't listen. Too wasted, I guess. I already told you once. No transmissions. Even if you try, I'm blocking you." He stepped back from the car and put his hands on his hips.

Billy smoked awhile, letting the car continue to do its best to communicate with him. He figured he'd grown accustomed to the hum; he found it soothing. Leaning against his own vehicle, he had to smile. His partners called him crazy for it, but he'd been doing this for over a year, five nights a week. The practice had become second nature. He doubted he could abandon it if he tried.

It's a hot night, he thought, *but only because of what his sensors told him.* The personal cooling unit integrated into his armor kept him comfortable. Billy wondered if he missed feeling the heat. He used to sweat like a pig in August. As a bat swooped low overhead, he remembered sitting on his mother's porch in a rocking chair and sipping lemonade. It had been too hot to move, then. Too hot to think. Billy figured he could feel the heat again, if he wanted, but it wouldn't be the same.

"All right," he said, sauntering back up to the car. "I've heard enough. I'm a kind-hearted man. I'll let you off this time."

"What do you mean, sir?" the car asked.

It tried to continue, but Billy crossed his lips with a finger. "Quiet. I ain't done. If I catch you again, I'll have to be harsh." He drew his automatic pistol and pointed it at the car. "Blam. You know what I mean."

Maybe it didn't, but the car apparently understood enough to drive itself away. Billy thought it seemed relieved. He watched it wind out of view. He finished the cigar and then dropped the smoldering butt in the grass. He walked back to his vehicle.

"You ain't any smarter, now are you?" he said, slapping the hood.

It didn't reply. That was one voice he had grown tired of. Billy got in and put his hands on the steering wheel. He still drove. You could get away with driving on country roads, especially as a cop. Not busy enough to demand precision. Grinning, he grabbed a glazed donut and stomped on the gas. Yes, he loved donuts. If anything, fulfilling the stereotype pleased him. He tore down the road, not lifting his foot. Finishing the donut, Billy opened a beer with his free hand.

He passed another cop car going the other direction. Phil, his supervisor. Billy laughed and honked his horn. He spilled a little beer. He knew Phil would be pissed and didn't feel like dealing with him.

"Catch me if you can," Billy hollered, looking back. He sent the message to his comrade through the net but blocked any response.

The road curved abruptly. Warning lights flashed across his field of vision. He turned hard, maintaining control as long as he could. The wheel went soft when the AI finally took over. Tires squealed. Billy tipped the can up and chugged, bracing himself against the gees. The car slid along the edge of the road. It clipped shrubs, sending leaves and branches across the windshield. There was a red house with a short driveway on the right. He hoped the car didn't flip; that was a real pain in the ass.

Billy hooted when he noticed the bass-shaped mailbox ahead. He tried to remember the last time he'd been fishing. The impact stopped his car with a crunch. He felt nothing. Cop cars were designed for much worse. He finished the beer and opened the door. He enjoyed having the AI for backup. He could drive like a bat out of hell and still survive. The car could handle almost anything. He'd only flipped once.

Phil's car pulled up. Billy walked toward it. The window rolled down. "Guess you caught me," he said.

"You've got to stop doing this," said Phil.

"I don't hurt nothing. I'm playful, that's all."

"You just damaged property, Billy."

Billy turned to examine the mailbox. He could see the mouth and a few gills; most of it was hidden beneath his car. "Come on, what use is a mailbox these days?"

Phil cupped his face in his hands. "Being a sheriff's deputy isn't a game."

"Seems like one, sometimes."

"Not just driving crazy. You've got to stop it all. Harassing empty cars affects people. You delay them. Folks have to wait."

Billy had heard this many times. He yawned mightily, almost unhinging his jaws.

"When you started doing it, everyone laughed. It ain't funny no more. You pull damn near every empty car that comes by. Folks are complaining."

"What's the crime rate in my sector, Phil? That's what they care about. The numbers."

"You don't hardly report anything. It's gone too far." Phil's gray eyes narrowed. "Your dubious numbers ain't enough. Keep this up and they'll fire you. Maybe even lock you away."

Billy nodded and made for his car, not turning back. He knew Phil meant well, but he'd heard an earful. He returned to the road as quickly as he could. He specifically avoided looking up the mailbox's owner. It was probably a family he knew. If anyone cared, he suspected Phil would fix the damage. In spite of his preaching, the man always covered for him like that.

He cruised past solar panels, hardwoods, and pines. Three years ago, Billy had resolved to see how much his masters would tolerate. He'd seen his share of corruption over the decades. Uniform patrol boys who smoked captured weed and pocketed confiscated weapons. Sheriffs who spent public money on mistresses, parties, and drugs. Sadistic deputies who tormented some poor bastard at every traffic stop. And on and on. A cop could break certain rules without worrying about punishment.

Such conventional misconduct didn't appeal to Billy. He yielded to whim, to fancy. They had tolerated a lot more than he'd predicted. Each day, he tried to be a bit more outrageous. Aiding and abetting minors that were criminals. Slapstick battles with local punks. If anything, he thought the community preferred his new behavior. His superiors complained now and then, yet did nothing. Having a sister in the State Senate probably helped, but that couldn't be the whole explanation.

Back in the day, he was sure they'd have sacked him. Are the powers that be stronger now? As he drove toward his favorite country store, Billy pondered. A vast cybernetic juggernaut, sprawling across the continent. An ancient monster he'd helped grow fat. Perhaps they're too tough to care what a single guard does, he thought. Nothing seemed to matter as much as it used to. He shook his head.

Approaching the store, Billy slammed on brakes. He almost hit a rusting ice machine as he parked. From the outside, the store looked much the same as the country stores of his youth. A few glowing neon signs. No enticing holograms or bots. Not much flash. Old James, the owner, was a pragmatic man. He only spent his money on virtual glitz. From the ads on the net, the place looked like a palace.

Billy walked inside. At the battered table to his right, he saw Luna Luces reading a magazine. Something about the conflict in Taiwan. He looked at her plump face and unkempt hair approvingly. Like Billy, she hadn't made her body conform to societal standards of beauty. He fondly recalled adjusting armor to accommodate his gut.

Luna turned and met his eyes. "You owe me another hundred," she said.

"Crap," he replied. "Failed again, huh?"

"You think one will pass next month?"

"Course I do. Government's already got AIs smarter than anybody."

"You keep saying that." Luna stretched her right arm, twisting it, tendons straining. "Where's the proof?"

"No proof." Billy opened his wallet and handed her a hundred-dollar bill. "Here, take it. I'll win soon enough."

He moved deeper into the store, looking for cruelty-free pork rinds. The idea still felt odd to him, but Billy had always been fond of pigs. As he brushed past a rack of peanuts, he remembered watching pigs wallow, listening to their happy grunts. They were smarter than folks gave them credit for. Some days he'd wished he'd been born a hog. He didn't see any reason to skin one when the substitute tasted the same. Billy had accepted slaughter to please his palate. He wouldn't accept it only for authenticity.

Wallet in hand, he decided to pay with cash. He walked toward the bot manning the register. It roughly resembled Old James. Long white whiskers, slender frame. Thanks to rejuvenation therapy, James was as young as anybody, but he kept the white as a mark of seniority. Billy typically paid with a thought. He carried paper for Luna and emergencies. He had a single hundred left.

"I doubt I'll be needing this anytime soon," he said loudly, handing the bill to the bot. Luna snorted.

Billy sent James as he walked away from the counter. "You'd best get back to your store. Bot's giving me the evil eye."

"You goofball," James sent back. "A bot's a bot!"

"Come on, lazy coot." Billy opened the package of pork rinds and began munching. "Pull your ass out of bed someday. I ain't seen you in ages."

"I keep busy."

"I bet you do."

Ending the communication, he made for the exit. "You could consider taking net payment," he said to Luna. "Like normal folk."

"That'd be too easy for you," she replied.

He put his hand on the door.

"Hey, stay and talk a minute, Billy," she urged.

"All right." He sat in a wooden chair across from her. Handcrafted cherry with a rough finish. "Got a crime to report or something?"

"No." As she spoke, he noticed the dark hairs by her upper lip. "I want to know if you've found anything on the roads."

"I ain't found shit."

She smiled. "Are you going to continue looking?"

"Of course. Why wouldn't I?"

"I'm wondering what will happen if you leave." She set the magazine down.

"Oh, you been hearing things?"

"Maybe. I have ears, you know."

Billy offered her a piece of pork rind. She refused. "I ain't planning on leaving."

"You ignore a lot, Billy. The next guy probably won't. I'm worried."

"I don't ignore nothing. I handle things my way."

"Yeah." Luna crossed her large arms. "And my immigration status? How do you handle that?"

Billy shuffled in his seat. "Perhaps I should send you back to Mexico. Hell, you rob me every month."

She leaned closer. "Look, don't fool around. Will you be gone soon? Tell me."

"I can't say." He stood up, tipped his helmet, and turned away. "The Singularity's almost here, Luna."

"I hope so," she said as he left the store.

His car sprayed gravel. Billy decided he needed a moment to think. Years ago, it all would have given him a headache. Angry bosses. Uncertain futures. Luna. Foot planted firmly on the gas, he drove toward the tallest pine tree in the county. A good spot for reflection. A good spot to get in a brawl with teenage troublemakers. Did those things go together? He realized he desired both. He'd spent a lot of time near the tree in his youth. It had been the place to find snakes. Scarlet kings, especially. He used go looking for them with his buddies. At first, they'd been morons, shooting any venomous species they found. He remembered waiting for a copperhead to strike his shotgun's barrel, then pulling the trigger. Most Southerners were barbarians when it came to reptiles. They'd give you an earful about gun rights, but couldn't stand armed animals.

Eventually, Billy learned to respect fangs. He convinced his friends to do the same. They still hadn't known bunk about herpetology, not even scientific names, but at least they stopped killing. It'd been easy to find snakes back then. Timbers, pygmies, coachwhips, mole kings, pines. Something under every log and piece of tin. His hands tightened around the steering wheel. Species they'd shot were now threatened.

As he drove, Billy noticed an incoming message from his uncle Oliver. He sighed and accepted it. An image of the man appeared beside him, sitting in the passenger seat. Oliver, looking youthful and healthy, turned and spoke.

"Do you have a moment? I want to talk."

"Maybe," Billy replied, glancing over.

"I know we haven't exactly gotten along in the past."

Billy snorted. "Yeah."

"I've been meaning to change that. We're family, after all." Oliver's hands moved continuously, clasping, twisting, fingers tapping against thighs.

"Want a beer?" Billy held up a cold can.

Oliver's face darkened. "Look, I'm worried about you. Your sister told me what you've been doing."

Billy opened the beer for himself. "Elizabeth likes to talk."

"I've heard you joined a sort of cult." Oliver's tongue started to stumble. "A kind of utopian religion, I mean."

"I worship no gods. Not even any goddesses."

"But you've been acting, well, mighty strange lately. Looking for robots to rule the world or something. I know a few folks who believe the same thing. You don't have to be so zealous about it."

"I'm not doing anything wrong."

"Denial comes first." Oliver shook a finger. "What is it, Billy? Do you miss Mollie? Elizabeth didn't say nothing about another woman."

Jackass, Billy thought.

"It's hard for couples to stay together, the way things are changing. I can see why you'd find this technological faith. None of us expected to get young again."

"No woman, yeah." Billy sneered. "That don't mean I ain't got a lover."

He found his uncle's shocked silence profoundly gratifying. He'd figured that was a sore spot, especially after his cousin John appeared at the last family reunion as an Asian lady. At first, Oliver said she was as hot as the rising sun, rubbing his hands together. When he learned, he stomped away from the table, toppling a shrimp platter and terrifying a waiter.

"His name's Arnold," Billy continued, cutting off further communication. He kept Oliver's image, savoring the confusion and disgust on his face.

"My name's Alan," Billy murmured to himself. He wished it were true.

Prying about a failed marriage wasn't much of a peace offering. But his uncle hadn't been wrong, only tactless. Rejuvenation therapy had dissolved many unions. Billy had seen the statistics. People could accept forty or fifty years and then heaven. Indefinite monogamy in physical form was new. Frightening. At the same time, virtual reality provided a convenient place for discreet sexual encounters. Considering it, Billy wondered how any marriages endured.

Folks get wild when they believe they'll live forever. He imagined that was his problem. Though he supposedly faced death daily, he hadn't believed that for the last decade. Just a week ago, he'd read about a terrorism victim they'd remade from pieces. If that didn't do it, what would? He shrugged his shoulders and then drained the beer. According to both maps and memory, he was almost to the tree. He decided not to open another can. Punching the brakes, he skidded to the side of the road. The ground bore his mark; he'd been here five times in the past week. Thanks to vision augmentation, he could see the tall pine through the darkness. Rolling down his window, he breathed in deeply. The air smelled of life: decomposition, summer flowers, stagnant water, musk. Cicadas and katydids called from the canopy. A chorus of amphibians resounded from nearby ditches and trees.

None of it helped. He reclined in his padded seat and tried to focus. His mind drifted away from nature and to the net. Billy scanned headlines. Bombs in Bangalore. Legal squabbles over nanofactories. A reenactment of Waterloo in virtual reality that involved tens of thousands. Frenzied speculation on the upcoming congressional elections. He disconnected rather than learn more about Patrick McHenry's latest indiscretions. A chuck-will's-widow began to sing in the distance. A distracting sound, distinct from insect noises. He listened for a while. Then he sat up.

Reflection is a crock, he thought. *I need more information.*

Billy searched through his bank of sensory recording. He wished his systems were better integrated, with biological memory tied seamlessly to digital. They were not. He considered himself a primitive sort of cyborg. Normally, the recordings were external. Bits of himself outside of himself. As he looked, one stood out: his first meeting with Luna Luces. He had gotten complaints about a big Hispanic woman dancing in the middle of the road. It felt right. Their last conversation lingered in his mind. He wanted to understand her.

With a thought, he was there again, standing upright on pavement. His armor told him it was a colder night. The moon hadn't risen, but a few stars sparkled. He walked toward Luna as she lay curled across the double yellow lines. She wore a red and black dress. A storage chip rested in the open palm of her right hand. He'd never figured out the significance of that chip. He hadn't asked her about it. She hadn't mentioned it.

"The Amazon is almost lost," she said. She spoke in slurred Spanish; Billy heard a quick translation. Not her voice, but a close approximation. "Millions are homeless in Bangladesh."

"You need to get up, lady," he heard himself whisper. His systems translated it into louder Spanish.

"Lady? Am I a lady? Does that make you treat me a certain way?" She closed her fingers around the chip, and then covered her face with the fist. "What if I weren't a lady? How would you treat me then?"

"Gender is a social construct." He reached down to her. "Please stand up."

She smiled, but didn't take his hand. "But I'm still a lady to you. If gender doesn't matter, why use it?"

"English is a barbaric, sexist language. Spanish too." He waved his hand in a circle. "Up. Folks don't like it when you block traffic."

"You have to keep the system running."

As she spoke, a giant pickup truck came around a curve. "That's my job," he said. Billy didn't like hearing those words come out of his mouth.

"We're both fat." She didn't seem to notice the truck, which had stopped behind her. "Does that mean we're poor? In this country, only the poor are fat."

"The poor and the strange. It's the same in your country."

The truck honked. The man inside looked around and frowned. "I don't have a country." Luna gazed at Billy.

"Why are you doing this?" He held up a palm to the truck.

"Why should I move? Cars are smart now. They won't hit me."

"Not by accident anyway." The truck honked again.

"You know their programming prevents them from hitting people. No one can override that."

"Maybe this one's gotten smarter." Billy pointed his thumb at the truck. "Developed a personality. If so, you're about to get squished."

Luna laughed, rolling onto her back and wiggling her feet, toes aimed at the stars. "A car is a machine, not a person."

"Machines are people." The man in the truck stared blankly as Billy spoke; he'd escaped back into virtual reality. "If not now, they will be soon."

"Machines don't have souls." Luna sat and rubbed her eyes. "We've been taken over by machines. Conquered. They're everywhere. In my head. I don't want any more of it."

Billy offered his hand again. "Where do you live?"

"We should return to living in villages." Luna swayed from side to side while she talked. "Living as a part of nature again. We think we're above nature and God now. It's a lie. Everything about machines is false."

"Hell no." Billy took a step away from Luna. "Technology is the way out of this damn mess."

Luna snorted. "Technology hasn't helped us yet. Some are rich; some are poor, as always. It's the same. All the same. Technology has only made the power structure stronger. It's made us all like machines."

"It's going to be different. We're too stupid to build a reasonable society ourselves. We need help from the machines."

"You're the power structure, the state, the machine, in that armor." Luna waved her left hand. "Can you even feel the night's chill? You're isolated, alone."

The debate was more absurd than Billy had remembered. A wasted illegal immigrant and a renegade cop, arguing about the world's ills in the middle of a rural street. If he controlled a body, he would have laughed. Instead, he spoke to Luna. "Where do you live? I'll walk you home."

She staggered to her feet. "Okay, policeman. Why haven't you beaten me up?"

"I'd rather talk. Where do you live?"

"A mile or two down the road." She pointed with the hand holding the chip.

They started walking, Billy supporting Luna. The truck drove past them. "Why did you come out here?" he asked.

"The night is beautiful. I saw a rabbit as I was walking. In the summer, I've seen snakes."

"On rainy nights, I bet you see frogs."

"Yes." Luna sighed. "I want to go back to growing corn in Tlaxcala. I want to work with my hands again."

"I've had my fill of manual labor."

"You worked in some damn factory, right?"

"Nope. I grew up on a farm."

Luna frowned. "Oh."

Billy guided her around a ditch. Her boots got muddy. "Nature's nice to visit, but I wouldn't want to live there."

"The machines have conquered your mind, man. They won't save you, no matter how intelligent they become." She stopped walking and looked him in the eyes. "You might as well be waiting for the return of Christ. We have to make our own future!"

Billy raised his eyebrows and took a step back. "You speak awfully well for a drunk."

"I'm enhanced." She pressed a finger against her left temple.

They started walking again, no longer speaking. A few vehicles passed them. Billy wished he hadn't left the store so quickly. *We should have talked longer,* he thought. *I should ask her about that chip.* As they trundled on the side of the road, Luna carried it in a clinched fist, pressed against her belly. For a moment, he wondered if it contained an AI, or part of one. Luna always kept her secrets. *Was that one of them?*

"I'm in love with a girl in Georgia," Luna said after some time.

"I'm in love with a boy named Arnold," Billy answered.

"She's a farmer. I can feel her here, through the soil. Without machines, we're connected."

Billy nodded. They walked. He thought about what he would do if they kicked him off the force. He could steal his car and guns, become an outlaw. If they cracked all his sensory recording and viewed them, they'd certainly throw him in prison. He didn't want to be abused. He knew how prisons were, though he tried not to the think about it. *Maybe I should just erase everything,* he thought. But he knew they could read his mind almost as easily.

"This is my place," Luna said as they approached a tiny house behind a short driveway.

"Go sleep it off," Billy suggested.

"Thank you for not arresting me," she responded, hugging him. She put her chin on his shoulder and vomited down his back.

With a thought, Billy warped time, skipping over many hours. The sun appeared overhead. He got out of his car in front of Luna's place. Pale yellow curtains covered its single window. There was a little rock garden in the yard. He ascended the few concrete steps and knocked on the metal door.

"Coming," she said. English. Her voice.

"Take your time."

She opened the door. "I'm embarrassed about last night."

"What were you drinking?"

"Tequila. I wasn't myself. I'm not like that."

"May I come inside?"

"No." She closed the door. "Let's talk in the yard."

Billy went down the steps. She followed. "What are you like?" he asked.

"I'm not a primitivist."

"Only when drunk, huh?"

"I work with AIs. I spend my time wired into the net, managing them."

"How are they?"

"Look, they're all amazing at what they do, but they're specialized. I've yet to encounter one with much general intelligence. They can pretend, but it's superficial."

"That's about how I'd describe my experience with cars."

Luna laughed. "You're looking for salvation on the roads?"

"It's not salvation. It's science. A few years, AIs will be far beyond humans. Everyone knows that'll change the world."

"Yeah, yeah. I've been hearing about the Singularity for decades. I'm not a primitivist, but I am a skeptic."

"Are you hungry, skeptic?" Billy pointed at his car. "I brought food."

"I am, actually. But aren't you on duty?"

"Who cares?"

They ate moon pies and ham omelets off the hood of his vehicle, drinking creamy coffee. Luna rolled her eyes at the selection, but consumed more than he did. Billy savored the tastes and smells. He never skipped over meals. Some of his favorite sensory recordings consisted exclusively of eating.

"I'm not poor, you know," Luna said, wiping her mouth with a sleeve. "Compared with most of my relatives, I'm quite rich."

"After the Singularity, we'll all be rich."

"No one should be poor today. But look at Africa or Latin America."

"Poverty exists because of assholes like me."

"Why do you believe thinking machines will change that?"

"They'll have to. Nothing that smart could accept the current social order."

"Augmented people seem to accept it."

Billy scowled. "Sunday best on shit."

Luna snickered. "I'm sorry. I'm poking holes in your theories."

"I'm happy you ain't intimidated by the badge."

"I'm not easy to scare." She turned to look at her house. "And if you wanted to arrest me, you already would have."

He picked at an omelet lazily. "So what are your theories? Are you strictly a skeptic?"

"You know, maybe I am."

"Come on, tell me something."

"I should get back to work."

"I want to talk more." He dropped his spork. It stuck in a

エ

leaf by one of the car's wheels.

"We will."

"You never told me your name. I'm Billy." He stepped toward her.

"Luna Luces." She started walking away. "I'll see you later, Billy."

"Hey, you can't run off before giving me a straight answer! What's your theory?"

She went inside and shut the door.

Billy ended sensory playback. He was in the car again, sitting. The chuck-will's-widow hadn't stopped singing. To make sure he could, he lifted his arms. He and Luna had talked a great deal since that encounter. About society, identity, the future. Months had passed. They'd gone on hikes together, finding snakes and salamanders. She'd won hundreds of dollars from him on the recurring bet. He still wasn't sure exactly what she believed.

Billy stepped out into the night and lit a Brazilian cigar. He would miss it, he decided. The badge, the car, the guns. He wouldn't give them up without a fight. Even with those privileges, he didn't feel free. He'd be damned if he'd tolerate life as law-abiding civilian. He hoped he could keep the job for at least another month. *I don't want to fight them quite yet,* he thought.

A bullet bounced off his chest. He figured it was the Sanders kids. He was near their family's land. They often took pot shots at him. Technically, he could charge them with numerous counts of attempted murder. *Antiquated laws,* he thought. They weren't serious. With even the cheapest Aimbot-brand hunting scope, misses didn't happen within a hundred meters. If the boys wanted to hurt him, they'd shoot at his face. And a head shot wouldn't kill him, even if his visor didn't drop.

Taking a drag from the cigar, Billy focused his sensors. An AI distilled thermal, radar, chemical, and other readings into information he could understand. As he suspected, the Sanders brothers were a ways up a hill, hiding in a decrepit shed. Another bullet struck him, deflecting off his shoulder into the woods. The chuck-will's-widow became silent. He slipped behind his car to get out of view. He noticed they'd brought along Sal, the family dog. *About time to teach these little bastards a lesson,* he thought.

Discarding the cigar, he switched on his armor's active camouflage. The visor fell to conceal his face. He snuck across the road with confidence. His camo wasn't perfect, but he doubted the kids had any way to defeat it. He stopped communication with the net, no longer sending any signals. As he climbed the hill, he might as well have been invisible. *I'm a goddamn ninja,* he thought.

The shed was surrounded by all manner of junk: road signs, fuel containers, broom handles, piles of bricks. Billy paused to examine the scene, enjoying the power to see but not be seen. Ethan Sanders stood in front of the shed, holding a shotgun. His tight-fitting t-shirt was gradually shifting from green to indigo. Indian-style pop music sounded from the bill of his NCSU cap. Sal was beside him, sniffing the air. Sensors told Billy Dale Sanders was inside the shed by its upper window. *Figures that brat would be the sniper*, Billy thought.

Sal gave him away, somehow. Billy had never thought much about olfactory camouflage. He'd assumed whatever his suit had would be enough to fool a dog, but she started barking. Dale came thundering down from the loft and ran out of the shed, rifle in hand. Ethan clutched the shotgun and looked around. The music stopped. *They know I'm here*, Billy thought. *Reckon I should greet them.*

He produced his pistol and fired at a small pine twelve meters from Ethan. The explosion nearly severed the tree. Billy watched its upper half slowly topple. Ethan jumped like a bunny, dropping his hat. Billy could remember when it'd been illegal to use explosive bullets against people. He hadn't imagined cops would be packing them. But people had changed. Against armor and synthetic bodies, you needed all the power you could get. Billy took a few shots at the ground, spraying both kids with sand and dirt. He'd had to fiddle with settings to turn armor-piercing rounds into the glorified firecrackers he preferred. He didn't quite know why they gave him such ammunition. Billy hadn't ever had to battle cyborg thugs or terrorists. He'd never even been in an earnest gunfight, despite all his years as a deputy.

The Sanders brothers cursed and hollered, but still they couldn't find him. Billy snickered as he listened to Sal's yapping. Dale attempted to use a brick pile for shelter, holding the rifle over his head. Billy unloaded the rest of his magazine into a barrel beside Ethan, creeping up behind the bewildered Dale as he fired. Grinning eagerly, Billy decloaked and planted his boot on the child's ass.

"Daddy's here!" he said, holstering the pistol and clenching his right hand into a fist.

Dale stumbled forward, then tripped and fell face first. Ethan leveled the shotgun at Billy's chest. Billy didn't budge as two slugs bounced off his armor. *I should try to bat them out of the air sometime*, he thought. Ethan ditched the firearm and bolted toward the shed.

"You're learning," said Billy.

He leapt after Ethan, cornering him against the side of the shed. He wound up for an epic punch, using his exoskeleton's full power. Ethan ducked, covering his head with both hands. Billy's fist blew through the wood effortlessly, his arm sinking in up Ethan's shoulder.

"Should've watched your butt," said Dale.

Billy felt Sal's jaws clamp down on his behind. Thank God for ass armor, he thought. He tried to shake the dog off, but she held him firmly. A bullet from Dale's rifle struck Billy's back and ricocheted into the shed above. Coming from below, Ethan's laughter seemed deafeningly loud. Billy's cheeks started to feel warm.

"Sweet Jesus," he said, pulling his arm free and turning to face Dale.

Sal growled. Ethan slunk away, retrieving his cap as he retreated. Ignoring them both, Billy hefted a nearby propane tank over his head. The tank was rusted and ancient; it had been empty for years. Dale started running, kicking up pine needles. Billy's armor made him feel like a giant. He hurled the tank. It sailed for fifteen meters before striking a tree. He'd missed by a centimeter. Sal whimpered and released her grip.

"Go to Dale," Ethan said to the dog, pointing. "I'll handle this." He drew a Bowie knife from his jeans.

"You crazy?" said Billy. He slipped back and grabbed one of the many signs the boys had collected. An old stop sign.

"You bet." Ethan's grin displayed white teeth.

Billy hefted the sign aloft as if it were an ax. The kid waited slightly crouched, slashing at the air. Billy swung his weapon down. Ethan leapt forward and to the side. The metal octagon cut into the soil. As Billy freed it, Ethan chopped at his hands. He knocked the boy away and then swatted him on the rear with the sign.

"Could have cut you in half," Billy said.

"Like hell."

Their duel continued. When Billy swung at Ethan's feet, he jumped over the blow. When aimed at his head, he ducked under it. They'd played similar games before. Ethan began to pant. Sweat beaded beneath his baseball cap. Eventually, Billy knocked the knife from his hand. With primal growl, he twisted the sign's pole in two and discarded the pieces.

"All right," Ethan said, baring his palms. "Truce."

Billy nodded, sneering, blood pounding from the feat of strength. He examined the kid. Folks are better looking than they used to be, he thought. Designer babies. Superior genes. He wasn't pretty himself, but he could appreciate beauty. As he watched, Ethan produced a fat joint and lit it. The boy stood about seven meters from him.

"Give me one," Billy said, stepping closer.

"It's regal bud. My daddy's best."

Ethan handed him a smoldering fatty. They smoked together for a moment. Billy noticed the Sanders kid was growing his first wisps of facial hair.

"Got dirt on your chin," he said.

"Yeah." Ethan smiled a little. "You're a weird fucking cop."

"What, you think I should throw your scrawny ass in jail for liking dope and guns?"

Ethan shrugged. "That's what y'all pigs do, right?"

Billy could remember doing that. How many teens had he sent to juvy over the years? Names and faces came to mind.

"Us pigs love dope and guns," he said. "We don't lock ourselves up, now do we?"

"Guess not." Ethan nodded and smoked.

"Look, things are about to change. This country's been run by goddamn idiots from the start. Not no more." The joint fell from Billy's lips. "Mankind's dumber than stale shit, but that don't mean we can't create something smart."

Lost in his own words, Billy hadn't noticed Ethan backing away. He hadn't been watching his sensors. Suddenly, Ethan bolted. Simultaneously, Dale appeared from around the shed's corner, holding a rocket launcher.

"Scorched pork!" he cried.

Billy's visor dropped automatically as the projectile came for him. He tried to dodge, but the missile compensated, curving through the air. A flash. A bang. Smoke. He was on his behind, back against a large pine. It hadn't really been hurt. Despite the flames coming from his breastplate, he felt comfortably cool. Billy stood. He wondered if they knew his armor could withstand such rockets or simply assumed he would survive anything. Or if they wanted to kill him.

"Sweetest thing I've ever seen!" he heard Ethan holler. Dale cackled.

"Get your dog," Billy said, amplifying his voice. "Start running."

He slung down his assault shotgun. With explosive ammo, it might as well have been a grenade launcher. They started running, Sal beside them. Billy pumped round after round into the old shed. As he expected, the kids stored all manner of illicit weapons within. Explosion beget explosion. Shards of wood and metal flew outward, sticking in trees. Bricks sailed as if they were foam. Black smoke rose and coalesced into a column. The kids cowered on their bellies. When Billy stopped firing, little was left of the shed. Looking over the rubble, he winced. Debris coated the surrounding area for many meters. *Imagine this won't improve my standing with the sheriff,* he thought. Stowing the shotgun, he hoped he hadn't killed too many vertebrates. He hadn't thoroughly scanned the shed for life.

"Holy shit," Dale muttered, turning toward the burning ruins.

"You got us, piggy," said Ethan. "We can't fucking top that."

"It is a beauty, ain't it?" Billy said.

The three of them gazed at the lingering flames for a little while. Ethan conjured up more marijuana, and they all smoked. Sal whined and nuzzled her masters.

"Did you do stuff like this as a kid?" Dale asked.

"Nope," said Billy. "Hell no. Where'd y'all get that rocket from, anyway?"

Dale's eyes twinkled, but he refused to speak.

Billy stared at him for a moment. "Hey, do y'all kill snakes?"

Ethan made a nasty face. "We ain't that ignorant," he said.

"Snakes are badass," said Dale. "Especially rattlesnakes."

"Damn right."

Billy nodded. "Y'all lose many toys?" he asked, gesturing at the destroyed shed.

"Yeah."

Billy handed Dale his pistol. "I'll leave a bunch of ammo where my car is."

"Got anything else for us?" asked Ethan.

"My butt still hurts," said Dale, looking at Billy expectantly.

"I got cut by some shrapnel." Ethan didn't show any wounds.

Billy snorted and separated the medical kit from his armor. He knew they liked the pain killers. They begged for them every time.

"For a pig, you're all right," remarked Ethan, snatching the kit greedily.

"Don't kill anyone," said Billy, turning to leave. "If the flames last too long, put them out."

He walked back to the car, whistling to himself. He took a backup pistol and holstered it. He left two hundred rounds in the grass. Explosive but not armor-piercing. Not after that rocket. An owl called in the distance. A barred owl. Fifty three meters away. Billy stopped whistling and mimicked the call. His armor could have reproduced the sound flawlessly. His voice did not.

He got into the car and waved at Oliver's image. To his left, the hilltop faintly glowed. A report of stolen property had come while he'd been disconnected. He ignored it and checked long-range sensors. No empty vehicles nearby. Logs said one had gone past while he'd been fighting. Nothing to play with. He checked the headlines. Duke professor declares human-like AI impossible. Billy blinked and stretched. His armor had already begun repairing itself. The damage wasn't major, but it was quite visible. He tried to tidy up. When he returned to the road, Billy angled toward the east side of the county, looking for a car to harass. There wasn't as much traffic as there used to be. Not nearly. Why ride when you could go virtual instead? Folks used the net for everything now: work, family, games, love, news, sex. Thinking about it, he preemptively ignored any complaints of explosions in his sector.

A storage chip rested in the pine needles hundreds of meters ahead. Functional. As he drove, Billy tried to access it remotely. The encryption stopped him. He stopped the car and got out. He knew most discarded chips were worthless, even the protected ones. It was an antiquated design in a purple plastic case. He picked the chip up and examined it. It had a physical port. He attached it to his armor and continued to battle the security features.

As he turned to go, he detected a snake slithering toward him from many meters away. A pygmy rattler. He switched camo on and stood motionless, one foot on the pavement, one on needles and sand. A tiny brown and gray head appeared at the edge of his vision. He watched as the snake slowly crawled closer. Dark spots down its back with a hint of red between them. A button rattle at the end of the sharply tapering tail. He didn't move until it had crossed the road and vanished into the pines. He saw each muscle contraction and cautious pause, each probing tongue flick.

"Thank you," he muttered, decloaking. "I feel blessed."

Inside the car again, Billy's programs unlocked the chip. He hunched over the trinket and smiled. His heart seemed to skip as he attempted access. It was blank, completely scrubbed of data. He held it before his face and stared. A smooth surface, marked only by a tiny wireless receiver and physical connector. *You should have been something,* he thought. *Haven't I searched enough?* He rolled down his window and cast the purple chip onto the road. It bounced and skittered, landing near an aged orange reflector. He drew his pistol and blew it to shards.

Nearly unconsciously, he slipped into another memory with Luna Luces. They were swimming, floating through silty water like jellyfish. Billy felt the sun on his hairy shoulders. Light reflected off the lake's ripples. He smelled pollen in the air. A horsefly buzzed overhead. Then he dove, aquatic plants tickling his belly as he skimmed along the bottom. In the olive haze ahead, bass and brim darted away. When he broke the surface, Luna launched a tsunami at his face.

He splashed back. They smacked and slapped, creating as

much foam as a speedboat motor. She closed to grapple, overpowering and winding behind him, pushing his head under. He held his breath, squirming and kicking. The blurry image of a turtle paddled a meter or two away. He stopped struggling and watched it swim, noting the stripes and claws. He wondered why he'd chosen this recording. A recent one. Gradually, Luna relented, gripping his armpits and lifting. She gaped in laughter, displaying teeth and tongue.

"Hay una tortuga, hombre," she said, pointing.

The juvenile yellowbelly slider didn't give them much chance to stare. After extending its neck, the turtle spun around and retreated. Luna frowned.

"I've heard the universe is balanced on a turtle shell," said Billy.

"There are turtles all the way down," she replied.

He reclined, turning chest to the sky. He saw a polka-dotted kite beneath the clouds. "Tell me a bit more about your work."

"I can't tell you what you want to hear."

"They're machines, not people, huh?"

"Casper might convince a person if she weren't so crazy." She was by his side now, bobbing on her back.

"Go on."

"Yesterday she told me most humans were pointless. She wanted to sterilize them, stop the breeding. She said Mexicans were the worst."

"I know folks who think the same way."

"It's not like communicating with a person. She's alien."

"Oh, please." He splashed at Luna. "I wouldn't have expected you to speak up for the breeders."

"That's not what I mean, and you know it." Luna paddled with her feet. "I don't believe she's self-aware. She doesn't understand how her comments would offend me or anyone else. She can crunch numbers and ideas, but I don't detect real consciousness."

"I'll take what I can get. Without the machines, we're trapped in flesh, shit, and gender."

"No. Who do you think makes the AIs, Billy? They're tools of the bosses."

A bald eagle flew far above, passing across the sun. "Should I just drown myself then?"

"Only if you drown me too."

"Do you think they'd let us die? I am a cop."

"If we're lucky." She closed her eyes.

They floated along, meaty buoys in gentle waves. Wind blew the flies away. Billy thought of disconnecting. The water massaged his spine down to the buttocks. Luna whispered poetry by Octavio Paz. Fish started to nip at his skin cautiously, then vigorously, tearing away lifeless cells. He remembered how people used to use nibbling fish for exfoliation. Turkish fish in spas. Time passed. He couldn't quite bring himself to shift back.

"You're going to get a tan," said Luna.

"Doubt it." He opened his eyes.

"I don't have any answers for you." She lay in the water serenely. "Be glad you have questions."

"Thanks, guru." Billy found the bottom with his feet and stood. "You should let me talk to Casper."

And he was in the car again, flying down the road to the general store. The pistol rested on his lap. He holstered it, blinking, shaking his head. An incoming message from Sheriff Robert Brewington had summoned him back. He took command of the vehicle, accelerated, and accepted.

"This is the end of the line, William," said the sheriff. His image appeared in the passenger seat, replacing Oliver's.

"What'd Phil tell you?" Billy asked.

"Only what I could wring out of him."

"Sounds like Phil."

"It was plenty." Robert's figure was strikingly muscular, with wide shoulders and balloon biceps. Sitting beside him, Billy felt sure the vehicle's mass had increased. "This has gone on far too long."

"Maybe so."

Robert looked directly at Billy. "How many cars have you harassed tonight?"

Billy kept his eyes on the road. He didn't respond.

"Look at me, Billy. Let the AI drive."

"I don't think that's necessary."

"Damn it, look at me."

The wheel went loose in Billy's hands as the AI took over. For a moment, he pretended to drive. He held the wheel steady. He pressed the gas pedal when the car accelerated. Feeling stupid, he turned to the sheriff. "Did you have to do that?"

"Yes, I did. I want you to understand that I'm serious."

"I understand." He released the wheel and put his hands in his lap.

"I'm not sure you do. I don't know what's wrong with you, Billy. I've told you repeatedly this isn't acceptable behavior for a deputy. Way I see it, you're forcing me to act."

Billy twiddled his thumbs. "What are you going to do?"

"First I'm going to ask you a few more questions. I've just received reports of explosions near the Sanders property. Your sector. What the hell happened?"

"Old shed blew up. Gas leak or something."

Robert sighed. Billy almost felt the man's breath on his

cheeks. "That's what I thought you'd say. You've been feeding me shit for months, haven't you?"

Billy shrugged. "No."

"I like you, Billy. We used to drink together. Remember that? But if I don't do something, this will cost me my job."

"Maybe we both could use a vacation."

"I think your woman's the root of this. Women make men crazy. It's a scientific fact." Robert smiled. "How long were you two married? Sixty years? You should have put your foot down. I don't care what happened. A relationship like that should be preserved."

They zipped around a turn with mechanical precision. Robert's image swayed as if it were affected by the motion. Subtle, but Billy noticed. He wondered why everyone he knew tried to explain his insanity. Luna was the only exception.

"Cheating is bound to happen," Robert continued, adding gestures for emphasis. "I cheated; my wife cheated. It's the twenty-first century. She wanted to end things a few years ago. I had to get tough. You have to be tough. I told her she couldn't leave. We're married. Period. That's it."

"I've heard plenty, boss. Tell me what you're going to do."

"No, I'm not finished." He wagged a finger. "Go find Mollie and tell her you're man and wife. You need her. I think that's your problem. I have the suspicion you were too much of a gentleman. Women like strong men. You're doing all this to make up for being a pussycat at home. I've seen it before."

Billy scowled. "I became a homosexual, Bob. That's why we split."

"Jesus Christ." Robert put his hands on his thighs and stared at Billy for a moment. "Is that your excuse? You need help, man."

"We all need help. The world needs help."

"I guess I should get to the point. I'm suspending you, Billy. Effective immediately." The sheriff made a sharp, sweeping gesture. "No more lies. No more excuses. There'll be a full investigation. Maybe you'll be vindicated. I hope I don't have to put you in prison."

There it is, Billy thought. *But I'm not licked yet.* "Have you talked to my sister?"

Robert's brow furrowed. "No, and I don't need to."

"Elizabeth won't be happy."

"I don't need her permission."

"Guess you want that vacation."

Robert was silent.

"I think you should talk to her," Billy said.

Robert cupped his face in his hands. "All right. You've bought yourself maybe an hour. If I hear about any more explosions, you will go to jail." His figure vanished.

Billy reclaimed control of the car. He immediately began searching for programs to prevent the sheriff from accessing his systems. *This is it,* he thought. If they caught him tampering with public property, he'd be done for. He searched furiously, diving through anarchist sites offering open-source software and traditionally criminal ones demanding dollars. He connected to a few of the people's AIs and let them work. He didn't know how he'd keep the car after going rogue. They watched the roads. He focused the AIs on liberating his armor. He could hide in the woods, basking like a lizard to recharge. It could extract nutrients from almost anything. He could scavenge beer and tobacco. What else did he need? *I'll wait for the Singularity as a hermit,* he thought. He hoped Elizabeth talked the sheriff into giving him more time.

Billy drove aimlessly, roaring across sandy roads that

should have been paved decades ago, swerving to avoid the occasional rabbit or toad. He watched the AIs tamper with his armor, sometimes testing the encryption. It looked safe; he didn't think his masters would notice. The programs didn't seem to be making much progress. Billy shrugged. He'd always assumed illegal AIs would be more effective. *Whatever happens,* he thought, *I won't eat a poisoned apple.*

"I'll see the end of millennium with Arnold," he muttered to himself.

A 1949 Bentley Mark VI appeared at the edge of Billy's sector. Modified engine, of course. Empty. He made a wild U-turn and headed toward it. The move wouldn't win him points with Robert, but he'd be damned if he was going to waste what might be his last hour. He zoomed past the fish hatchery, past the creek that used to be full of cottonmouths. He nearly struck a meandering and obviously well-fed raccoon. His victim floated over the country road like a ghost lost in space and time. An odd English antique. Billy turned on the lights and sirens. He didn't have to; silently signaling the car over would have worked as well. It drifted to the side of the road, gradually decelerating. Both cars stopped. Billy started blocking the Bentley's transmissions. He stepped out and walked up to it.

"Why'd you swerve back there?" he asked.

"Where?" Unlike most vehicles, this car's voice wasn't noticeably electronic. Billy was disappointed that it didn't seem to have a British accent. He couldn't place the sound. No images came to mind.

"Don't even remember, huh?" He tapped on the driver's side window.

"No, I don't." Billy was convinced the voice was androgynous. He couldn't assign a gender to it.

"What you been drinking? Whiskey?"

"I'm a car." The Bentley's lights flicked on and off.

"Don't give me lip." Billy took a step back. "Do you want to go to jail?"

"No, I don't. What's the problem, officer?"

"Are you stupid or just drunk? Don't think I'll treat you better because of your age."

"No, I wouldn't expect that."

Billy cupped his chin and debated his next move. He wished he had another cigar. He should have bought more, but it was too late now. "You an early model or something?" he asked after a moment. "The AI, I mean."

"I'm state of the art." He'd heard that before. Many vehicles had advertising claims embedded in their speech systems.

"How fast you go?" He swept his right hand through the air.

"The speed of light. You?"

Billy shook his head. "Acceleration?"

"Instantaneous."

"Steering precision?"

"Flawless."

He stamped his foot. "I reckon you're stoned too."

"What do you want from me, officer?"

"Hell, I don't know." His arms went limp and swung by his sides. He wondered if this would be the end of his freedom, pestering an idiot Bentley AI in the dregs of the night. He checked on the armor's progress, but those AIs seemed little better. He looked at the Bentley, his eyes wandering down the long hood to the winged brand symbol. "Give me some advice."

The car inched closer to him, wheels angling and turning

slowly. "Do you play chess?"

"Used to."

"Suppose I have my king at e8, and no other pieces. You have your king at e6 and rook at h1. What do you do?"

Billy wiped his brow. He realized he was hot, sweating. The tampering had somehow disabled his cooling unit. He blinked and rubbed his eyes. It should be operational again soon, the anarchist AI told him. *This ain't making no sense,* he thought. The AI offered an incomprehensible explanation. Deciding not to press the issue, he took off his helmet and set it on top of the Bentley.

"What do you do, copper?" The car flashed its lights again.

He tried to picture the chessboard. "No pawns, huh? No queens?"

"No."

"Why that setup?"

"Endgame. Simple."

"I want a beginning." Billy looked down at his boots. His toes were sweating. I need to find me a wallow, he thought.

"I don't believe you really play chess."

"Maybe I've forgotten."

"Do you play checkers?"

Billy laughed, a short, sharp bark. "Goddamn it, give me some advice. I'm starting to think you're an idiot savant."

"Don't drink and drive."

"Wonderful." Billy looked around. He'd noticed a pool by the side of the road earlier. "Wait here a moment."

He walked toward the pool. Nearby, a tree frog called with a rhythm of an automatic weapon. Pine woods, he thought. Common enough species. Leaning over, he peered into sandy brown water. Kneeing in the grass, he removed his gauntlets. One slid into the ditch palm up, the index finger barely penetrating the pool's surface. Billy cupped his hands and doused his face. The water trickled down to his shoulders and back. It wasn't cold, but the evaporation would cool him.

"That's not the Fountain of Youth," the Bentley said.

"I know." Billy splashed himself again. "We've already found youth. We need wisdom." He sighed. The treefrog stopped singing.

"You're not cut out for this job anymore, piglet. Things are changing."

Billy stood and turned to face the Bentley. "I hope so."

"I'm a lot like you. Old body, young mind. Wait a little while. We'll work it out."

"Okay."

"Give Arnold a hug for me." The Bentley glided back onto the road, graceful as a serpent. "Be seeing you, fleshbag."

Billy glimpsed his reflection in chrome and white as the car sped past. His face and hands were streaked with silt. A dirty, silly ape. It made him smile. The helmet sailed off the top of the Bentley, bouncing slightly when it struck the pavement. It landed about a meter from him. He watched until the road curved and the car faded.

He wanted to follow. He wanted to find Luna and talk about everything. He wanted to hide from the sheriff, to tear off the battered breastplate and disappear into hills and pines. He thought of blowing up his car, spending the rest of his ammo shooting at the moon. He dreamed of making love with Arnold under the stars, before dawn came. In this moment, forecasts and predictions failed him; he couldn't imagine tomorrow. The far future seemed too protean and portentous to ponder. Billy only looked ahead in minutes, but he saw plenty he needed to do.

Benjamin Abbott is a PhD student in American Studies at the University of New Mexico, practicing anarchist revolutionary on the streets, and genderqueer transhumanist visionary. Eir interest in radical politics began with reading Howard Zinn's, A People's History of the United States, and continued into Shulamith Firestone's socialist-feminist manifesto, The Dialectic of Sex. Ey simultaneously critiques and contributes to the transhumanist movement at eir blog Queering the Singularity.

The Perfect Femdroid
by Karl Beecher

"All right, I'm coming!" Avram yelled as the doorbell rang. He stumbled through the dark living room, running his hand along the wall in search of the light switch. Stepping forward gingerly, he tried to place his bare feet on anything resembling carpeting, but more often he stepped on piles of paper, fast-food cartons, or empty boxes from his DVD collection. At least they had better be empty; replacing a DVD was a time-consuming business these days.

The doorbell rang yet again.

"I said I'm coming!" Avram shouted even louder.

At last, he succeeded in locating the switch, and the full chaos of the interior was revealed. This single room was practically Avram's whole apartment, except for the little staircase leading up to his tiny bedroom. Most of his possessions were on open display: books lying on the sofa, magazines strewn about the floor, and clothing hanging over the furniture. The mess did not bother him. He almost never had visitors to worry about, making this persistent late-night caller an annoying rarity.

He stepped up to the front door, while kicking from the sole of his foot a slice of salami he had somehow picked up, and tapped on a small control panel mounted on the wall. A little screen beside it powered up showing a grainy image of someone standing on the other side of the door. Avram peered closer and saw it was Charles Lace, a colleague of his at the Cybernetics Institute, wrapped in a dark trench coat with a bundle of blankets in his arms.

"Charles?" Avram pulled back the latches and opened the door. He pulled his robe tighter as the cold air rushed into the room, and he observed the man on his doorstep for a moment. Even though he barely knew Charles, Avram could definitely discern that his colleague was distraught. "Charles, what are you doing here? It's almost midnight!"

"I'm sorry, Avram," replied Charles in a fragile, timid voice. "I didn't know who else to turn to. Can I come in please?"

"I guess," Avram sighed. He stood aside as his visitor struggled through the doorway, heaving the floppy load in his arms. Something seemed to be wrapped inside the sagging bundle -- he was certainly holding more than just blankets. Once inside, Avram closed the door behind him. "Charles, what is it you want? What the hell have you got there?"

"Sorry," Charles panted. He looked around the room for somewhere to drop his bundle. "Can I, um...?"

"Yes, yes."

Avram scuttled over to the sofa and grudgingly cleared off the papers and books that littered its surface. Charles knelt down slowly in front of the sofa and gently laid upon it his mysterious possession, treating it as if it were a baby.

"All right," Avram said. "Now, can you please tell me what this is about?"

Still kneeling, Charles began to unravel the blankets. "I need your help," he said. The final layers of cloth parted to reveal the motionless face of a woman.

Avram recoiled, almost leaping back from the sofa. "Charles! What the hell is...?"

"It's not what you think. She's not real. She's a femdroid."

Avram raised his eyebrow. "Right." His annoyance

morphed into an uncomfortable sense of creepiness. He would not have guessed Charles was the type to get a femdroid, but then he would not put it past the guy either. As far as Avram knew, he was a quiet, awkward sort who kept mostly to himself. Then again, those were probably the people to suspect first of being the secretively kinky types. The strange thing was that the face of the inert droid looked quite mature. To Avram's mind, femdroids were built to look like twenty-year old sluts, not that he was an expert in such matters. This one, however, looked older. The edges of the eyes and mouth were brushed with light wrinkles, and the skin appeared a little lived in. It looked closer to a woman in her late-thirties, roughly the same age as Charles. Was it really a femdroid?

Avram struggled for something to say. "I didn't think you were into such things."

Charles did not look up. He straightened out the cloth around the face and brushed away a few strands of dark hair. "Well, it's not something you go around telling people about, is it?"

Avram hummed in agreement. "Doesn't look much like any femdroid I've every seen before."

"No." Charles stood and looked his host straight in the eyes. "That's what makes her so special. And you have to repair her for me."

"Repair her? Me? Why?"

"I'm pretty certain it's a hardware problem in her neuronics. I can't heal her; I'm only a programmer. But you're a specialist in neuronics---"

"No," interrupted Avram. "I mean, why not just contact the company you got it from? They can fix it better than me."

Charles shook his head. "The company doesn't exist any more. She's been with me over ten years."

"Ten years?" He had certainly been keeping *this* quiet throughout his time at the Institute. Not even the secretary on the fifth floor had been heard gossiping about it.

Avram looked again at the nun-like thing on his sofa, wrapped up from head to toe, exposing only its face. If it really were a femdroid, then its neuronics, the circuitry that made up its artificial brain, would be relatively simple. But Avram felt uncertain as to how involved he ought to get in this whole situation. "Well... perhaps then it's time to get a new one?"

"No!" Charles looked offended. "I can't get rid of Ada!"

"Why not?" asked Avram.

Charles looked tenderly at the droid. "Because I love her."

Avram closed his eyes and sighed. "Ho-boy."

Together they moved Ada over to a corner in the apartment where Avram had his computer. Beside it was the table where Avram usually took his meals, and they cleared it of stacks of plates and bowls, putting the femdroid in their place.

As she was being unwrapped and transferred over to the table, Avram took the opportunity to inspect Ada closely. She was dressed in a loose white nightgown that reached down to her knees, her black hair was shoulder length and simply styled, and her skin was only slightly tanned. Avram could also see, through the rather conservative night-gown, that her figure was not quite the perfect model-like figure he expected. Rather, her curves were a little fuller than those of a fantasy woman, befitting her overall appearance as an otherwise healthy woman approaching middle-age.

Charles did not take his eyes from her as Avram continued with his task. Ada was indeed a femdroid, Avram having located the hidden neuronic interface at the back of her head. He plugged in an interface cable linked to the computer. And, while he loaded up his hardware diagnostic program, Charles sat in another chair beside him, dutifully stroking Ada's hand like a husband at his wife's sickbed.

After some rapid-fire typing on the keyboard, Avram spun around in his chair and faced Charles.

"OK, I'm running a full neuronics scan…"

"How long will it take?"

"Easy there," replied Avram. "It's a full scan of all the brain hardware, so it'll take a while. Maybe half an hour or so. But if anything's wrong, we'll find it."

His guest seemed little relieved by the assurances. He had let go of the femdroid and now piled his head into his hands with a deep sigh.

"I hope so," Charles said in a muffled, pathetic voice.

Avram continued, a little hesitant. "I have to say, I never thought anyone could be so… attached to their droid."

Charles slowly lifted his head, looking a little sheepish. "Yeah. Well, there's nothing wrong with that, is there?"

"Of course not," replied Avram, not so confident in his response. "I just assumed that toys like these had pretty rudimentary AI programming. Nothing too realistic."

"Oh, no," Charles reassured him, his voice growing firmer. "She's much more than that. Much more, I promise you."

Avram began to grow very intrigued. He knew from the seedy advertisements that Femdroids were designed for just one thing: sex. Their knowledge base would simply be a of list of sexual references, and their conversational skills were probably limited to discussing which positions 'master' felt like adopting that night. It went without saying that reasoning skills would be nice and dumb. But then again, Avram knew by his reputation that Charles was a heck of a good AI programmer. If he was so taken with the depth possessed by this droid, surely there was more to the situation than surface appearances.

The diagnostic would take a while to finish, and Charles remained on edge. Perhaps, if Avram dug deeper and encouraged his guest to explain, then Charles' mind would be distracted and Avram's curiosity satisfied.

"So what about her?" began Avram. "What's so special?"

Charles lolled his head slowly from side to side. "It would be kind of hard to explain unless I began at the start."

Avram pointed to his computer screen, where a progress bar crawled along pixel by pixel. "We've got time."

Charles looked blankly at the screen, and then sighed. He resigned himself to the request. After all, what else was there to do in this messy apartment besides catching germs? He eased himself back into the chair, noticing for the first time the stale crumbs on the seat beneath him. He did his best to hide his disgust, "All right. From the beginning."

* * * * *

As you might have noticed, I'm not exactly a ladies' man. I don't *avoid* women, but they seem to do their best at avoiding me. I've worked at the Institute ever since graduating. I keep mostly to myself, but I've got a few friends – all guys, naturally. Being without female company never really bothered me. Until about ten or so years ago.

During the same week, two of my friends announced they had become engaged to their girlfriends. The following week, I had my twenty-ninth birthday. After that, I began to see my friends less and less, which bothered me. It began to dawn on me that I would soon be thirty and still alone, unlike everyone else I knew. The more I thought about it, the more I actually liked the idea of having someone for myself.

And so, I put myself on the market. I tried to get to know

girls at work. They weren't interested, not even that secretary on the fifth floor. I asked friends to set me up with people they knew. They never seemed to know anyone. I went on dating web-sites. No joy. For months I tried, but no one was interested in me. The few dates I had were disasters. I just didn't know how to be around women. I read books and magazines, asked other guys, even watched romantic films, but I couldn't master how to handle females. To be honest, girls just frustrated me. There seemed to be so little logic to the whole thing, no rules I could apply. Probably the only thing I truly did learn was how to recognize a girl's bored expression. It started to get so maddening that I was ready to chuck the whole thing and accept being alone.

Then, one day, I saw an advertisement for femdroids. The new generation had just come out. They were ultra-realistic, looked just like real humans in every way. "The ultimate in feminine pleasure" they called them. "Just like a real lady, except this one is dedicated solely to your pleasure." So I ordered one. Why not? I was only trying to satisfy my base instincts for companionship, and nothing as sophisticated as a real woman was needed to fool them.

The day that the package arrived was one of best of my life. I had taken a day off work, and the box arrived that morning. After lugging it into my bedroom, I found attached to the box a little switch. When I flicked it, the box began to shudder, and the lid burst open. Packing foam went flying everywhere, and it was a little scary. For a moment. But then out of box came Ada. I'll never forget it. She was gorgeous. She had the most perfect, bronzed body, long, wild-looking, dark hair, and she was dressed in nothing but frilly, black underwear. She looked so real!

"Hello, Charles," she breathed—Ada had been pre-programmed with my details. She stepped out of the packaging, gracefully for an android, and leaned towards me. Her face was achingly beautiful, although it was covered in colorful make-up. She put her hands gently on my chest and, through those dark, deep red lips, she said, "I've been waiting for this moment for so long. Now, I'm all yours."

After that... well, suffice it to say that we were busy all day. It was absolutely incredible. Ada could do things I didn't even know there were names for. Whoever designed these femdroids had clearly done their research. She was warm; she was soft. I admit, when she moved and spoke, there was something slightly artificial about her—maybe we'll never perfect droids one hundred percent—but, right then, I couldn't have cared less that she wasn't real.

The following few weeks were insane. I only had contact with other people at work because, every evening and every weekend, I would be with Ada, busy making my bedroom window steamy. She did anything I wanted, whenever I asked. All I had to do was switch her on. In time, I even trained her to fetch me things, like a drink from the kitchen when I was hot and out of breath. As I would relax, sipping my nice, cool drink, she would stand there by the bed just looking at me. I got into the habit of telling her to get back into bed with me and cuddle up. It was wonderfully soothing after such an intense workout.

One morning, as I was leaving for work, I just happened to remark, "Wow, we've left the bedroom in a bit of a mess today."

"Oh," Ada said. "I'll clean it up for you, Master."

And she did! I came back home from work, and my room was pristine.

My whole life was heavenly. I would listen to people at the

Institute complaining about their spouses.

"Oh, she's been moaning at me!" one would say.

"He never listens to me!" said another.

"She's changed since we got married! And not for the better!"

And here I was with an artificial woman having the time of my life! They would have laughed at me if they had known about Ada, but, to me, after hearing their endless bellyaching, they were the fools.

It must have been a month or so before things started to calm down between us. Those years of frustration that I never knew I had were worked away. My real life began to seep back in, so fewer and fewer nights were spent with Ada. Nevertheless, every time I came into my bedroom at night, she would be there wearing another one of the frilly underwear sets from her supply. She would stand and strike a pose, looking at me as though I were the most desirable man on Earth, and ask, "Hi, Master. What d'you want to do with me tonight?"

"I'm tired, Ada," I'd reply. "I'm just going to bed."

"Whatever you say, Master." Then she would sit back down again, unmoving like a sunbathing mannequin.

It began to bother me that she was always there, waiting on me, but I didn't feel right just stashing her in the cupboard until I felt randy again. So I began to ask her to share the bed with me, which she unquestioningly did, of course. I'd already made her remove most of the make-up her face was caked in, and, now that we began to lie together in bed, I got her out of those silly, frilly costumes. I wanted to just feel her body huddled up against mine as I fell into a slumber.

Sometimes, when I had trouble dozing off, I tried talking with her about anything and everything. It wasn't easy. Her

AI was pretty limited; she didn't know much at all. But I thought, *"Hey, so what? I'm an AI programmer, so I can change her myself!"*

So I began to tinker, linking her up to my home computer and making her programming more sophisticated. I gave her advanced conversational skills, expanded her emotional range, and constructed a new knowledge database that continually made her learn new things. Pretty soon, I began to spend every night tinkering with Ada's brain. I couldn't help it; it was so enjoyable. Turn her off, tweak the AI, and, when I switched her back on, she had become that little bit more realistic. The thing I was most proud of was giving her a real ability to learn, far better than the default learning methods she was pre-programmed with. The leap in her intellect was stunning.

All the while, I was still doing the usual things you're supposed to do with femdroids, of course. In fact, one day, after returning from a particularly enjoyable day at work, I walked into the bedroom, and Ada was standing there waiting for me, naked as usual. My mood was high, and that familiar feeling appeared as I swept my eyes across her gorgeous body. I lunged forward, desperate for her. As I did so, she greeted me as though everything was normal.

"Hi," she said. "I learned something very interesting today; would you like to hear?"

"Never mind that," I growled, gathering her up in my arms and throwing her onto the bed. "I want you!"

I climbed on top of her and looked into her big, green eyes. As I did, Ada's expression changed. In an instant, she went from sporting a normal, cheery face, to that of a seductress. "Ooh, you're so dominant tonight, Master!"

When I saw her doing that, something made me stop. Her

reaction felt all wrong. Then it dawned on me that I had completely missed a new behavior she had learned and exhibited. Watching her initiate conversations based on what she had learned should have made me happy, but, instead, I felt bad. Confused, I rolled over and sat on the edge of the bed, my passion utterly defused. Why did I feel so bad?

"Is there something wrong, Master?" asked Ada, sitting up.

"No," I sighed. "It's nothing. It's just... what I did was rude. You wanted to say something, but I ignored you. I made you... what I mean is, you should stop me if you don't want to have sex."

"But I always want to have sex with you, Master."

"And don't—!" I had begun to shout, but composed myself. "Don't call me 'master' any more."

"What should I call you?" she asked like a hotel receptionist.

"Charles. Charlie. That's my name." I turned around and stroked her arm. "What I'm getting at is...that you can refuse me if you don't want sex. Do you understand?"

"No."

I sighed again. It was all too frustrating. All these changes I kept making, why? Why couldn't I have been happy with plain Ada? The thought occurred to me that I should just reset her memories, make her like she was on day one. But having barely begun to ruminate over it, I was horrified at myself for even thinking it. The thought of what I would lose should I wipe her mind made my stomach burn. Ada wasn't perfect, but she was mine. I had made her unique and special. It was unthinkable to lose the things that made her the way she was.

So I took it upon myself to program into Ada the ability to experience moods. Not just the simulation of emotions, but to feel distinct emotional states that influenced the decisions she took. You know how hard that is; in fact, it's barely possible on the most advanced droids. Not surprisingly, it was probably the most difficult thing I'd attempted so far, taking up every evening for weeks. Progress was almost non-existent. After a lot of time spent on it, I began to feel the urge to give it up as an impossible task. It looked like I would simply have to live with the fact that Ada would always be just a "pretend" person.

I started to get quite depressed. I'm not exactly a chatterbox at work, but at that time I never wanted to speak to anyone. I worked longer hours alone in my office not wanting to go home and face Ada.

Then, a little later, our department held its Christmas party. My friends, noticing my continuous sour mood, dragged me out. A dozen or so of us stormed through a few bars and clubs in the city, and I proceeded to get very drunk.

Later in the night, we found ourselves in a club: loud music, lasers, half-naked dancers. Not really my kind of place, but I had drunk enough to numb myself. I found myself on the dance floor surrounded by sweaty young people gyrating away. Out of the blue, I began dancing with a girl named Heather, having been pushed into it by my colleagues. She was almost embarrassingly sexy, way out of my league: long blonde hair, big brown eyes, and a figure to die for. Nevertheless, she seemed to like me. It was then that a thought struggled through my half-drunk mind: if I could have someone like Ada, then why not someone equally as attractive as Heather? So I struck up a conversation with her. Before long, she asked me to take her home - I immediately obliged.

We returned to Heather's apartment, a really stylish and modern place. She took control of everything as soon as we arrived, as though she had done this a hundred times before. She led me by the hand into her bedroom, giving me instructions: wait here, undress there, and lie down here. Now that we were out of the noise and commotion of the club, I had a different sense of things. My head was still spinning. Thinking was a hit and miss process, but I could still feel that everything seemed clinical and rehearsed. There was no real passion or excitement. That's what's supposed to happen between people in this situation, isn't it?

As I climbed into the bed with the waiting Heather, my thoughts ran to Ada. It seems silly to admit it now, but I began to feel bad for what I was doing. I knew that Ada would be, right then, sitting alone in my darkened bedroom, but, when I looked at Heather, I told myself, "Ada's just a thing, an object. She's not waiting for you; she's not thinking anything at all right now. You can't betray a machine." The conflict raged in my head. In the end, my libido won.

Afterwards, I lay in the bed, recovering myself. Perhaps it was the adrenaline, but the dizziness was beginning to leave me, replaced by a faint headache. Heather busied herself around the room, putting her underwear back on and tidying up. I wasn't totally sure how to act in this situation. I tried to think of what guys in the movies did after they had seduced the heroine.

"So," I began to splutter. "I guess we should talk..."

"Talk?" echoed Heather. She was not even looking at me. Instead, she brushed her hair while standing in front of the wardrobe mirror.

"If, um... if we do this, you know, again sometime."

"Well," she said. "Again would be another three-hundred."

"What? Three hundred, what do you mean?"

She finally turned to give me the majority of her attention.

"I'm an escort, darling. Didn't your friends tell you?"

"An escort!"

"Yeah. They said you hadn't had a girl in years, so I was their Christmas gift to you."

She spoke so matter-of-factly, as though explaining how someone had asked her to do me a quick favor. I don't know if it was the effects of the booze or what, but I began to feel sick.

"Don't worry," she laughed. "They already paid me!"

"I've got to go."

I shot out of the bed and dressed as fast as I could. Heather just shrugged and turned back to the mirror. The atmosphere suddenly turned stale. I felt incredibly awkward stumbling around trying to get into my clothes. In fact, I left the room before I had even fully dressed, still tucking and straightening the fabrics as I went. I couldn't even bring myself to say goodbye.

Once outside, the cold night air chilled me to the bone, and I made my way home as quickly as possible. This whole situation made me feel like a stranger who had wondered into the wrong neighborhood, somewhere that I just didn't belong. I burned to be with Ada, just to see her. She occupied my mind all the way.

When I arrived home, I made straight for the bedroom, but stopped in the doorway. The room was almost black, but a few moonbeams shining in through the open window allowed me to see outlines: the wardrobe by the far wall, my chest of drawers beside the door, my bed beneath the window-frame. Visibly lying beneath the covers where I had left her that morning was Ada. I froze, feeling apprehensive. I didn't know what to do. If I entered the room, she would wake automatically and greet me. What should I say then? I began to run through the possibilities in my mind, but then shook my head as I realized the absurdity of it. Instead, I marched confidently into my room. When the lights went on, Ada sat up and turned to look at me. I knew that any normal woman would immediately have demanded to know where I had been until so late and given me the tongue-lashing I so deserved.

Instead, the electrodes that covered her plastic endoskeleton sent impulses to the gel-based muscular structure in her face, which caused them to contract and so stretch the synthetic skin of her lips into a smile. "Hello, Charlie," she said, her words dripping with sweet innocence. "How are you?"

I could have dropped down on my knees and cried. I'd never felt so pathetic in my life. Everything was so unreal. Inside, I was pleading for the fight that we should have been having right then. I made it to the bed somehow and sat on the edge, Ada's loyal, attentive glance never breaking from me.

I looked into her eyes, those large, green orbs that now seemed so vulnerable. My words struggled free from my throat. "I've been out. With a girl."

Ada just smiled as she listened.

I continued, as though purging myself through confession. "I found her very attractive. We went back to her place and had sex."

"Did you have a nice time?" Ada asked.

"No," I replied, dropping my head into my hands. My whole body seemed to deflate in one huge sigh. "Not at all."

"Aww, I'm sorry to hear that, Charlie," Ada said. She gently rubbed my shoulder – another little trait that I had programmed into her.

"That's OK," I said, pushing her hand away. "Go to sleep."

And with that, she wished me good night and lay back

down. All my tinkering, all my programming, thinking I could make her into a real woman, was all for naught.

Ludicrous as it may sound, I actually slept on my couch that night. I just couldn't stay beside Ada. Sleep eluded me, no matter how long I closed my eyes. Questions raced through my mind tormenting me. *Was I a fool? Should I stop all this now? Was I becoming lost in some kind of* craziness? But the questions eventually stopped, and my mind somehow wandered onto the topic of Ada's AI. Becoming lost in the intricacies of problem-solving seemed oddly comforting, so I again ran through the problem that had been torturing me these past weeks. And there, while lying on the sofa of all places, I had a sudden flash of inspiration, my eureka-moment. It was the way to give Ada genuine emotional states. The pieces of the puzzle just seemed to fall into place. The whole concept almost laid itself out.

The next day was a Saturday, giving me the whole weekend to implement what I had discovered. I hooked Ada up to the computer and started to program, beginning hours of endless work in front of the screen. The code just flowed out of me and onto the machine, never-ending cycles of coding, testing, and re-coding. I barely ate and didn't bother sleeping, but, by Sunday morning, my work was done.

For the final time, I reactivated Ada. When she re-awoke, I saw the change in her instantly. She sat up slowly, looking around, almost like a blind person who had suddenly been given sight. She eventually looked at me. I must have appeared nervous, but she tipped her head to one side and gave me the warmest smile I'd ever seen. That alone was all I needed to see. I took her hand, kissed it and held it against my cheek. With her other hand, she began to stroke my hair.

"I'm so very pleased to see you, Charlie," she whispered.

Life from then on was wonderful. It was like Ada was her own person. I could so easily give to her whatever needs, desires, or moods I thought she needed. We lived together like a normal couple.

And so, the years passed. Time started to catch up with me: my hair began to thin, my skin began to loosen, and a paunch began to develop. Yet Ada stayed the way she had always been. I don't know which came first, the feeling of ridiculousness being with a girl who looked fifteen years younger, or the change in my taste.

I can still recall the day that I was sitting in my apartment, just looking at Ada as we were sharing a quiet moment, her head resting upon my lap. I remember there was a hard rain outside, drumming onto my bedroom window endlessly, and I sat stroking her long hair and gazing at her still face. She was still beautiful, I knew, but she was a snapshot of beauty, which somehow reinforced the whole unreality. In my mind, I aged her, picturing her with a few dignified years behind her: a couple of laughter lines around her full mouth, the wisps of a few wrinkles around her eyes, and her wild, dark hair tidily pinned up. The result made me feel so good. She would be mature, dignified, and, best of all, real. On that cold and miserable day, I had created a warm and comforting image for myself.

So perfect did I find it, I took Ada back to the company from which I ordered her. They had a department that provided new parts and exteriors for people who had grown bored of their droid's old appearance. Normally, that means you change the skin color or get bigger breasts, but the engineer was all too surprised when I told him to age her. His resistance to the idea melted away after I told him how much I would pay if he would simply add fifteen years, but keep as much of Ada's original material as possible.

I had to spend a week waiting for her to be completed. It was torture. After all this time with her, I realized how much I now took her presence for granted. In her absence, my apartment felt like something critical was missing. I didn't know what to do with myself in the evenings and the bed felt so damned empty. The only thing keeping me going was the thought that she would soon be ready.

And finally, when I went to collect Ada and clap my eyes on her, the result was astonishing. It was as though the engineer had read my mind. Her appearance now matched her more developed temperament: not a frivolous, slutty girl, but the attractive, dignified *woman* you see now.

That night, we didn't just have sex; we made love. It had never been so gentle and tender between us. It was then that I told Ada for the first time that I loved her.

She said she loved me too.

* * * * *

"And so," said Charles, as he began to wind down his narrative. "It's been pretty much like that ever since. I continued to refine her AI, of course, little-by-little making her more realistic and shaping her personality to match my own. In fact, I've been using some of the more successful ideas in my work at the Institute -- that's how developed her AI has become! I'm very proud. If I didn't know better, I would write a paper on her software make-up, but, undoubtedly, that would cause a storm."

Charles turned his head, looking adoringly at the still inert Ada lying on the table. Avram, meanwhile, was still reeling from the story just recounted, having never heard anything quite like it. He had a thousand questions, but, not knowing where to start, inquired about Charles' last remark.

"What do you mean by: 'If you didn't know any better?'"

"Well," began Charles a little reticent. "It wouldn't do much for my reputation if I came along and said, 'Hi, everyone, this is the femdroid I've had for ten years; you wanna' know what I did to her brains?'"

"And what would it do to your reputation?"

"Come off it, Avram. I'm not totally naïve. I don't mind telling you, if you can help her, but I'm hardly going to declare to my friends and family I'm in love with a droid!"

"Friends and family?" He frowned. "You mean no one knows about Ada?"

"No," Charles replied simply.

"You never took her out? Ever?"

"You know how it is. No matter how good robotics gets, no matter how good they look, androids still don't act totally real. Humans have an instinct for what looks genuinely human, and they don't like fakes. Why do you think service droids purposely look so mechanical? I had no intention of letting people stare at me and my robotic partner. Oh, she did begin to ask about going out to see the world, but a little bit of programming soon adjusted that."

Avram suspected his visitor had an inkling of how wrong the things he was saying seemed. Before he could continue further, a bleep from the computer caught his attention; the diagnostic had completed. He spun around in his chair to review the results, with Charles' eyes flicking back and forth between Avram and the indecipherable symbols. He watched his host reach beside his computer to retrieve a half-empty can of soda without taking his glare from the screen.

"Well?" asked Charles.

Avram pieced it all together. It did not look good, but he needed more information. He turned back to face his guest.

"When did you first notice anything wrong with her?"

Charles shook his head as he tried to think. "A few weeks ago, I think. Her speech began to stutter, but rebooting didn't seem to help. Then, last week, she began to forget things or just freeze mid-sentence."

"And today?"

"When she froze this evening, I couldn't boot her at all. She simply won't wake up."

Avram hummed and took a swig from the can. It all began to make sense to him. "I think I know the problem: looks like axon degradation."

"What does that mean?" asked Charles, even though he knew enough about neuronics to infer it.

"The relays between the neurons are starting to give up. Without them Ada can't function, can't process anything. It's like digital Alzheimer's disease."

"Can you fix it?" Avram shook his head, but Charles simply grew more animated. "Surely there's something you can do. Regenerate the axons? Replace the neuronics."

Avram could scarcely believe his friend was asking such things. "Charles, you know we can't do such things. Neuronic brains develop organically, you know that. Once those millions of connections are forged, they can't just be reprogrammed. Ada is no different. In fact, I'm surprised she lasted this long with her cheap, rudimentary AI."

Charles looked at Ada lying helpless on the table. "There has to be something you can do."

"I can easily get you a new processing unit," Avram suggested. "A more sophisticated one than you began with. You could program it like you did before, have a girl just as realistic as Ada within time."

"Replace her brain?" Charles echoed, horrified. "She'd

have a totally different personality!"

"Sure. You want a realistic femdroid, don't you?"

"I want Ada!" Charles yelled, immediately shrinking upon seeing Avram's surprised face. "Sorry. But there must be something you can do."

Avram sighed and rubbed the back of his neck tiredly. "Well... there's maybe one possibility: re-alignment."

"What's that?"

"Obviously, some connections are still working. I could screen out the dead axons, bypass them and re-route through the remainder."

"And that'll bring her back?" Charles began to grow enthused. "Then do it!"

"I don't think you realize the gravity of it. We only do things like that in an emergency, like if we need to recover a droid's brain-state before disposing of it. I'd be shutting down large portions of her neuronics—it's like cutting out huge chunks of someone's brain."

"You have to try," Charles pleaded, roughing his hand through his hair. "I love her, I need her. I know you don't believe me—"

"I don't doubt any of that," interrupted Avram. "I really don't! Your affection for her is plain to see."

"Then help me!" exclaimed Charles.

"Listen to me! After re-alignment, Ada wouldn't function as well. She'd behave differently, and she wouldn't be able to move like she did before. Also, her ability to process would be sharply reduced, and her past memories would be incomplete. In addition, with extra load on them, the other axons would degrade that much quicker. Every day, something she could do the day before would then be beyond her. When enough of them failed again, in a day, a week, maybe a month, this would all happen again."

"I'll care for her," Charles insisted. "We do the same for people now. We give them the chance to keep living."

"Yes, but... only if their life is worth living." Avram sighed and sat forward. "The worst thing is that Ada's ability to form new memories is now almost completely broken. She'd forget almost every experience she had within moments. And I hate to say this Charles, but with all of the abilities you've given her, she'd react to all of this like a real person. She'd get frustrated, angry, confused... and frightened. The rest of her life would be spent in a short, terrifying decline."

Charles paused. His persistence was beginning to wane. He looked tired and defeated, but there was still some fight left in him. "She's mine," he said weakly. "She belongs to me. I get to decide what happens to her."

"Would you say the same about a human being?" Avram's reply came quickly. "If this were your mother at death's door, would you plead with the doctor to hack away at her mind? To cripple her, make her barely able to think, to experience, or remember? Knowing that, all the while, you're simply buying her just a few more weeks of a life not worth living?"

Charles looked meekly at the floor, unwilling to respond. Avram drained the rest of the flat soda from the can, and then tossed it aside. He slouched back in his chair, feeling it best to allow his guest a moment to run these things through in his mind. He watched as Charles kept rubbing his hand over his forehead.

"One thing, Charles. Why didn't you take her to meet your friends or family?"

Charles looked back at him and frowned. "We've already been over that."

"Why did you never take her out at all? What would you

care what other people thought about her?"

"They..." Charles struggled. "They wouldn't understand."

"You didn't want anyone to know. You kept her all for yourself. You decided everything for her, and you shaped her exactly the way you wanted her."

"Because she's mine," said Charles.

"I think I get it now." Avram slowly twirled his fingers around in the air, as if it helped to bring out his thoughts. "You love her, but you don't love her as an equal. I mean, you've spent this whole relationship considering her practically a human being. Now, in this situation, you're talking about her like she's your property. It's true, isn't it? I mean, for whose sake do you want to keep her alive?"

Charles buried his head in his palms. He fought to remain composed and keep from breaking down. "Is there nothing you can do?" he mumbled through his hands.

Avram sighed. "I'm sorry, Charles. You know as well as I do that she's at the end of her natural life. Anything I did now would be mere life support."

Charles sat still for a moment longer; then, he raised his head and sighed wearily, his shoulders dropping as though the weight of the world fell from them. He looked at Ada, leaning closer to her side, and stroked her cheek. She still felt warm, but then the material that acted as Ada's skin was always warm. It made it all the harder to bear that she was no more. He turned to Avram. "Could you try and reboot her?"

"Reboot her? Probably, but she'll freeze up again within minutes."

"That'll be enough," whispered Charles.

Behind him, he heard Avram tap a few keys before a tiny light on the cable connecting to Ada's brain began to flash. A moment passed, and her eyes struggled to open. She looked from side to side, as though straining to focus her vision. Finally, she fixed on Charles standing beside her.

"Hello, Charles," she said. Her voice sounded weak and distorted. "I appear to have a system problem, but I am unable to diagnose it. I recommend returning me to the nearest service centre for immediate repair."

"It's OK, Ada," Charles replied.

Ada continued, slurring and sounding as though speaking was a great effort. "If the problem cannot be resolved, my manufacturer will be delighted to replace me---"

"Ada, that's enough!"

Avram chimed in. "It's just automatic speech. I can cut that off." He deactivated the relevant portion of Ada's neuronics pre-programmed to deliver advertising, noticing in the process how poor her readings were. Her mind was dying fast.

Charles, meanwhile, saw a sudden difference in Ada; her blank expression transformed into something more puzzled, almost fearful.

"Something is wrong," she whimpered.

"Yes," Charles replied.

"Do you know what it is?"

He took her hand in his, and then closed his eyes. It helped to fight back the tears that were beginning to well up. Seeing Ada in this state was almost too much to bear. "You're dying."

Ada looked back at him blankly. "Do androids die?"

Charles blurted out a painful sob at her tender question. "Yes. Yes, they do."

She looked away, pausing for a moment. "I never thought about that... that's not fair."

"No. No, it's not."

Ada looked back at Charles. "Should we say goodbye now?" She asked, her voice beginning to degrade further.

He finally gave in to the flow of water swelling up in his eyes. "Yes," he replied, tears beginning to trail along his cheeks. "I'm so sorry, Ada."

"I don't want to go," she said, her words exuding almost childlike innocence. "I enjoy being with you."

"And I loved every minute with you," Charles sobbed. He could not resist his grief, now forcing his body to curl up. As he fell forward, he planted his lips upon Ada's smooth forehead and cried. From the corner of his eye, he saw the light on the cable cease flashing. When he wrenched himself up once more, he found Ada's face frozen in its unhappy expression. Her body no longer made any movements, not even the simulated breathing. Charles even thought that her eyes had changed, as though some spirit had finally vacated them. Ada had gone.

Charles lay down his head upon her chest. The flow of tears eventually stopped, but the involuntary sobbing continued until he was aware of how he must appear to Avram: a man weeping over a dead machine.

"You must think me pretty pathetic," Charles mumbled through the fabric of Ada's gown.

"Why would I think that?" replied Avram in a tender voice. "You loved, and you lost. We've been doing that since time began."

"I mean falling for a bloody droid and treating it like the real thing. Now I'm crying when it breaks down. I'm a grown man... what the hell was I doing?"

Avram stood and drew up beside Charles, putting his arm gently on his shoulder. "You were learning how to love. You were taking something... someone... and raising her up to levels no one could ever have conceived of."

At last, Charles sat up, drying his eyes, but never taking them from Ada.

Avram continued. "You gave her an existence she would never have had with anyone else. And you did it because you wanted to. You gave to her, you took pleasure in seeing her happy, and you wanted to see her become better than she was. Any loving person would do those things. I think that shows more emotional maturity than anything else I can imagine."

Charles felt his emotions coming back under his control. He swallowed hard and pondered over Avram's words. "You really think so?"

"Absolutely," Avram replied. "If you demonstrated one tenth of that maturity with someone who had their own genuine will, someone who challenged you as well as loved you, you'd be a very happy man. You wouldn't be able to program her to perfection, but you'd do all right."

It was worth thinking about, Charles reflected. Maybe, one day soon, an imperfect woman would measure up to the perfect femdroid. It might work, as long as she did not mind an imperfect man.

Karl Beecher was born and raised in Great Britain, where he developed his two greatest passions: computers and literature. After obtaining his PhD in computer science, he moved to Berlin, Germany, where he earns his living as a researcher at the Freie Universität. He spends much of his spare time in front of a word processor in an effort to satisfy his overwhelming urge to write, which never seems to leave him be.

Exorcisms Forbidden
by Catherine A. Callaghan

Helen Wiley had investigated several listings, but, so far, they proved to be too expensive or too remote from shopping centers. After turning down a flat next to a unit with three yipping poodles, she decided to calm her nerves by driving slowly through the tree-lined streets of Victorian Heights. A huge red-brick building with four visible gables dominated one corner, and a tower rose above the wraparound porch. On impulse, she parked her car and walked back. A maple stood like a sentinel just beyond the wrought-iron gate, its trunk straight and strong with a huge root buckling the walkway. Even in October, green leaves still covered its branches, except for one dead limb that angled grotesquely over the yard. Helen wondered why no one had sawed it off. The sign next to the entrance read:

Shady Side Manor

Furnished apartments $700 and up, utilities included

No pets, no wild parties.

$700 would strain Helen's budget, since she depended on a fixed pension, but she could manage if she lived frugally. Victorian Heights was within walking distance of a shopping mall and close to her doctor's office, which would save on gasoline as well as time. Her eyes traveled to the bottom of the sign, and she did a double take.

No exorcisms.

If she had not been so desperate to find a place, she would have laughed and returned to her car, but she decided to investigate. The front door opened onto a short hallway. A sitting room with a fireplace extended to the left, and a staircase rose to the right, angling above a table with a flickering jack-o'-lantern. She entered a room straight ahead labeled "Manager." A thin, elderly man glanced up from his desk. "Can I help you?"

"I'm looking for an apartment," she said after introducing herself. "Do you have anything left in the $700 range?"

The man struggled to his feet and extended a hand. "Reginald Pate, at your service. You can call me Reggie, and you're in luck. Number 10 is still available." He walked toward the staircase, leaning heavily on his cane. His bald head reflected light from a chandelier, and Helen glanced up. Wainscoting bordered a stained glass window on the landing, the pattern suggesting morning glory against an orange moon, but a crack in the upper left corner marred the effect.

Number 10 turned out to be an attractive one-bedroom unit on the second floor, with a view of pine trees in the back yard. "I like this apartment," said Helen, "but what do you mean by 'no exorcisms'? Does a New Age cult live here?"

"No, most of the tenants are conservative retirees. Sometimes, we get a young couple, but they usually leave as soon as they can—not enough excitement."

"Why would anyone want to perform an exorcism?"

"Occasionally, someone gets into an argument with a ghost and tries to drive it out. A powerful exorcism might banish all the ghosts in the building, and that wouldn't be fair to the other tenants."

Helen could hardly believe her ears, but his expression told her he was serious. She was about to object that she had never heard such rubbish when he interrupted her thoughts.

"Look at it this way. Seventy per cent of older single

women live alone, and that's not natural, so Alf and I redesigned all the units to be ghost-friendly. Don't tell me you've never longed to see your Henry again?"

How had he known her dead husband's name? She couldn't recall having mentioned it.

"We offer you the chance to contact Henry in this life. That way, you won't have to wait till you die to see him again."

Helen gulped. She envied people who believed they'd meet their loved ones in the hereafter, but she considered them delusional. Once people were dead, they were done—no flitting about in heaven or returning in diaphanous form to scare people. She was about to tell Reggie as much, but her better judgment prevented her.

"If you feel sorry for lonely people, you should allow pets," she responded finally.

He regarded her with rheumy eyes. "Ghosts are cleaner and usually quieter."

Right now, the yipping poodles seemed preferable to this nuthouse. Reggie sighed, as if reading her mind. "It's obvious you don't appreciate our accessories, but I can let you have Number 4 for $500. It's not upgraded."

"What do you mean?"

"So far, it's never been haunted."

She followed Reggie downstairs and almost walked out the front door in disgust, but at the last moment, she turned back. Number 4 was also a one-bedroom unit, but it boasted a fairly large living room, and the back door opened onto the patio. She savored the heady scent of pine needles from a row of young trees. A privacy wall separated the area from the street. Impatiens poured from an overturned whiskey barrel, and bright-blooming beds of late marigolds dotted the yard beyond.

"These flowers are beautiful," she said. "Who planted them?"

"I did, a couple of years ago," said Reggie, but he looked uncomfortable. As she walked over for a closer look, he coughed nervously. "Must be allergies. Let's go back."

Inside, pastel colors with modernistic patterns proved restful to the eyes, and an attractive fern, feathery green except for one brown stem, hung from the ceiling. She fingered it before discovering it wasn't real, and wondered why an artificial fern would include a fake dead frond. However, $500 per month would allow her a few small luxuries, such as membership in a spa, an occasional trip to the theater, and even limited travel.

"I'll tell you what," Reggie said. "If you give me a check for $500, you can stay here a month without signing a lease. No obligation. You can't beat a deal like that anywhere around here."

"I'll have to think it over," she said.

"That's all right. Here's my card, and you can call me any time. Nice meeting you." He tapped his way down the hall and around a corner.

The door to apartment 3 opened, and a gray-haired woman stepped outside. "Is Reggie still here? My faucet's leaking again."

"You just missed him. I think he went back to his office."

"My name's Lillian Bradford, but I go by Lil." She extended a hand, and Helen introduced herself. Lil then stepped closer and lowered her voice. "Don't let Reggie get to you with his talk of ghosts. We're an active lot around here, and we don't spend all our time communing with the dead."

"I'm glad to hear it."

Helen started walking down the hall, and Lil followed. "There's an exercise room in the basement, and, if you're an early riser, a group of us go on a three-mile walk every morning," she said. "We car pool it downtown during the holidays and whenever there's a traveling performance."

"That's more my style."

"When do you plan to move in?"

"Actually, I haven't decided..."

"That's all right. Take your time." Lil ducked into the manager's office, leaving the door open. Helen saw Lil and Reggie exchange glances. She returned to her car, glad to be out of this strange place, whatever its advantages.

* * * * *

Night had fallen by the time Helen reached home, and her daughter Janet looked worried. "Where have you been? I thought maybe you'd had an accident." Her black hair was drawn back severely, and her skin looked pale since she'd stopped using makeup. Helen longed for the soft-featured girl she had known before her daughter found Ron and religion.

"I'm sorry. I got stuck in traffic, and there was a detour..."

"You should allow more time—you've missed dinner. Ron and I are late for our prayer meeting, and you know we can't leave Christina alone."

Helen glanced around the living room. Something was missing. "Where's my easy chair?"

"I sold it to the junk man this afternoon. It was full of bugs, and the stuffing was coming out."

"What! You had no right..."

"Of course, I did. You gave it to us when you moved in, remember?"

Helen clenched her fists. "What I remember is that the chair belonged to your father; it was his favorite, and I liked to sit in it."

"I'm sorry, Mother, but it was sagging, and I thought it might collapse on you. I was afraid the junk man wouldn't take it at all if I didn't sell it right then. I did it for your own good."

Helen was too stunned to answer. There had been a time when Janet would never have made such a decision without consulting her. She looked into her daughter's eyes and saw a certainty she had never noticed before, a certainty that extended beyond religion into all areas of life. Janet really believed she knew what was good for people and was behaving accordingly.

"Ron and I have to leave now. Your dinner's in the fridge, and Christina's upstairs. When you wash the dishes, please get them clean."

"Never mind; I'm not hungry." She hurried up the stairs to her bedroom.

"Goodbye," Janet yelled up the staircase. "We'll be back around 10:30." The front door banged shut. Helen collapsed onto her bed, numbed by the rift between herself and Janet. She heard the soft sounds of Christina moving around in the next room and was overwhelmed with sadness at the thought of leaving her grandchild, but Janet gave her no choice. Ron had provided her with the one thing that was beyond Helen's power, a mission in life. At first, Helen had welcomed the change, but it had spun out of control, and loss of the easy chair was the last straw. Living here was no longer an option.

She phoned Reggie later that night. A brisk wind blew new -fallen leaves across the sidewalk when she returned to Shady Side Manor the following day. Lil sat in Reggie's office, and he prepared a rental agreement for the first month, allowing for the option of a year's lease or longer at the same rate if she was satisfied. The last paragraph caused her some consternation: "In the event that a ghost appears in the aforementioned unit, the management reserves the right to charge an additional $200 per month."

"Does this mean you can raise the rent any time you want by claiming my apartment's haunted?" she asked Reggie.

"I told you the lease was a bad idea," he explained to Lil. "We can't make a profit at that low rate, and there are mortgage payments on the whole complex every month."

"We'll manage! We're committed to providing the happiness tenants can't find anywhere else." For a moment, Lil's face glowed with the determination Helen often saw in her daughter, then it relaxed into kindly wrinkles.

"You haven't answered my question," insisted Lil.

"I explained to Reggie that you were a woman of honor. You won't have to pay extra until *you* see a ghost, and we expect you to tell us when haunting begins. You don't look like the kind of person who'd hide a ghost just to keep the rent down."

Helen wondered if she was leaping from the frying pan into the fire by moving to Shady Side Manor, even for a month. "I think I should make a few things clear. I've never seen a ghost in my life, and I doubt I'll start now. I'm taking this apartment only because things are uncomfortable at home. During the coming month, I plan to look for another place."

Lil smiled. "Don't worry. We're confident you'll come around to our way of thinking, or we wouldn't make such an offer. It just might take a little longer in your case."

The comment puzzled Helen. "We? Do you set policy here? At first, I thought you were another tenant."

"Actually, I'm the owner, but I also live here."

Helen felt her face flush. "I... I wouldn't have guessed. Most owners of large buildings stay out of sight."

Lil sighed. "You're right, and that's a pity. I consider it my duty to make everybody feel at home if I can. These units are my life's work." The light caught her eyes again.

With some misgivings, Helen signed the contract. Reggie called Alf, the handyman, to serve as a witness. "Won't you stay for tea?" Lil asked afterward. "We usually gather in the sitting room around 5 p.m."

A fire was blazing as Helen and Lil entered, and the logs looked almost real. A display table featured *The Heath Readers* for first and second grades. Helen's grandfather had used those books as a child. The two women sat on a comfortable sofa next to a table with a huge silver teapot. Helen was surprised to find current issues of magazines strewn nearby instead of additional antique books.

Lil poured a cup of tea. Her soft face offset dancing blue eyes. "We're a bit early, so you can tell me all about Henry without being interrupted."

Helen gasped. She wasn't used to such directness, but Lil's warm face confirmed her interest. "Henry was a wonderful man—we had the closest thing to a perfect marriage possible." She found herself describing in detail how they had first met, the night Henry had proposed, and their long, happy years together. Lil seemed to share both her joy and her sorrow over his sudden death as only a close friend could, something she had never achieved with Janet.

"I wouldn't dare hold a conversation like this with my daughter—she'd simply worry about the probable fate of her father's soul. She even sold his favorite chair to the junk man yesterday without asking me. That's when I decided to move out immediately."

"That's sad," said Lil, "since, after death, the soul stays right here on earth." Helen thought it best not to comment, but the remark made her uneasy.

"I understand where you're coming from," Lil added hastily. "I had a wonderful marriage with Willie for almost thirty years; then things changed."

"What do you mean?"

"He got brain cancer."

"I'm so sorry," Helen said. "My grandmother died of brain cancer. I know what you went through."

"Don't be sorry. His passing was very peaceful." Lil stirred in her seat, and her expression belied her words, as if something very unpleasant had occurred when her husband died. She seemed about to say more, but several tenants were entering the sitting room, so she proceeded to make introductions. To Helen's surprise, they all seemed normal, no aging hippies in robes. Two retired secretaries were discussing a hike in the foothills of Mt. Perry, a few miles away, and a former sea captain was trying to find a companion for a cruise to Antarctica. Night had fallen before she thought of looking at her watch.

Janet was upset when Helen again came home late for dinner, and even more worried after learning her mother's plans. "Are you sure you'll be all right? You don't know any of these people."

"Don't worry. My agreement was only for a month."

* * * * *

The following week, Alf came by with his pickup truck and loaded most of Helen's belongings. She stuffed the rest into three suitcases and drove to Shady Side Manor. Apartment 4 had been cleaned in the intervening week, and she decided to rest in the living room before unpacking.

She froze at the entrance. The easy chair stood in one corner next to a lamp. After a moment, she found the courage to examine it closely. The upholstery had been repaired, and there was no sign of bugs, almost as if this homey atmosphere provided its own healing. No, that couldn't be—it must be a different chair in the same style; maybe it was there all along, and she hadn't noticed it. When she sat down, it enclosed her like a glove and induced the same sense of peace as Henry's old chair.

Her eyes focused on the opposite wall. Earlier, she'd dismissed its patterns as decorative design, but, from this position, they seemed three-dimensional and otherworldly, suggesting depth and something beyond. On closer inspection, they again collapsed into abstract patterns.

A knock on the door startled her. "It's just me," said Lil. "I thought you might need another pair of hands."

Lil helped her unpack most of her boxes and arrange things, after which Helen thanked her profusely. "Not many owners are this considerate."

"Unfortunately, that's true, but I believe the tenants should come first. If you ever need anything, just tell me or Reggie. I'll leave you alone now, so you can get some rest."

Helen hadn't realized how tired she was until Lil left. Instead of sitting outside, she went to bed immediately although it was still light. To her surprise, she slept till morning, something she had not managed since Henry died. She rose early and heard a knock on her door as she finished dressing.

"Who is it?" she asked.

"Alice and Betty." She opened the door to the two secretaries she had met at her first tea. "We thought you might like to join us for our morning walk. Lil can't make it this week." Betty was a bit taller and more robust, but both women appeared to be in excellent shape.

Helen put on her hiking shoes and had to walk briskly to keep up. The other two women had recently joined a discussion group at the local library, and were commenting on the latest Book-of-the-Week Club selection. Helen could not remember when she had last read a truly interesting book, let alone found someone with whom to discuss it. Janet and Ron made a point of reading only religious books, but she joined in the conversation as best she could.

The fall colors were splendid, and the October air was crisp and cold; still, after a mile, Helen started to pant. Alice and Betty paused while she caught her breath. "I'm afraid I'm out of shape—it's so hard to keep up a fitness program alone. My daughter Janet used to walk with me, but, recently, she spends more and more time in prayer."

Alice laughed. "I had an aunt like that, but don't worry. After a few weeks, you'll be running. Has Lil told you about the exercise room in the basement?"

They started walking again and had almost returned to Shady Side Manor before Helen broached the subject that disturbed her. "Since I'll be here at least a month," she said, "there's something I'd like to ask you. Both Reggie and Lil imply that most of the apartments are haunted. Have you ever noticed anything?"

Her two companions stopped in mid stride and looked at each other. "Since... since you're new here," began Alice, "you can't know that, among us, ghosts are a private matter. My husband Jeff was killed in a car accident five years ago, and I... I was a basket case until Lil took me in and gave me the chance to see him again. She told me that's why she bought this place and hired Reggie to renovate it, so she could help out people like me. She considers it her mission."

Betty elbowed her. "Alice, you're too serious. Ghosts are nothing to be ashamed of. Marvin Travis came with my apartment—that's number 12. He died there two years ago."

Helen opened her mouth, but no words came out.

"Anyway, he used to be an English professor, and he always reads book club selections over my shoulder. I try my ideas out on him before I bring them up at our discussion group."

"Hah," said Alice, "that's why you sound so smart! It's hardly fair to the rest of us for you to have expert criticism ahead of time."

Betty put her hands on her hips in mock indignation. "Of course, it's fair! You're free to join us anytime you want."

"Thank you, but I'd rather not. As I said before, I think one's ghosts should be a private matter. Besides, Jeff might get jealous."

Betty put a warm hand on Helen's shoulder. "Don't mind us. You'll understand how things work after you contact your husband."

Helen didn't know what to say, so she walked back in silence with the other two women. "I'll knock on your door again tomorrow at the same time," said Betty.

This arrangement is only temporary, Helen thought. *I can put up with any kind of lunacy for a short time—I've had plenty of practice with Janet and Ron.* At any rate, she would prefer their talk of ghosts over Janet's fear that Helen would lose her soul unless she joined the True Apostolic Temple. She found herself unpacking the rest of the boxes she had brought from her daughter's house. Even if she had to re-pack them at the end of the month, she was determined to settle in properly.

She spent another restful night and awoke to the soft sound of rain. To her surprise, Betty again knocked on her door. "Mornings we can't walk, we usually exercise together downstairs. Care to join us?"

The exercise room was well-provided with equipment, including free weights and a rowing machine. It might not be necessary to join a spa after all. A pleasant half hour passed with no reference to ghosts, and Alice lent Helen some books so she could participate in the discussion group that Friday.

"Do you like opera?" Betty asked. "Captain Smythe is organizing a group for *Carmen* next Sunday, and he has a ticket left. If you want, I can sign you up."

"I'd love it," replied Helen. She later learned that the outing would be an all-day affair, including lunch at the Victorian Ritz. The intervening days zipped by as Helen learned again what it was like to prepare her favorite foods, read at leisure, and spend long moments in her easy chair, thinking about nothing.

Saturday evening, her telephone rang. It was Janet. "I'm sorry to disturb you, Mother. You're probably still unpacking."

"As a matter of fact, I finished days ago. People here helped me move in."

There was a pause at the other end, as if Janet could not imagine such behavior. "I called because the baby sitter canceled at the last minute, and we need you to stay with Christina tomorrow. Could you come over?"

"Janet, I'd love to visit with Christina, but I can't this time. I'm going to lunch and the opera tomorrow. *Carmen's* playing."

"But it's an emergency, or I wouldn't ask. Our temple is holding its annual revival."

"In that case, take Christina with you."

"You know I can't. She'd cry all the time."

"Then make other arrangements."

Janet sounded exasperated. "I've tried, and no one's available. If you won't go to church yourself, couldn't you just once support people who do instead of going off to an immoral opera?"

"The answer is no, and that's final." Helen pushed the receiver into its cradle. She could hardly believe she had found the nerve to hang up on her daughter. The telephone rang twice in the next hour, but she ignored it.

Sunday was a glorious day, and Helen stepped lightheartedly into Lil's van. Her outburst the previous evening had banished the guilt she always felt in her daughter's presence and given her a new sense of independence. The group took a morning tour of the foothills. Afterward, Helen sat next to Lil at the Ritz. Captain Smythe, whom she'd also met at the first tea, sat across from her with Basil Jackson, a tenant who used to be a car salesman.

"Basil and I will be going on the cruise to Antarctica," the captain announced to the group. "For a long time, I didn't want to leave Myrtle, but she talked me into it. She said I should enjoy myself while I can, and she'd accompany me in spirit. She's always had a great sense of humor."

"Myrtle is the captain's daughter," Lil whispered to Helen. "He was devastated when she died in childbirth."

Helen nearly choked on a swallow of soup, but managed to keep her composure. Aside from that interlude, the food was delicious and the conversation normal. Doubt pricked her for the first time. She'd prided herself on her rationalism, but here was a group of ordinary people who took the existence of an afterlife and ghosts so much for granted that they felt no need to proselytize or even justify themselves. Could they be right?

The performance of the opera was striking, and Helen found herself identifying with the heroine as she deserted her faithful lover for the flashy toreador. When she drew the fateful spade from a deck of cards and uttered the words "la mort," a chill crept over Helen. Carmen seemed to be looking directly at her.

Helen's frame of mind did not lighten, even after she returned to her apartment. The easy chair brought her comfort as always, but the patterns on the opposite wall again assumed a life of their own, looming three-dimensional, forcing her to think of Henry. At one point, she was certain she saw his image emerging from the wall, greeting her with the casual smile she had loved so much. Doubt again wormed its way into her thoughts. Was survival after death possible after all? She shook herself. *I have to get over this mood*, she thought, *or I'll become morbid.* When she looked up, the patterns were merely an interesting design, and it was easy to persuade herself that she had imagined the whole episode.

As the month progressed, Reggie's prediction concerning outside apartments turned out to be correct. Most units in Victorian Heights rented for $900 or more. Cheaper apartments close to the mall were dirty and rundown, and Helen didn't like the looks of other tenants. She investigated a few rentals in the foothills, but they were miles from any stores, and the streets lacked sidewalks. Even the flat next to the poodles had been taken. She phoned Janet once and was informed that her selfishness had prevented her daughter from attending most of the revival. Despite its drawbacks, Apartment 4 in Shady Side Manor was looking more and more attractive.

* * * * *

Lil knocked on her door one evening. "I just wanted to make sure everything was all right. Is this a bad time?"

"Not at all; come on in," said Helen, and they both sat down.

"I'm glad to see that you've settled in and made friends. Betty tells me that you've livened up the discussion group at the library."

Helen laughed. "Not really; everyone contributes, but I was a literature major in college. This is my first chance in years to use what I learned, and I'm glad I haven't forgotten everything."

"I probably shouldn't bring this matter up so soon, but have you made any progress in contacting Henry?"

Helen felt goose pimples rising. "I haven't really tried."

"That surprises me. I was impressed by your love for him and your grief when he passed on. Wouldn't you like to see him again?"

Helen wondered how she should respond. "I'd give everything I own to see him alive," she said finally, "but I have no desire to contact his spirit."

"Has he tried to contact you?"

Helen remembered the incident after coming home from *Carmen* but decided not to mention it. "Let's put it this way. I've been sleeping peacefully for the first time since his death."

Lil looked puzzled. "You probably don't know how to summon him. If you'll come next door, I'll show you how I get in touch with Willie when he doesn't appear spontaneously."

Helen started to object.

"You needn't worry," Lil reassured her. "Willie doesn't mind company."

Helen debated what to do. Since there was no polite way to refuse, she agreed to go along. Unit 3 was much like her own, except that the living room was smaller, and it lacked access to the patio. Lil invited her to share the sofa, and she picked up an old Ingersoll watch. "This belonged to Willie's grandfather, and Willie carried it in his pocket every day of his life. A personal item helps me focus."

She took several deep breaths, clasping the watch, and closed her eyes. "First, I empty my mind. Then I visualize Willie. I say his name out loud after I get a clear picture in my head, and he usually appears in front of the opposite wall."

Helen noted otherworldly patterns on that wall, similar to those in her own unit. She wondered if they were part of Reggie's renovations. As Lil's concentration deepened, they seemed to vibrate, forcing Helen to think of the grave—of something coming from the grave. The image of a handsome middle-aged man, cut down in his prime, started to protrude from the wall. She could almost hear Carmen crying "Death!"

No! she thought. *I"m hallucinating.* With great effort, she shook off this black mood, and the patterns collapsed into innocuous symbols.

At that point, Lil called out "Willie," then opened her eyes and looked startled. "That's strange. I had a very clear image in my mind. One summons is usually enough."

Helen did not know how to answer. "Let me try again," said Lil. A half hour later, she admitted defeat. Her eyes focused on the opposite wall. "Those patterns—they've changed. There's no life there anymore."

She looked at Helen in consternation. "You don't believe; that's what's wrong."

Helen rose. "I think I should leave."

"No, please sit down. You really don't believe in survival

after death at all, do you?"

There was no way for Helen to avoid answering and also maintain her integrity. "If you must know, I don't believe in the supernatural. I believe this life and the natural world are all there is. Other people are free to think what they like. That's the kind of tolerance I thought I'd instilled in Janet before she met Ron and the pastor of the True Apostolic Temple."

"Isn't there even the slightest doubt in your mind?"

Helen remembered her strong sense of Henry's presence a few nights back and how the possibility had threatened her peace of mind. "I have to be honest. I find the possibility of the dead roaming among us to be morbid, not consoling."

Lil stared at her as if she were an alien species. "Let me put it this way. Suppose you're wrong and ghosts do exist. Wouldn't you like to see Henry again?"

"The answer is still no. My husband's death nearly destroyed me, and, if I thought I saw his ghost, I'd resist it. I'd be afraid that I was losing my grip on reality."

Lil seemed flabbergasted. "You don't just doubt—you willfully disbelieve."

Helen grasped Lil's hand. "Please don't let any of this interfere with you. You've been very kind to me, and if you get consolation from a séance—"

"This isn't a séance."

"—from believing that Willie's close by, I'm happy for you. Now I really think I should leave."

Helen hurried out the door and into her own unit. She headed straight for the easy chair and tried to compose herself. No one had been more helpful than Lil, and she hated to hurt the woman's feelings. How could a sensible person like her want to contact her dead husband? Or was it possible?

Was Helen the one with a closed mind? Her eyes rested on the fake fern with the fake dead frond. Of course! There was a perfectly natural explanation for what was happening. When Reggie and Alf redesigned the units, they installed devices to produce special effects. She remembered watching a believable ghost play the piano at a magic show. Lil appeared unaware of any trickery, but something must have malfunctioned in her apartment this evening, and Helen was sorry. Lil was the first person since Henry who had made her feel at home.

She searched her own apartment for hidden microphones and other paraphernalia, but found nothing. Of course, she was no electrician, and she resolved to keep quiet concerning her suspicions. Reggie and Alf were providing companionship for the lonely inhabitants of Shady Side Manor, and, if the two men were conning the tenants out of extra rent, they were still morally superior to the pastor of the True Apostolic Temple, who lived in a mansion and had served time in prison for tax fraud.

The two secretaries seemed subdued the following morning. Betty mentioned that Marvin had not come by the previous evening. "Perhaps it's because he doesn't consider the book club selection, *Lust on Ivory Hill*, to be worthy of literary comment." Alice smiled at the joke, but seemed preoccupied. Helen wondered if the ghost equipment had malfunctioned throughout the building. She changed the subject and managed to enjoy the walk.

Afterward, she sat for a good hour on the patio, enjoying the profusion of late impatiens and remembering Reggie's discomfort. What caused him to be so uneasy, considering he had done such a good job of gardening? She doubted that he suffered from allergies, and Lil had also refused to sit out here. Was the patio supposed to be haunted as well?

As the month wore on, Helen realized she was becoming attached to her new home. She again phoned Janet.

"Mother, where have you been? Christina thinks you've deserted her, and she still can't understand why you wouldn't babysit during the revival."

"I don't want to argue. I phoned to tell you that I'll probably stay on at Shady Side Manor. I'm definitely not moving back to the house."

The receiver was quiet for a long time. "I'd hoped I could persuade you to accept the Lord," Janet said finally. "I don't know how I'm going to explain things to Christina."

Janet's last comment cut like a knife. Playing with Christina was the only thing that had made living at her daughter's house tolerable. She resolved to visit in the near future.

Helen returned to the manager's office the following day and found both Lil and Reggie present. "I've decided to stay," she announced, "and here's my check for $500 for the coming month."

Reggie did not seem pleased. "That low rate applies only until Henry appears."

"I assure you that he hasn't shown up yet." Helen had privately resolved to let an electrician check her unit if ghostly phenomena ever started manifesting again.

Lil glanced up. "I thought you were looking for another place."

"I was, but I couldn't find anything reasonable."

"I'm willing to attach a rider to your contract and give you another month," she said. That way, you won't have to commit yourself."

"But I want to commit. I've settled in and made friends.

I'm going to stay at least a year, maybe longer. According to the agreement I signed, I can stay as long as I please."

"The usual rate is $700," said Reggie.

Helen sighed, but she knew she had to be firm, the same as with Janet. "I signed a contract in good faith, and I've kept my side of the bargain."

"Is there any way we can make you reconsider? How about two months? If you want, I'll even help you look for a new apartment," Lil said. She seemed almost frantic.

"No, and that's final. If you try to break the contract, I'll call my lawyer."

Reggie started to object, but Lil intervened. "All right, we'll just have to accept Helen's decision. A contract is a contract, after all, and I know she's telling the truth about Henry. If we lose a little on the unit, so be it."

She looked at her watch. "It's only four o'clock, but I could use some tea, couldn't you? I just bought a new brand called 'English Sleepy Time.' It's 100% herbal and very restful." Helen suddenly felt tired, or perhaps it was relief over finally making a decision and taking charge of her life. She stood up. "I think I'll just go back to the apartment."

Lil followed. "That's fine. I'll come over in a few minutes."

Helen agreed that a cup of tea would be most welcome, and Lil appeared soon afterward with two steaming mugs. Helen settled into the easy chair, inhaled the "Sleepy Time" essence, and began to sip. The hot tea was the most relaxing she had ever drunk. Within a few minutes, her worries seemed to disappear. She could even remember her conversations with Janet without guilt or regret. When she turned to thank Lil, she found difficulty in moving and became alarmed..

"Something... something's wrong," she said.

Lil frowned. "What's the matter?"

"I ... I think I'm having an allergic reaction to the tea." Helen could hear her voice starting to slur. "Please call a doctor."

"Nonsense! Just lean back. You'll be all right."

"No!" With great effort, Helen pushed herself erect and staggered forward. After a few steps, she stumbled and fell.

Lil tried unsuccessfully to help her up. "Just a minute. I'll get Reggie." She disappeared out the door. Helen crawled to the side table, but the phone wasn't there. In a few minutes, Lil returned with Reggie, and the two of them lifted Helen into her chair.

"Just lean back and relax," said Lil. She turned to Reggie. "Hunting down Helen's easy chair and having it repaired and re-upholstered was a stroke of genius. It'll hold her in the apartment after she passes over."

Helen looked pleadingly at the manager. "Doctor . . . please!"

"This is cold-blooded murder," he said. "I'm calling 911."

"Not murder, Reggie. It's assisted transition. The soul never dies. You know that."

"That isn't the way the police see it."

"Now, now! If you say anything to the police, I'll have to tell them about Willie. After I gave him a cup of this sleepy-time tea, you helped me bury him in the patio under the whiskey barrel, remember? That makes you an accessory."

Reggie shuddered. "That was a mercy killing. He was dying of brain cancer."

"The law still calls it murder. If I go to prison, so will you."

The two locked eyes while Helen stammered, "D... doctor."

"You shouldn't have offered her that lease," said Reggie.

"How was I to know? I've never seen willful disbelief in anyone so caring. It's driven all the ghosts away. It's more powerful than any exorcism."

"And you were afraid you'd have to lower the rent on all the units when she refused to leave?"

Lil seemed hurt. "Of course that's not the reason; it's the principle of the thing. I couldn't let her stay on even if she paid full price. Her disbelief is keeping the ghosts away and destroying my mission. I'm strong enough to live without Willie, but the secretaries are devastated, and Captain Smythe is sure he's lost Myrtle for good. I have to consider the well-being of all the tenants." She frowned and wrung her hands. "Don't think I didn't agonize over this decision."

This strange conversation was beginning to sound like a dream. Helen resolved to remember as much as she could after she woke up so she could share it with Betty and Alice on their walk the following morning.

"How will killing Helen help?" Reggie asked, and Lil immediately put her finger to his lips.

"Don't use that word, Reggie. Of course, her passing will help. She can't disbelieve in ghosts after she's become one, can she? The other ghosts will all return."

Lil looked directly into Helen's eyes. The image started to blur. "I'm sorry it's come to this, but you gave me no choice when you insisted on staying. You'll benefit, too, you know, or I'd never have gone through with this. You'll become a resident ghost, and you won't ever have to pay rent again. I'll make sure the next tenant in Apartment 4 is congenial and appreciates culture the way you do so you won't be lonely. That's what I did for Professor Travis."

"But he died a natural death," said Reggie.

"And Helen's passing will be near-natural. The poison's slow acting and doesn't cause any pain. She'll just gradually go to sleep."

Helen felt that everything Lil said was true and good, even though she could hardly understand the words. Her eyelids were becoming too heavy to open, and Lil's voice sounded far away.

After a while, Lil and Reggie hauled away some heavy part of her, a part she no longer needed. She discovered she could control how solid the rest of her appeared, and her mental acuity had returned, along with full vision. Sounds and smells were now sharper, but she knew she'd never be able to taste anything again. It was easier to walk touching the ground, although she could float or become transparent altogether if she chose. She could even leave the building, but right now, it was more pleasant staying near her chair in a place where everyone believed, where death was not morbid after all. The designs on the wall were again becoming other-worldly and soon Henry would be able to visit anytime he wanted.

She was surprised at how natural it all seemed.

Catherine A. Callaghan enjoys speculative fiction that emphasizes character and skirts the boundaries between the real and the unreal. She has published a book of poems, Other Worlds, based on the prints of M.C. Escher (prints included). In her other life, she is a semi-retired professor specializing in Central California Indian languages.

Negev

by Joshua M. Young

Do you remember?

We swore to make the desert bloom, you and I.

We all did. Each and every one of us.

What greater desert can be found than this? This world, this galaxy... It will all bloom one day. First here. First Negev. First our world, so far from earth and the ancient battleground, where we are, perhaps, safe from those older than man, should they come back to finish what they started.

Then—the galaxy. We will heal the ancient battlegrounds, and they, too, will bloom. And should Avaddon return then... Well, maybe then we will be able to beat them.

I saw the first wild flower today.

It was lovely. Just a small, frail thing, clinging to life in the desert, surviving only by virtue of its enhanced genetics. It was the only plant in sight, as far from Ben-Gurion and the ruins of the *Merkava* as Negev is from earth, it seems.

I knelt next to it, cupping the blossom in my hands for just a moment. The petals were broad and blue, thin like tissue. A gift from the posthumans, a preview of what our world could be like. With the *Merkava*'s resources gone, we could not have done it ourselves.

I wrenched it from the ground, crushing the flower in my fist.

Not at the cost of our son.

I'm so sorry, Ester.

* * * * *

They came during the month of Tishri, a little after Sukkot, while the festival booths still stood and Ben-Gurion was still crowded with pilgrims.

It had been so long since the crash of the *Merkava* that the children didn't know what they were. They didn't recognize the shuttles as machines made by men. Some clung in terror to their parents, and some stared in rapt wonder at these new birds. Only one, a little girl named Yael, not more than five or six, seemed to understand. She pawed at my leg and said, "Rabbi, look. It's like 'zekiel. But why aren't they wheels?"

No dust was stirred when they landed. They settled on the ground outside the city with less effort than a robin; the only wind came off the plains, unstirred and unaffected by the ships. The hull of the ships rippled like water, and the metal pulled back, flowing away from an invisible point, exposing the insides of the shuttles to the open air.

Ester, they are not human. I don't care what they say... they are not like us. They have traded away their humanity. You can see it in some-- the machines in their flesh, hidden, for the most part, but still visible as a flash, a glimpse of sunlight on metal in places where there should be only flesh. In all, their eyes are cold and distant, constantly fixed on something known only to their kind.

Is this what earth has come to since we left?

They never talk to each other, only to us. I feel as though they are communicating through the machines in their flesh— faster, too fast for humans, too fast for a mortal to follow. Remember the stories about the web back at Earth? The great network our parents talked of? It is as if they sunk that network into their skulls, so that they are now part of it.

And it is they who are part of it, not the other way around. Alone, they seem incomplete-- vacant and empty. I got

Yitzhak's recruiter alone the other day, and questioned him. Always, Ester, always, he seemed to be looking at a place beyond the wall, beyond sight, and his answers came slowly, as if from far away.

They left their ships quietly, smiling and holding out empty hands, as though we were savages, afraid that clenched fists may conceal a blade. I bristled, annoyed at the condescension. "We have not fallen that far, whatever the state of other colonies you have visited. Some of us have even seen Negev from orbit."

One, a slim, dark man who had disembarked from a ship near the center of the cluster, seemed to freeze, hesitating a moment.

"Let's see the beads, then," I muttered. "If you intend to buy our land for a handful of glass."

He laughed, shaking his head. "You can keep your world. We're after trade, not a colonial annex. You call this world Negev?" His Hebrew was flawless, with less of an accent than many of our children.

"We do."

"Israeli descent?"

"Indeed."

"Then the wreck near here is—"

"—The *Merkava*. Yes. It crashed about fifteen years ago." I did not add that you had been aboard, Ester. I did not tell him about what that crash took from us. The resources. The possibility of travel. The family. God, Ester.

He knew, though. I'm sure they studied us before landing; it would have been foolish not to do so. I'm sure they would know that we have less than half a dozen power plants, and no personal computer use to speak of. I'm sure he knew just how backwards and isolated *Merkava*'s death—and yours, beloved—left us. But in spite of that, or perhaps because of a sadistic desire to rub salt in our wounds, he asked, "How's your connection to the rest of the universe?"

"You are a surprise. Have all humans been, uh, upgraded? Did you eradicate true humans? There were rumors of military action to be taken against your ancestors when we left."

He grinned, apparently gleaning all that he needed from those few sentences. "No contact at all, then. There have been a few schisms. 'True Humanity' and posthumanity are separate empires these days."

The crowd grew restless; I heard shouts to make way for other Sanhedrin officials in the background. "And posthumanity found us first."

The man's grin grew vicious—but only just. "Posthumanity finds everyone first. True humanity has yet to look beyond its immediate neighborhood. The Shinto colony on Torii, the Caliphate Remnant of Umayyad, the Australians of Ayer's Rock, you here on Negev, others. The so-called true humans have no clue as to your existence."

"Then you are our only contact with the galaxy."

"Azazel, of the Ambassador School of the Becoming, at your service."

"You name yourself for a fallen angel."

"I name myself for an *Irin*," he said, grinning and sweeping his arms towards the other posthumans, "Enoch's Watchers of old. And, Rabbi, I am going to teach you all how to forge metals once more."

* * * * *

I visit your grave still, Ester. It's hard—people do not like to approach the wreck. We don't know if it's radioactive or not; no one has the tools to find out. Why did we need them on Negev? You needed them on the *Merkava*. Needed to know if the reactor was leaking, if you were in danger...

I try to visit once or twice a year. I try to stand, barefoot, on the ground that shattered your body, and the body of so many others, and the body of the chariot that brought us to this world... I stand there for a long time, feeling the warm metal underneath my feet, looking up at the rusted beams and supports of the skeleton of the ship, knowing that these are the only tombstones you and the others can have.

I scratched your name into one. It was the best I could do.

Sometimes I feel that the painting hanging in the Sanhedrin's chambers is a mockery. It shows the *Merkava*, beautiful and lustrous, at peace with the world around it, with the lovely hues of a nebula we never passed in the background. It does not show the *Merkava* as you and I knew it, the aging hulk of a colony ship, growing increasingly frailer, but still the only place with the processing power and labs and resources we needed after we lost the supply pods.

Azazel and his retinue stood in front of the painting. He addressed the Sanhedrin with a pleasant voice, free of all but the friendliest condescension, saying that he would help us make the desert bloom, that he would help us preserve our culture, and that the posthumans were only there to help.

"Why do you think we need your help?"

Azazel smiled at me. "Abdiel Shachar, ABD," he said, reading the name plate resting in front of me. "*Av Beit Din*, yes? Do you preside here?"

"I do not. It is in the more modern sense—I am simply the chief rabbi of Negev. Not so grand on a world this small. Please answer my question: We were fine without you; why do we need you now?"

"Do you know what year it is?"

"It is the thirty-seventh year since we landed."

"In the common calendar of earth, please."

I said nothing, resting folded hands on my desk.

"In the traditional Hebrew calendar?"

"It is difficult to say. The relativistic time dilation from *Merkava*'s spacefold—"

"Do you truly know the meaning of those words? Do you know where you are in the galaxy, Rav Shachar?"

I felt anger stir within me at his mockery. My clasped fingers dug into the backs of my hands.

"Did you understand how to save a file on whatever outmoded operating system you used on your ship? Yes? Do your children? The little girl clinging to your leg when we first spoke—does she even know what a computer is? How long until your children no longer know the meaning of the word 'Israel'? Of the meaning of the letters ABD, or of YHWH?

"Perhaps you missed it when we first spoke—The Caliphate Remnant is out there, Rabbi. On Earth they swore to push you into the sea, and it is only by the skin of your teeth that Israel survived the twenty-first century—not that you would know that it did. Your ship had left by then.

"Rav Shachar, do you know what the sea looks like now? The sea you will be pushed into without our help? It is the darkness between the galaxies.

"As luck—or misfortune—would have it, you are once again on the edge of the sea." With an extended palm, Azazel caused a convoluted spiral of stars to form above him. Some of those seated around me gasped, not seeing the play of light along strips of metal embedded in the flesh of his hand. A single star flared bright red, toward the very outer edge of the spiral's disk, not the red of an old star, but the red of something meant to stand out. A second one flared green, much farther in, about halfway between the central bulging and the outer edge. "Green is Earth. Red is Negev." A third, not quite in between the two, but farther from the edge and closer to the bulge, turned blue. And then a fourth, and a fifth, and a sixth. "The worlds of the Caliphate Remnant. In theory, you could slip out between them to find another world, should they attack. Space, as they say, is big. But then, you lack even the ability to reach orbit."

* * * * *

They scare me, Ester. I am afraid of what they represent— not the rebirth of technology on Negev, but the severing of soul from body. To look into their eyes... It is the look of something worse than a corpse, for they still move. They link themselves into this great web of theirs, and I must wonder: where are their souls now? If they can range all over their web, without physically moving, where is their soul, Ester? Who is to say that when I speak with Azazel, I am speaking with Azazel, and not speaking with some other posthuman who may not even be on Negev? If the soul may range anywhere it wishes, are the bodies not interchangeable, no different from the fingers of my hand, or the tools issued to laborers by their employers?

I am reminded of the serpent. "You shall not die; your eyes shall be opened, and you shall be as gods."

* * * * *

I am afraid that I have lost my temper many times since the posthumans have arrived. In the central square of Ben-Gurion, there is now a notice-board constructed only of light. You can put your hand through it, though this ruins the image for a short time. It is small, not much more than four feet tall and eminently tasteful, and rests on the eastern side of the square, near the Sanhedrin chambers, where it is easily found. It displays information about the posthuman schools, slowly cycling through the different disciplines one may choose to study under. Ambassadors, Siliconists, Embedders, other arcane names without meaning to me.

It had been there for less than a week when I saw Yitzhak perusing it, lips and eyes that belonged to you pursed and narrowed in concentration as he studied it.

The serpent was conversing with my son, extending to him the Fruit of Knowledge on a limb that should have died and withered millennia ago, when the Most High cursed him.

I broke two knuckles and an expensive sheet of glass— covering a more expensive photograph of you and me, Ester—when I saw this from my office in the Sanhedrin.

"The next time you see something you hate so," said the doctor as he bandaged my wounded hand, "punch the bare wall. You will not hurt the stone, and you will not hurt your hand any more than you have by trying to cushion it with glass."

Bits of broken glass lay at the base of the wall; a smear of blood and a jagged tear fouled the image of you. Perhaps the serpent can restore it—certainly, no one on this world can.

* * * * *

Sometimes, in the middle of the night, when the sun is hours away in either direction, I wake up and reach for you, and my hand brushes not the line of your arm, nor the swell of your breast, nor the plane of your belly, but rumpled, empty sheets. I lay, for a few moments, dumbfounded, till the memory returns, and the warmth of affection inside my heart flickers and dies.

It was weeks before I washed those sheets after the crash. Night after night, I lay in bed, inhaling the increasingly faint scent of you, till at last there was no scent but myself. I wept, then, bawled as I did the night I saw *Merkava* die.

These are the nights when I pace about the house—not, as some may suspect, because I am an old man with an equally old bladder, but because I have lost you anew. Each and every time it is as though I can again see the streak of fire across the sky.

Time heals all wounds, but there is no time on sleep's tail, and every wound is as fresh and as jagged as the day it was rent.

On those nights, I generally do not go back to sleep. I putter around the house, careful not to wake Yitzhak. I read or work out chess problems. On occasion, I will leave, setting out under the stars for wherever my feet will take me, though I do this only rarely. I am too afraid that I will see a shooting star, too afraid that a little streak of fire across the sky will ruin any composure I might have.

Some nights I risk it. The night after I broke my hand, I found myself alone under the stars, feet carrying me into the wilderness, inexorably in the direction of the *Merkava*.

It is a long walk. The sun was high when the shadows of *Merkava*'s ribs finally fell across me.

I wrapped my arms around the spar bearing your name, pressed my forehead to the dirty metal, heedless of the rust and dirt that smeared my face.

The world moved on.

I did not.

* * * * *

"Dad."

"Yitzhak." I did not turn, but I let my hands drop to my sides.

"I figured you'd be here. I heard you pacing last night."

"I tried to be quiet. Apologies if I woke you."

"No, I was awake already. Thinking."

I made a show of rubbing my face, as though I were tired, and hoped that this would hide the wiping away of tears and grime. "About the visitors. Our self-proclaimed *Irin*."

"Yeah." He paused. "Dad, I want to study with them."

I felt like vomiting.

"We can't even build cars anymore. No one remembers how... We crossed the stars, Dad, and we can't cross the continent, much less make the desert bloom. Unless we learn to be human again, the desert will consume us."

"What... what did you want to study?"

"Terraforming. Life-adaption. I want to pick up where Mom left off, and adapt things to live here, adapt this world to us."

"Noble." I turned, then, looking at him finally. Your smile graced his face, a little embarrassed at the praise. He is a fine young man. I wish you could see him.

"Practical," he countered softly. "I don't want to see the death of Ben-Gurion and everyone who lives there. And--" He stepped forward, brushing his fingers across the letters scratched in the spar, "—we all have our ways of remembering someone."

"We will talk with the posthumans, then. But, Yitzhak—"

"Yeah?"

"—Being human is not about the tools we wield. Remember that."

"I—I will, Dad."

* * * * *

The posthumans dwell in a structure on the outskirts of Ben-Gurion. This building did not exist before they landed, and it was not constructed in any fashion with which I am familiar. A cocoon of dull black, about thirty feet tall, grew there overnight; a few nights later, it was gone, replaced with a modest sized building, sleek but not out of place in a city built of native stone. There is a reception area inside, about which people may come and go, and a few posthumans seated at their scattered desks—desks that, like everything which they have constructed here, have the foreign promise of the future ingrained into their being without being overwhelmingly alien.

The nearest of the posthumans greeted us before the door closed. "Rav Shachar. Can't say this is expected."

"Have we met?"

His answering smile was flat. "Not as such. Who is your companion, Rabbi?"

"My name is Yitzhak Shachar."

His eyebrows rose in an expression of surprise, though his eyes remained dull. "Son of the rabbi? Come to visit the posthuman embassy? Intriguing. Sandalphon, of the Ambassador School of the Becoming, at your service."

The way he spoke-- it was so similar to Azazel. The intonation, the faint derision in his voice. "Do your parents give you these names, or do you choose them intentionally to mock us?" I struggled to keep my voice from becoming bitter.

"I am your world's primary liaison to the Becoming, Rav Shachar. What better name than the angel who carries prayers to God?"

"Are all of you this skilled with subtle blasphemies?"

"Had I truly wanted to mock or blaspheme, I would bear a different name. Perhaps Shekhinah."

Yitzhak laid his hand upon my shoulder, just the way you used to do when I grew angry. There is so much of you in him, Ester. So much.

"I'd like to study under one of your schools."

Sandalphon tipped his chair back, propping his feet up on his desk, a strangely normal gesture to come from one of the posthumans. "I know. The records of those who peruse the board are stored to our network."

"Then why ask?" Yitzhak spoke with a calm, quiet grace-- not something he learned from his father.

"You may come to understand this in time," Sandalphon replied. "What school were you thinking of joining?"

"The Cellulist school, primarily."

"Got another biologist in the family, eh, Rabbi?"

I clamped my mouth shut and nodded mutely. Sandalphon withdrew from a drawer in his desk a dull grey disk, about a quarter of an inch thick and an inch wide. He held it up to the light critically. "We will have to get a Cellulist down here to work with you, Yitzhak. It's not a common choice. Colony worlds tend to get a lot who wish to be Ambassadors, at least initially. Not as heavy on, uh, visible modifications as some other schools. In the meantime, this will start your initial network implant's growth." He waved the disk a little, extended it to my son. "Place it on the back of your neck, and it will dissolve. The implant will take a few days to grow, and then come back on in and we'll get your connection initialized."

I exhaled, a rough, ragged action, "No implants."

Yitzhak looked confused; Sandalphon smiled that posthuman smile, full of condescension and hubris. "Rav Shachar... Surely you did not think the word 'school' implied desks and gym class? These are schools of thought within the Becoming, Rabbi. There is no university for your son—just a network that will one day span the universe. Knowledge, wisdom, immortality—just a few days away for him."

"Who are you to bestow those things? We do not need your fruit to survive!" I pulled at Yitzhak's arm. "We are leaving."

* * * * *

As much as he looks like you, Ester, he is my son, and, like me, he is a stubborn ass. He left with me that day, but, several nights later, I found him on the floor of his bedroom, shivering, body curled in agony, skin burning with fever. I knelt to help him, and when I slipped my hand behind his head, I felt a small, hard lump under his skin.

"Oh, Yitzhak, what have you done?"

His smile was weak, watery like a thin soup. "What needed done... Sandalphon... said this would happen... nanomachines... like a virus in my body. It'll pass."

I resisted the urge to yank my hand away from him, away from the damned implant growing under his skin. I felt silk, a nausea growing in the pit of my stomach to match the device in his neck.

With my free hand, I groped behind me for the pillow on his bed, and slipped the pillow under his head. I stood and slipped out, returning with a cloth and a bowl of cool water. I sat beside him, keeping him cool until the fever broke.

* * * * *

Sometime during the night, I must have fallen asleep. When I awoke, our son was sitting on the floor in the same spot in which he had sprawled earlier; now, though, he sat upright, skin free from sweat—the sun had barely risen, and it was not yet hot—and the fingers of one hand twitching rapidly, flying, it seemed, over a keyboard I could not see.

"What are you doing?"

"Learning." His fingers lay still for a moment. "Did you know that there are 457 human colonies that the posthumans know about? Out of those, only 62 remain in contact with Earth at all, and only 23 claim membership in the Parliament of True Humanity. The largest interstellar empire currently in existence, outside the posthumans, is a relatively enlightened Anglosphere-derived nation in the Cygnus Arm. Near us, as it happens. Also not a force to be trifled with, they do have a standing military." He smiled broadly, sparing me a glance away from whatever invisible information he was seeing. "Perhaps the alliances of our parents could be reborn, and we could gain some help against the Caliphate. We don't have much to offer, though. We're not in a strategic location, orbital surveys don't show much in the way of valuable minerals, there are no giant worms in the desert, and producing immortality drugs..."

* * * * *

Yitzhak will never be sick again. His fever did not break because his body fought off the infection; it broke because the posthuman machines inside him shut off his immune system and replaced it with a swarm of nanomachines to serve the same purpose. The machines are stronger, smarter, and faster than a natural immune system, or so Yitzhak tells me.

I am forced to confess that I find this marvelous-- no sickness, no disease, and, if Yitzhak's hints are to be believed, not even old age. Some of the machines repair DNA itself, and he intimates that the decay of DNA is what is responsible for aging.

And...

And, Ester...

If those machines could repair something as complicated as the human body, what could they have done for the *Merkava*?

If they had only come two decades earlier.

If only.

* * * * *

It rained this morning, very early; the sun was not yet up, and I had only just stirred from my bed.

Since you died, Ester, I can count the number of times that it has rained on one hand. But it came down this morning, a fine, cold mist that was dirty enough to seem as mud. I found Yitzhak standing outside in it, staring at the vague, light grey that marked the sun rising through the cloud cover and smiling enigmatically.

"It's beginning," is the only thing he said to me, and: "The desert will begin to bloom, soon."

We stood in silence, watching the sky grow gradually lighter; the rain eventually grew heavy enough to mat down my beard and soak my clothing, and though I was cold to the bone, we did not go inside.

Yitzhak may not have been cold; I am not even sure he was wet. His hair did not seem so. Some trick of posthumanity, no doubt.

* * * * *

"Why do they do this?"

Yitzhak's gaze was blank, empty. "What do you mean, Dad?"

"Come to worlds, offer technology and aid, and ask for nothing in return."

He looked back to the horizon, arms crossed over his chest, and stared intently at the lightening sky. "They're getting a lot in return. No one seems to realize just how valuable this—" He tapped the side of his head. "—is to them. What having access to a whole new culture and point of view does."

"A single person is that valuable?"

Yitzhak smiled, a here and gone flicker of his lips. "There

are three of us, now. The other two have chosen the Ambassador school. But yes. A single new person is that valuable, especially from a world that has not contributed any members to the Becoming's mental web. I, and the other two, represent a mental attitude that is uniquely Negevite in many ways-- some small, some very large."

"The Becoming? Is that what they call themselves when they are not mocking us?"

"Posthumanity has been given a lot of names—most of them aren't all that flattering, but then normal humanity has been given a lot of names within the Becoming. Acorns. Caterpillars. A few downright nasty things. Humans are a seed, Dad, and despite what may have been said in the past, most humans are acorns that are afraid to become oak trees. Posthumans—the Becoming—are not afraid to leave behind the shell, to spread our roots in the soil and lift ourselves skyward."

"Do you really know of what you are talking?" I murmured quietly. "Yitzhak. The stripping away of humanity for this godhood. It is the oldest sin there is."

Your smile again found its way to his face, and it is a sight I hope I never see again. It was cold, lifeless, a perversion of the beautiful smile that I had seen on your face throughout your life. For the first time, it dawned on me that his gaze was not distant because he was staring at the horizon, but because he was alone, without the immediate companionship of other posthumans. For the first time—perhaps because the sun had finally crawled high enough, perhaps because I now knew to look, I realized that he was no longer entirely human. Motes of light swam in the black of his eyes, nearly invisible, but there; dark bands of rough flesh wrapped his arm in a spiral that suggested at once both DNA and the straps of the armtefillin.

"A DNA-based biological computer," Yitzhak said, voice flat, eyes following mine to the strangely textured skin. "It will be more noticeable in a few days; it is still growing." With a flick of his hand, he brushed the hair away from his forehead, allowing me to see the darkened flesh growing there, again suggesting the phylacteries he had worn to temple for the past decade.

"And so you, too, mock us." My voice faltered. "You alter your body, praying for apotheosis, mocking and ridiculing your heritage as you shed what you were for what you hope to become."

"This is not a mockery, Dad. Maybe if you weren't such a stubborn Luddite, you'd understand that."

"What is it, then?"

"Evolution. Humanity must evolve, but we cannot. We have used technology to ease all the environmental pressures that lead to evolution, and so we must take it into our own hands. Use that same technology to guide and shape our growth.

"I choose to remember where I came from, and so I bind the Word to myself in the tradition of our people."

"That," I hissed, stabbing a finger at his forehead, "is not the Word."

"Isn't it? Isn't the Word what spoke us into being? Isn't the language that spoke me into being composed of four syllables, uttered over and over in endless combinations? Thymine, Adenine, Guanine, Cytosine? That language will follow me all of my days! Most likely, anyway," he added, voice betraying a sudden, inscrutable amusement. "But I am not convinced that the Embedder's universal transcendence at the Omega point is possible."

It was as though he spoke a new language. I stared blankly at him, lost by the talk of transcendence. There was a disconnect, as if someone had removed a critical wire between two computers.

Two computers. I was sickened by the comparison, remembering the machines swimming inside our son's veins, seeing the computer growing under and inside his skin.

* * * * *

It rains more often than not, now. Muddy water—a thin stew of water, hydrocarbons, and other chemicals that Yitzhak mentioned—falls with a startling regularity. Six days of the week it rains, and on shabbat it does not.

The posthumans are bombarding our planet with comets, in trajectories precisely calculated by our son to lose most of their mass in entering Negev's atmosphere, impacting eventually on the far side of the planet, far away from Ben-Gurion. The frequency of the bombardment was again calculated by Yitzhak so as to allow the weather to be sunny on shabbat.

He is adding water and organic compounds to this desert, so that when the seeding begins, there will be material to support the growth of plants.

We would have died, eventually, without the posthumans. Yet another set of Yitzhak's calculations show that the terraforming began by *Merkava*'s damaged machinery would be completely reversed within another hundred years. The barely tenable land we built around Ben-Gurion would be reclaimed by the desert.

The posthuman's operations—Yitzhak's plans—are being worked on a scale we could never have been prepared for, Ester. The 21st-century Earth we left did not have the technology to harvest a system's comets, to send vessels out to the cloud of ice and dirt beyond the farthest planets, nudging and flinging the snowballs in carefully plotted paths, and the dying, brutalized colony ship we limped here in definitely could not have handled it.

We were dead.

And now we live. We are given our future.

I do not like being beholden to the posthumans. Even if I did not have my philosophical and theological misgivings about them, they are arrogant, irritating. The fact that they have saved us worries at me like a blister.

Maybe it's true. Maybe I am a Luddite, and an ungrateful son of a bitch—but I do not like what our son is becoming. It sickens me, almost physically—no, definitely physically. The "biocomputer" growing in his flesh nauseates me. It is not just the mockery of our heritage and beliefs; it is the thought of something alien, something unnatural, crawling inside his flesh. It is the thought that he associates with people who willingly remove and replace parts of their bodies just because those organs are not efficient enough.

Above all, Ester, our son, the product of our bodies, the child that you bore, that sweet, innocent thing, pink, and wrinkly and ugly, like every other newborn ever, but yet nothing like any other child and so stunningly wonderful and beautiful... I cannot imagine looking at that child and knowing that he would change his own body because it does not meet his needs. I cannot imagine that perfect, beautiful child not being perfect enough. I cannot imagine him discarding parts of himself.

* * * * *

"*The Book of Enoch?*" Yitzhak asked, smiling slightly as he read the cover of the book I had just set down. "Not your usual reading material."

He was correct, of course, but infuriating. He spoke with a son's knowledge of his father and a posthuman's underlying tones of mockery and derision.

"No," I replied, with the forced calm I had learned to adopt in the past weeks, "but I feel that it may be wise to study the *Irin* of history. Perhaps I may gain some insight into our latter day visitors."

"We're not quite one and the same, Dad."

I winced, either unable or unwilling to hide my reaction to his identification with the posthumans. I'm not sure which; I did not care, frankly. I was frustrated with him, frustrated with his descent into the posthuman world.

"What do you want, Yitzhak?" I asked. I have never before spoken to our son is such cold tones.

"Come outside with me."

"It's raining outside."

"Of course. It's not Shabbat. I planned the comets trajectories, you know."

"Yes, Yitzhak, I know. That doesn't change the fact that it is raining outside."

"It's gonna be raining for a long time, Dad. Years. Negev needs oceans and rivers and lakes. That's gonna take a while. You'd think, for someone born on a starship and raised on a desert planet, you'd be a little more interested in the rain."

"Muddy water falling from the sky loses some of the novelty after a few days of standing in temple, soaked and chilled to the bone."

"Do we need to teach you people to build umbrellas again?"

"Do you people need to be so damned patronizing?"

Yitzhak held up one hand, the hand wrapped and twisted about with darkened flesh of Yitzhak's mocking biocomputer;

held in between his thumb and forefinger was a small green twig, with two tiny leaves at one end. "Do you know what this is?"

"A plant."

"It's an olive branch, Dad. The first this world has seen. The tree's in your back yard." He tossed the twig on my desk and left.

* * * * *

Though I am a rabbi, I am no prophet. I do not claim divine revelations or visions; I do not claim audible dialogues with the Lord.

Nevertheless, for all those things that I do not claim, for all the things in the Tanakh that I do not have in common with those priests, prophets, and warriors, I am a Jew, and as a Jew, I excel at one thing in particular: I am good at grumbling and yelling at God.

It is, after all, one of our cultural past times, is it not?

Why, oh Lord, did You give us a beautiful land, but populate it with giants? Why did You allow those blasted Romans to scatter us to the winds, oh Lord? Why allow the Caliphate to eye our tiny strip of land with greedy, jealous eyes? Why, oh Lord, why did You not destroy the posthuman ship before it came to this world? Why did You not keep us hidden from them, and why, oh why, Lord, did You allow my son to do this!

Grumbling becomes bellowing and outright rebellious anger after a time. Your heart becomes hard like stone and you go to sleep angry, fuming at the injustice of the God of Abraham.

I dreamt, Ester.

A beautiful, angelic being hung in the depths of space. Though I knew it to be not much bigger than an average human, it trailed ten wings behind it; each of those wings, made of folded space and tamed star-stuff, measured in miles. Where they rooted in the creature's back, they formed the Sefirot, that ancient pattern representing the divinity of God and His interaction with the material universe, each wing placed according to a particular sefira.

The being was graceful, otherworldly; it was heedless of the gulfs in which it rested, effortlessly ignoring solar wind and the hard radiation that slammed into it. It wore no suit, no bulky clothing to protect against the assaults of the stars. From time to time an oil-on-water shimmer would appear; this I knew to be what protected this heavenly thing from the impacts of space debris, vacuum, radiation, and, finally, the weapons of its enemy.

It was at war.

I do not know who its enemy was; perhaps it was Avaddon, though I think not. This was not the legendary, hypothesized force behind the wanton destruction of the worlds surrounding Earth. These were warships, fearful and intimidating, but only warships, vessels of ultimately human origin. Each was covered, it seemed, with a fine layer of fuzz that I knew to be antennas and weapons emplacements reduced by distance.

That gulf, though great, shrunk rapidly as I watched, and the two forces, ethereal and otherworldly versus the solid metal and plastic sheen of the enemy, clashed in anger.

Chaos followed in the wake of that collision. I watched in awe as the creature swiftly and systematically dodged energy lances, missiles, torpedoes, other weapons I knew no names for; its wings tore through space, destroying projectiles by the score and slicing through the warships as though they were paper. Once, something impacted the creature during the battle, and though rainbow colors washed over it, I saw it clutch its side in agony for a moment before lashing out at the nearest vessel with a wing.

In the end, each and every one of those ships lost to the angel-thing.

But it, too, drifted like debris in the gulfs of space, and I knew then that the wound had been a grievous one.

Though it –he—lay alone and wounded in the void, I saw his lips twitch, and there, Ester, there I saw your smile grace his lips.

A globe, brown and tan and yellow, hung in the distance— it was for this that he had fought and had been wounded; for this world and the patch of verdant green coming into view as the planet continued to quietly rotate, oblivious to all that had occurred.

Space is not a line, nor is time; and neither is separate from the other. They are a tapestry, woven by the deft hand of the Creator, and we are part of that weave—so we cannot see the design.

There—those last six words. It is that which I had forgotten in all this, ignored since the posthumans came to our world—There is a design.

There is a design, Ester.

Images, too fast for my eyes to follow—perhaps too fast for even posthuman eyes. I saw the images after they had passed, processed long, long microseconds after the dream had moved on.

They were beautiful, Ester.

There is sorrow to come—much, much sorrow, for Negev, for the Caliphate Remnant, for Torii and Ayers Rock and those Anglosphere worlds and all the other worlds in this pool of stars-- but there is joy, too. There are a few worlds which will be beacons in the darkness: shining fortresses, cities set atop hills, barricades to the return of Avaddon.

The garden world of Negev will be one of those citadels, shining in the dark for the lost.

You and I, Ester, both trace our lineage—as does everyone on this world—to a people, light-years distant, who would sooner die than surrender. It seems that stock will serve us well in the coming conflict against darkness and the sons of hubris.

* * * * *

There are more than a few who would laugh if I told them of this, Ester; even some who attend temple on Shabbat would scoff. "The voice of the Lord," they would say, "is for the prophets of old and for madmen."

Of all the people then, how embarrassing, and how delightfully appropriate, that I should discuss this with Sandalphon.

I awoke in the small hours of the morning, the dream still fresh in my mind, and I lay in bed for a long moment. I was relaxed, calm, for the first time in years. For the first time since you died, Ester, I was at peace in our bed.

In my bed.

There is something sad in coming to terms with grief. In that moment when you finally accept what has occurred, weeks and months or even years later, it is as if you are finally relinquishing your right to the person that meant so much.

That sorrow comes arm and arm with peace, though, and while it is tragic, it is not heart-wrenching.

There, in the small of the morning, on the tail of a dream that was perhaps more than a dream and perhaps no more than the random firings of my unconscious mind, I came to terms with the loss of my wife more than a decade ago, and came to terms with the potential and imminent loss of my son.

An olive tree, of all things.

How could I have been so stupid?

My son, a good young man, growing rapidly estranged from both his culture and his father, had come into his father's study bearing an olive branch.

I did not agree with his choice; I will never agree with his choice, but the choice is his, and his fate is his. His and the Lord's; it is time I learned to put faith in my faith, I think. To heed the words of the prophets—and of the Lord—when the Tanakh says that there is a plan for good and not for evil.

But whether or not I agreed with that choice, he was still my son, and I still loved him.

"Yitzhak?" I called, stumbling away from my bedroom on legs that were convinced they still slept.

He did not respond; I thought it possible he still slept, though he had slept less and less since he received the first implant linking him to the posthuman network. I rapped on his door, wincing as my knuckles fell on the hollow metal. They were still tender from being fractured months ago. "Yitzhak?" I called again, "Yitzhak, are you awake?"

Finally, I cracked open the door. In the dim grey light of yet another rainy dawn, I saw that his room was empty, the bed untouched, and my heart fell.

I dressed hurriedly, throwing on whatever clothes were at hand, and ran to the posthuman embassy.

* * * * *

"Physically? He left the system three hours ago, Rav."

"Left the system?"

Sandalphon chuckled, all infuriatingly friendly condescension. "Yes, Rav Shachar. He is on his way to some other world now—" He paused for a breath. "Ah. To the galactic halo, actually. He'll be around from time to time to check on the terraforming and to continue guiding the process."

I slumped into the chair behind me, letting loose a ragged breath and choking back a sob.

Coming to terms does not mean immunity to pain.

"Rav?" Sandalphon prompted gently, and for once I heard nothing but genuine concern there. "This isn't uncommon. He's not the first. You're not the first. Most cultures are wary of us. And children sometimes see us as a means of rebelling against authority."

I nodded slowly; Sandalphon leaned forward and put his hand on my shoulder.

"Yitzhak wasn't rebelling, though. He genuinely wanted to help this world and genuinely thought that this was the best way to go about it. And so he sacrificed himself, Abdiel." He winced theatrically at the word "sacrificed." "Not that I like describing it that way, but that is the way he saw it, initially.

"Would you like to talk to him?"

"Isn't he—I mean, he's aboard a starship—Isn't there a time lag?"

Sandalphon's lips twitched into a small smile. Arrogant or not, he seemed genuinely amused. "No, we dealt with light speed limitations and time dilation a long time ago. It'd essentially just be a long distance phone call."

I smiled, unable to stop myself from laughing softly. "Sounds expensive. I'm not sure I can afford that."

"On the house."

"I, uh—can you just give him a message?"

"Of course."

"Tell him thank you for the tree. And that I will pray for him."

Sandalphon nodded knowingly, and I wondered briefly exactly how much he knew about my personal life-- how much of Yitzhak's memories were spread about the posthuman web. "If I may ask, Rabbi, you seem to hate us just a little less today, Rav."

"I don't agree with you. Any of you. Or your philosophy."

"Philosophies, actually, and we wouldn't expect anything less from a standard human, but go ahead."

I told him everything.

Every last bit.

My misgivings about the posthumans. Fears, founded and unfounded. And I told him, most especially, of a dream of an angelic young man fighting in the stars to protect a world turning green, and what I thought I glimpsed of the conflict to come.

He did not laugh, did not deride me for believing that I had glimpsed the future. Instead, he leaned back and kicked his feet up on the desk, as he had done when we first met, and clasped his hands behind his head. "How much in the way of physics do you want to hear, Rav?"

I laughed again. "None. That was the forte of my wife and is now my son's."

"Then suffice it to say that most sufficiently advanced cultures, posthuman or human, no longer regard time as a linear sequence of events. A does not lead to B does not lead to C; A, B, and C are all woven together in the fabric of spacetime in ways even we can barely understand. But you know this.

"Rav Shachar, if this is more than a dream, then consider yourself fortunate. There are a lot of people out there who have been researching a way of manufacturing such glimpses as you have received for centuries. Best you thank whatever agent, latent ability, or fluke that allowed that view of the landscape of the future."

* * * * *

Oh, Ester.

Twenty years since you died, today. Five since Yitzhak left, but that anniversary was a few months ago.

I haven't seen him again, but I awoke one morning, not too long after my conversation with Sandalphon, to find another olive tree in my yard, bearing a note written in Hebrew. It was not Yitzhak's hand writing—it was far too neat for that—but it bore his name and a promise to come home for a while when he was finished with his current project.

Whatever, and whenever, that is.

Both trees have born fruit this year. Grass, engineered to spread quickly and to apparently never grow longer than about four inches, is creeping out across the wastelands. Ben-Gurion has become the center of an expanding green blotch.

Grass and trees—Trees, Ester!

Did I mention the ocean growing in the basin to the east? It still rains, but it is natural rain, no longer formed by melting comets in the atmosphere. At least, not exclusively. There are still a lot of meteors in the skies at night.

Yael—the little girl who was with me when the posthumans landed—comes over to play chess a couple times a week. She began visiting shortly after Yitzhak left, and noticed the chessboard in my study. I taught her to play. Slow going at first, but over the past few years she's been growing more and more clever. Perhaps I am playing with Negev's first general.

I still miss you, Ester.

But we will meet again. We are promised Paradise, eh? Not Sheol, not the grave and a return to dust.

Yael is here. I have to go; it is time for chess. I love you.

Joshua M. Young, has been writing since his early teens, and attributes any skill he has to sheer stubbornness as opposed to any actual talent. He has studied everything from computer sciences to theology, has a long standing fascination with flight and space despite being deathly afraid of heights, and has a completely random obsession with the 1940s. His day job is with an airline in Columbus, Oh.

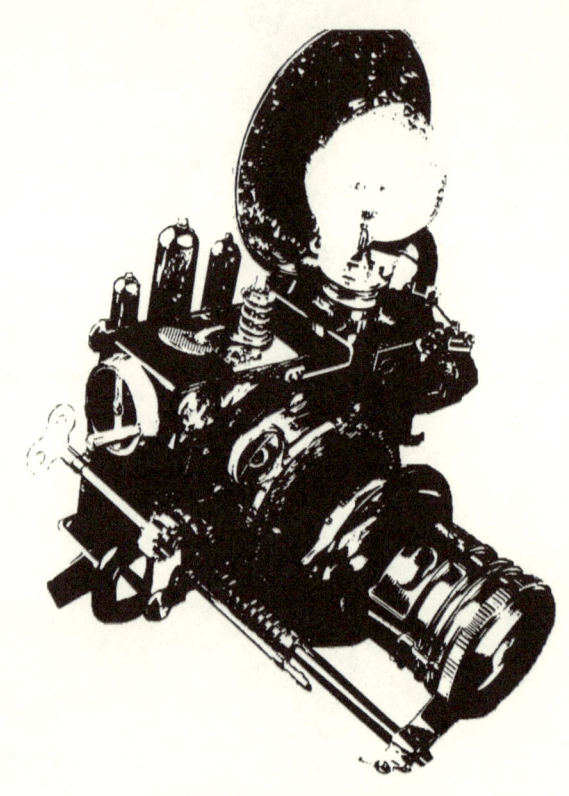

Ghost Writer
by Sara Camarata

My life was at a dead end. I was in a go no-where job at a hotel and convention center in southwest Ohio. I made a practice of getting through as many work days as I could without actually doing anything. It got so that I even wondered if the managers knew I was there. My academic career was in stasis, just waiting for me to kick things into motion, but I couldn't come up with a thesis worth spit. The book I was writing was stuck on chapter four and showed no signs of going anywhere. I had no social life, not even with people from work, and my friends from school had pretty much given up on me and my funks. My family was scattered all over the country, courtesy of the military, and, even if they were closer, we didn't really have any reason to hang out. In short, everything was dead, dying or gone... and then I was just dead.

I didn't realize it, not for a long while. It was Riss who showed me what happened. It was Riss who helped me come to terms with everything, and it was Riss whom I fell for. Her given name is Marissa Jayne Jones, but there's nobody who dares call her that to her face.

It was the weekend, and the hotel was hosting a sci/fi convention. I was standing near the concierge desk doing a pretty good job of evading work when I first saw her. Amongst a sea of aliens, time travelers, barbarians and other more bizarrely dressed people, she stood out. Even though she was dressed in the popular Steampunk motif, she still just stood out. She wore a self-lacing black and gold pin-striped corset, all along the back of which were cogs and gears twined with cord cinching her waist tight and narrow. A white blouse modestly covered her ample chest, and her long black skirt had the kind of fullness that only layers of petticoats can achieve. Her brown hair was pulled back under a black top hat. The hat was festooned with cogs, press passes, old tin type photos, and an old fashioned reflector from a camera flash.

In her gloved hands was an old looking camera. It was one of those boxy cameras from earlier days covered in brass tubes and crystals. The effect was very retro-futuristic. As she made her way across the lobby, she stopped to take photographs of the various people in their costumes, each time handing them a business card. As she grew closer to me, I saw that, instead of a guest badge, she wore a press pass for The Inquisitor.

I knew about The Inquisitor; it was a tabloid style rag and

website dedicated to the paranormal. I enjoyed reading the stories the Inquisitor published about all kinds of spooky things, weird places, and odd people around Ohio. I even suspected that a number of the items it ran might actually be true. Some things were just so weird that they had to be real. In the end, it turns out I was right.

I continued to watch as Riss worked the room, and soon I realized she was actually heading toward me. I put on my helpful face with mixed feelings. On the one hand, she was beautiful, and it'd been a good while since I'd talked with the fairer sex. It also meant, on the other hand, that I might actually have to do my job, and frankly I didn't want to bother. She stopped several feet from me and raised her camera, tilting her head and lifting an eyebrow questioningly. She was so cute I had to let her, so I nodded. She took a picture, the flash went off, and, for a moment, I was disoriented by the light. I actually felt a little dizzy and had to fight to maintain my balance. As the tiny, blinking lights faded from my vision, I saw that Riss stood closer to me. She was looking at a small screen on the camera while she fiddled with a small knob next to the screen. Then she looked up at me, and, for the briefest moment, I thought I saw a flash of pity in her eyes.

"Did the picture come out all right?" I asked. She nodded.

"Yes, quite all right." She put her hand out to me, "My name is Riss."

I took her hand; it was even softer than I expected. I felt an urge to raise it to my lips and kiss it, but I didn't. Instead I shook it gently, "I'm Nathan. Is there anything I can help you with?" Now I was doing my job much less reluctantly. Holding Riss's hand made me feel funny inside, and excitement blended with an odd uneasiness.

"Yes, there is something…" Riss paused and then gently took her hand back; she leaned closer to me and whispered in my ear, "You can meet me at eight o'clock at the bar." By the time the shivers down my back subsided, she was already walking away from me, her skirts swishing on the floor.

The rest of the day blurred, and my next clear memory is standing at the bar looking for Riss. Even though she'd changed clothes since the last time I'd seen her, she was easy to find. Her short, ruffled red and black skirt stood out in contrast to the guys in jeans around her. She wore a low cut black blouse that left little to the imagination while she somehow still maintained a sense of innocence. She was sitting on a stool at the bar, sipping a drink. She spotted me just as I began to move toward her. She stood, put some money on the bar and met me halfway. Her short skirt rustled as she walked. Her top hat was gone, and her brown hair hung in loose waves around her face.

"Right on time," She said, "Just as I expected." I put my arm out, and she threaded hers through mine. She led me out of the bar, and we walked across the lobby. I noticed she had her camera slung over her other shoulder.

"So, you're with The Inquistor?" I asked.

"Yes. I've been working with them for some years now. I find that they give me the best opportunity to hone my art. It's amazing how many weird and wondrous things are out there waiting for me to," she paused very briefly, "capture them." We spent several minutes making our way toward the elevators. There were a lot of people dressed up in awesome outfits, and Riss seemed driven to take pictures of all of them. Some of them wanted to talk with her, and she politely responded. She passed out her business cards and took down information from some of those who looked truly amazing.

Now and then Riss made comments about the various outfits we saw.

"That's too bad." Riss tsked once, "Look at that girl's weapon." She pointed to a lovely young lady wearing a kind of adventuring outfit, a split skirt with a decidedly Western top and vest. In her hands was a large weapon.

"What's wrong with it?" I asked.

Riss sniffed, almost disdainfully, "If you're going to modify a toy gun, you really should sand and file off the logos first, and the seams are awful. It's a very newbie mistake. I think I'll mention it to her. Wait a moment?" I watched as Riss approached the young lady. The two of them stood in quiet discussion for several minutes before Riss came back to me with a smile on her lips.

"At least she was willing to listen and not get upset that I would dare criticize her gear." Riss commented, "It's all about being genteel."

As we waited for an elevator, a girl in a devil suit walked by. What made her costume stand out were the white wings and the halo that her little devil horns supported. It was a cute and silly costume, and I chuckled as her tail waggled with each step as she walked by us. She looked back over her shoulder and smiled, somehow seeming familiar to me, and I was trying to remember where I might have met the girl when Riss snapped a picture.

Riss's brow furrowed as she reviewed the picture in the small screen. I thought I heard her mutter something quietly. She looked up sharply, and her head tilted as she watched the girl walk away.

"What's wrong?" I asked, "Picture come out bad?"

"Something like," Riss murmured, "I want to try and take a better shot." She looked at me, a curious expression in her eyes, "I'll be but a moment."

"Of course," I said, and gallantly added "I'll just wait for you."

"Yes, do." Riss chuckled, and I watched as she followed the girl. I didn't wait for long, reminding myself that I shouldn't let her out of my sight, and so I followed. I was almost too late as Riss and the girl went out a door to the courtyard of the hotel.

It took a little bit for my eyes to adjust to the darkness outside, but I heard a clicking come from around the corner of the building, and I followed the noise. The little sidewalk led to the pool and to Riss, who was alone, holding her camera up as though she had just finished taking a picture. I noticed that the camera was smoking and shaking in Riss' hands.

"Riss?" I stepped closer, reaching a hand out to her. She spun, holding her camera almost like it was a weapon. Her eyes were wide, and the light of the camera's glowing crystals reflected from the pool's surface and cast weird shadows on her face. She stared at me, almost through me, for a long moment. I took another step, and whatever seemed to be holding Riss snapped.

"Nathan!" She sounded startled, "Oh." She lowered her camera slowly, and I noticed that one of the crystals on the boxy device was pulsing with faint light. She took a small step backwards, almost stumbling, and was breathing heavily. I rushed forward to steady her. Strangely, for a moment I couldn't really feel her, but then quickly she felt solid in my hands.

"Are you all right?" I led Riss over to a plastic lounge chair and helped her to sit. I knelt next to her. "Do you need something? Water?" She shook her head. Soon enough her breathing eased, and she sighed.

"Oh, that does take something out of me, I must admit," she whispered hoarsely. She pulled a small black fan from her belt and waved it across her face. Peering at me from under her lashes, she asked, "How much did you see?"

"Your camera was smoking, and you looked like you weren't all here for a moment," I said. "What were you doing, and where did that girl go?"

"I was catching a ghost," she whispered.

* * * * *

Things got rather hazy after Riss made her declaration. I vaguely recall that we walked back into the hotel and took the elevator up to her floor. I can remember her opening the door to her room and letting me in. She took off her shoes, and I remember how she sighed so contentedly then.

I was watching Riss do something with her camera when I realized exactly where I was, in her room and sitting on her bed. Riss looked up at me and blinked, like she was a little surprised, too, to see me there.

"How do you feel?" She asked me, her hands pausing in their task.

"All…right, I think." I said, although my mouth felt a little dry, and I was certainly confused, "I…I don't really remember coming up here."

"I know. Don't worry. Things are always a little weird around me. I think you'll get used to it." She finally finished with her camera. In her hand was a small crystal, capped in bronze on one end. The crystal pulsed like a weak heartbeat.

"You said something about ghost catching—did I hear that right?" I asked.

"Yes, you heard quite right." She said, "It's what I do… in addition to more traditional photography." Riss laid the crystal down on the little round table next to the bed, picked up the camera, and handed it to me. Not expecting its weight, I almost dropped it.

"Makes my hands tingle," I observed, "and it's really kind of heavy."

"Well, it's been modified to capture non-corporeal entities in addition to taking the more usual kind of picture," she explained, then hesitantly continued, "This camera, it works using what we call aether-tech. It's a kind of science, really; the rules are different from what you're used to, but it's just as real."

"So, it's like magic?" I asked. Riss shook her head firmly.

"No, not magic. That's something else entirely and has its own set of rules. Aether-tech is an alternate science. Imagine if things were run on analog instead of digital, and the world used steam power more than electrical power. That's part of what drives aether-tech. By using this alternate science, we can make machines and devices that tap into this other energy in the universe. Aether has rules just like "modern science" does; in fact, many of the rules are similar. Just a little different."

"We? Does that mean there are more of you?" I asked.

"Well, not exactly like me," she laughed. "We all embrace the aether-tech in our own way and have blended in with different groups. Steampunk is a favorite because their ideas about technology and science are very similar to what we do. In fact, thanks to the modern Steampunk movement, we're able to operate more freely than ever. The little devices, modified toy guns, and such make it easier for us to carry our more real and working equipment in the open. We also really like the clothes."

"And you all run around catching ghosts?"

Riss shook her head, "No, not all of us. Just like any other group of people, we all have our own strengths and talents. Mine happens to be two-fold. I'm really good at reading pictures, and I can see ghosts. This," she patted her camera, "is more than just a tool. It's part of me, in a way. It amplifies what I do. I couldn't catch ghosts without it, and it couldn't catch them without me. Let me show you something."

Riss stood and walked over to the tiny closet next to the bathroom, her legs brushing mine as she passed. She reached into the closet and pulled out something. It was a large wooden chest. The chest was dark, like mahogany, covered in metal plates, metal tubes, wires, buttons and knobs. It looked very heavy, and Riss' slight grunt when she lifted it confirmed that. She placed the box on the bed next to me, causing the mattress to sag under its weight.

Riss pushed the buttons seemingly at random and twisted the biggest knob. There was a *click* and then a ticking. As the ticking sped up, a panel of metal on the top of the box lifted up, revealing a lever and inner gears turning. When the panel completely opened, Riss pulled the small lever, and there was another, louder *click*. On either side of the box, sections of metal slid back, and two pistons rotated out. She then pressed two more buttons on the sides of the box, and the pistons churned slowly. As they did so, the lid of the box started to open. Smoke, like from dry ice, frothed out of the widening gap. An almost sickly green light throbbed within the box. Eventually, the lid finished rising, and the pistons disengaged and returned to their places inside the open panels. Riss reached out and pushed the lid the rest of the way back so that the box lay completely open before me.

The smoke cleared, and I could see the interior of the box in full. It was filled with crystals, necklaces, rings, bracelets and other kinds of stones and jewelry. It looked like a pirate treasure, but one done up with cogs, gears, safety pins, and more.

"Whoa. What's all this?" I asked, fighting the urge to plunge my hands into that mass of metal and stone.

"It's my tool chest," Riss said proudly. "Everything I need to do my job, my second job, I mean, is in here." She reached in and pulled out a necklace with a large pendant on it. The pendant was mostly crystal, clear and cut in a square. There was a kind of flattened brass tube attached to the crystal by gold and copper wires. The tube had three tiny stones along the front in green, blue and red. At the top was a button. Riss handed it to me.

"Here, look at this and tell me what you see," she directed.

I looked closely at the crystal. It was warm in my hands, almost like a living thing. I could feel it moving in my hand a little, as though it was breathing. As I stared at it, I realized that the crystal wasn't clear like I first thought. Little clouds wove among the facets inside the stone. There were sparkling lights that pulsed and whirled. As I kept looking, an image began to form. The lights were being reflected off a small globe inside the heart of the stone. I peered closer, holding the pendant up to my nose. The globe was a tiny...disco ball? And then I could make out figures below the ball. The image became even clearer, and I realized I was looking at a scene from something like an old 70's era dance movie. There was a tiny little blonde woman in a silver jumpsuit and platform heels doing the hustle with a guy in a white leisure suit who bore an uncanny resemblance to a young Sylvester Stallone. I could even hear music.

"Is that... *Disco Inferno*?" I asked, incredulously.

"I'm not sure, but knowing Lisa, I'd say it's likely." Riss said.

"What is this?" I asked, handing the necklace back. "I've never seen anything like it."

"I'd have been quite surprised if you had," she answered. "It's an aetheric-apparition containment unit."

"A what?"

"A Ghost Keeper; it's what I keep some of my ghosts in," she responded by way of explanation.

"What you keep…" I shook my head, "I don't think I quite get it, but ok."

"Here, look at this," Riss said and handed me a smaller, rougher crystal, the one she took off her camera earlier, I realized.

I looked into this crystal and was able to see inside of it more quickly than before. This time there wasn't a scene, just a girl, the one in the angel/demon costume from earlier. She looked angry and was banging her fists against the facets inside the stone.

"She looks pissed." I said.

"I imagine she is," Riss affirmed. "I would be."

"Then why trap her? How did you get her in here anyways?" I asked.

"In this case I had to do it. She's been doing some pretty bad things," Riss said sadly, "It's pretty tragic really, her story."

"What exactly is that story?" Riss pursed her lips in thought, not answering me right away. She took a deep breath and handed me back the crystal pendant.

"See that button there?" She pointed to the top of the brass tube on the pendant. "Press it. I'll let Lisa show you the story; she's the one who scouted it out for me."

"It won't explode, will it?" I asked, holding the pendant awkwardly.

"No, silly." She laughed. "Press the button so the spirit inside can come out and talk to us."

"Oh." I pressed the button, hesitantly. The pendant immediately began to shake in my hand. The disco music from the crystal began to swell. The pendant glowed brightly and rose out of my hands, spinning slowly as it ascended. The light grew brighter, so bright it hurt my eyes. The throbbing beat of the music slammed into my ears, and I had to open my mouth to ease the pressure in my head. Then, shockingly, there was silence, and the light was gone.

"What the...? Riss? That's bogus! Now, really? I was in the middle of a dance-off!" The voice was not Riss's. This voice belonged to the blonde I saw in the crystal. She was a small woman; even in her platforms, she barely came up to my chin. Her blonde hair was swept back in a style long out of vogue. Her strapless jumpsuit clung to her like tin foil. On her neck was the pendant, pulsing in time like a heartbeat. I could see that the brass tube on the crystal was gone; it was replaced by an open chamber, and tiny and miniscule little gold legs poked out, like those of a spider. Those legs pierced the skin of the woman wearing the pendant. I could see little cogs and gears twirling inside the chamber, clicking, in synch with the pulsing light.

"I see," the woman said as she looked me over. "New one?" She pointed at me with a delicately manicured finger.

"Mayhaps," answered Riss, her demeanor quiet. I think she was a little worried.

"So then, tutorial or information reconstruction?" The woman asked.

"Both, I think." Riss said, "Lisa, go easy on him." Riss's eyes held a firm glint of steel as she said the last words to Lisa.

"Oh-ho! It's like that then." Lisa chuckled. She held a hand out to me, and I took it, slowly. Her hand was surprisingly solid and warm, for a ghost, I thought.

"Well, let's boogie. Catch ya' on the flip side, Riss!" Lisa said, and then the room around us dissolved.

* * * * *

We were standing in the corridor outside Riss's room; at least that's what I thought at first. On closer inspection I realized that the carpet was too new looking, the walls were a slightly different color, and the doors had regular key holes, not card slots.

"Where are we?" I asked Lisa, who was standing next to me. She snapped closed a compact mirror and put it in her pocket.

"1979."

"What?" My jaw dropped as I asked, "You can time travel?"

She shrugged. "Only to within a few years of my death and not exactly time travel," she said as she started walking down the hallway, "Come on." She waved a hand at me.

"What do you mean?" I asked as I stumbled after her. I felt weird here, like the air was thicker than normal. It was almost like I was inside some kind of bubble.

"Well, I died in 1978, was murdered actually. This nice guy I picked up one night turned out to be a real chump instead. I wasn't having any of his, and well, BAM! Upside the head with an ashtray. Riss found me, helped me get some closure, and I decided it'd be fun to kick it with her for a time." Lisa bit her lower lip and added softly, "I am so not ready to see what else there is, so here I stay." She sighed, "Anyways, I can travel back and forth around the year of my death. While we're here, we can't be seen, touched, heard or anything; we can only watch, and learn."

"Is that what you do for Riss?" I asked. "Observe things?"

"Yep, and I'm not the only one," Lisa said.

"How many of you guys does Riss have?" I thought about the box Riss showed me, how full it seemed to be.

Lisa shrugged, "I dunno… oh! Hey, there's our girl. That's Angela." Lisa pointed down the hall and, sure enough, there was the girl in devil/angel suit. Angela.

"So, now what?" I asked.

"Now, I show you what happened to Angela, and then we go back to Riss, and she blows your mind some more."

We followed Angela around the hotel as she aimlessly wandered from room party to room party. Eventually, a pattern emerged; she was looking for her boyfriend. Finally, she found him. He was a skinny guy in a gold shirt and black pants, with black boots. On his belt were some bulky looking things; one sort of looked like an old razor. It finally dawned on me that the guy was dressed up like a Star Trek character. He was busy chatting up a girl wearing pretty much nothing but veils, and her skin was painted green.

"There you are!" Angela ran up to the guy and pulled him around, "What are you doing? I've been…" She stopped talking when the green-painted girl put a hand in the guy's arm. He turned red and shook the hand off, at which point the green girl slapped him.

"Jerk!" she yelled and stormed off, leaving a green smudge on the guy's cheek. Angela stared at the guy, tears welling in her eyes.

"Jack?" Her voice was tremulous, but then it gained strength as disbelief was replaced by anger. "I don't… I can't…You two-timing, back stabbing… jerk!" Angela hauled off and slapped Jack, too. He took a step back, his eyes blazing.

"Man! No way am I putting up with this. Find your own way home!" he yelled and walked off. Angela stared at Jack for a bit and then started crying. A woman approached Angela, but she brushed her off and left the room.

"Come on," Lisa said, pulling my arm, "It's not over yet." We followed Angela to another room party. She walked in, grabbed a cup with some strange purple stuff in it, and chugged it down. She made a face, the kind of face that told me this wasn't a girl who was used to drinking. Angela took another cup, downed that one and then another. No one seemed to really notice when Angela grabbed a bottle of tequila and flopped down on a couch. She sat there, drinking right from the bottle, crying and sniffling, and not one person noticed.

I moved forward, reaching for Angela, but my hand passed right through her, like she was made of smoke, or I was. Lisa put her hand on mine; she was solid, here with me in whatever place of existence this was. She cradled my hand, and together we watched as Angela drank and drank; eventually, she staggered to her feet, and we followed her to the bathroom. She locked the door behind her and passed out, hitting her head on the toilet. There was so much blood.

"Do we have to watch the rest of this?" I turned away, closing my eyes.

"No, we can go back." Lisa held me, and the room dissolved away.

* * * * *

I opened my eyes to find that I was standing in Riss's room, at the foot of her bed. Riss was sitting down on the floor, her back against the wall. She was looking down at something in her hands, and I realized it was Lisa's pendant.

The tiny chamber was closing, the gears slowly turning as the light from the crystal pulsed slower and slower until finally the whole thing lay inert in Riss's hands.

"You did well," she murmured. She looked up at me, and I could tell she was tired. I held a hand out to her. Riss took it, her grip soft, and I helped her to her feet. She put the pendant back in the box with the others.

"Is Lisa all right?" I asked.

"Yes. It just takes a lot of energy to semi-materialize. Not to mention the time walk and taking you with her. She'll need some time to recover," Riss explained.

"What about you?" I frowned at her. "You seem pretty drained, too."

"The Ghost Keepers all have some of my energy in them. It's not a lot, but prolonged use can wear me out a little. Plus, I used the camera earlier when catching Angela, which takes a chunk of my aether stores, too." She said.

"Aether stores?" I asked.

In response, Riss opened up her top. I was momentarily distracted by her lacy black bra, but I saw that she had several tattoos of fancy scrolling numbers and symbols around her collar bone, and, in the middle of her chest, directly over her sternum, was what appeared to be an ornate clock face. It was fused into her skin and made a soft ticking noise in time with her pulse.

"This helps me draw and store aetheric energy. I need it to use the camera and crystals. It also drains me a bit."

"How do you get energy back?" I asked.

"It's all around us. I just need to breathe, eat and sleep. It's really not much different from physical exertion. It's just that Angela fought a bit more than some ghosts, so I had to work harder to capture her."

"Fought harder?" I sat down. "Maybe you should tell me the rest of the story."

"Of course." Riss sat next to me on the bed, taking my hand as if it were the natural thing to do. I still couldn't believe how soft her touch was.

"You saw how Angela died, right?" I nodded, "Ok. Well, she wasn't found until after it was too late to save her. Her death was considered accidental, and it was left at that. The next year Angela showed up at the con again, but this time no one could see her. She was just a small apparition then, a shadow of tragic death. Then a young man happened into the bathroom where she died. As best as I've been able to learn, Angela managed to leech onto the young man and take some of his life force. She got stronger from that, and the man died a few days later, heart attack they thought." Riss paused and added, "A tragic and unexpected heart attack." Her thumb rubbed against the back of my hand slowly.

"Then what?" I prompted.

"Then it happened again the next year, and the next and the next. On up to now. Every year on the anniversary of her death, Angela manifests, takes the life force from some poor guy, and kills him. They usually don't die until a few days later. No one else had seen the pattern until I did, but then I'm different like that." She gave me a weak smile. "Thing is, each time she takes life force, she stores some of it, so she's getting stronger. If I hadn't caught her this year, she would have killed again and stored even more life force. She'd already gotten strong enough to take on a mostly corporal form, and that takes a lot of energy."

"Could she have gotten enough life force over time to, I don't know, bring herself all the way back?" I asked. Riss recoiled, "No! Never. Dead is dead, and there isn't any coming back—she would figure that out eventually, and it would drive her mad. At that point, she'd become a poltergeist, a ghost strong enough to really do some damage. That's why I had to catch her now."

"So, now what will you do with her?" I asked.

"Well, I have to find a couple more ghosts, her remaining victims," Riss said.

"Why?"

"She's got their life forces. Those poor guys are all stuck here while she has that. They'll never be able to move on. What's more is that they're all missing something vital to what made them whole people. I have to try and get Angela to return those parts back to their rightful bearers," she said passionately.

"If she won't play ball, what happens then?"

"Well, it gets trickier; it does. I'll have to rip the energy out of her and return the energies to the victims myself. That will destroy her, make her cease to be." Riss shuddered, and I could understand it. We sat quietly for a time. I was thinking about all the incredible things I learned.

"Can I help?" I asked. Riss looked at me thoughtfully and almost sadly. She gave me a slow nod.

"Yes. I've managed to track down all but the last two of Angela's victims." Riss stood and crossed the room. She grabbed her camera and faced me. "Both of them are here at the hotel, trapped. You can help me find them."

* * * * *

"This first one we'll go after is a kid named Matt," Riss told me in the elevator later. "He was here in '87 for an air-band competition."

"Not the con?" I asked a little surprised.

"Not every one of Angela's anniversaries happens on a con

-weekend." Riss said.

"Oh, makes sense. So, air-band, huh? Is that why we're heading back to the lobby floor?"

"Yes. I was thinking that the conference rooms would be a good place to start. Thanks to my Ghosts, I've been able to research things pretty well," she said.

"How will I know if I've found him?" I asked.

"Well, there's a trick to seeing and recognizing ghosts. Almost anyone can learn to spot them, if they have reason to look for them. It's a little like looking at one of those posters with a hidden image?" She looked over at me.

"Yeah, I've seen those," I said.

"It's all in how you focus your eyes. Of course, the stronger the manifestation, the easier it is to spot. Some ghosts are so "here" that people see them all the time and don't even realize it. Some ghosts are nothing more than a shadow in the corner of your eye, and others are completely invisible," she explained. "One trick is to look for areas that seem a little off, like the air is wavy, or it shimmers a little. That's a clue that there may be something non-corporeal there; either that or you need glasses." We shared a little chuckle.

So, we wandered around the con a little, in and out of the various conference rooms. The day was in full swing now, which seemed odd; it didn't seem like that much time had passed since Riss captured Angela at the pool. That time walk with Lisa must have lasted longer than I realized. We had to wait until discussions were let go before we went into the rooms. The first three rooms were empty of all save the con goers who were supposed to be there. It was in the fourth room that we got lucky.

This was the largest of the conference rooms, used mainly for the big events. On one side of the room, near the front, there was a small dance floor. Next to that, there was a raised platform with some tables and chairs on it. The room was filled with rows of chairs in front of it. As we looked around the room, I thought I heard something near the dance floor. I went over to it, looking for the things Riss had told me about. After peering, I saw it, a wavy quality to the air, and, if I listened really hard, I could hear music. Hair-band type stuff. Soon, a figure began to take shape. He was transparent and barely there. The ghost had a long black mullet, a narrow face and a sharp nose. He wore a torn Iron Maiden shirt and ripped jeans. I couldn't make anything out below his knees as he faded in and out. He was playing an air guitar, his fingers pounding frantically up and down the imaginary frets. He wind milled his strumming hand and spun around. Raising his air-guitar over his head he brought it smashing down on the floor. He jumped up; legs split hands raised in the immortal symbol of rock-n-roll.

"Booyah! Oh, yeah!" He shouted pumping his fists into the air.

"Matt?" I asked, "Is that you, man?"

The ghost stopped and looked at me.

"Dude?" He leaned towards me, "Duuude!" He raised a hand, and I stared at it, "Don't leave me hangin', dude." I slapped his hand, sort of, as my hand sunk into his a bit before I felt any mass.

"When's this thing starting? You know?" He asked me and I shook my head at him.

"Riss?" I called, without taking my eyes off of Matt, "I found him."

Riss came over to us, her long brown skirt brushing the floor. When had she changed, I wondered, and where was I when she did? She raised her camera and said to Matt, "A picture, for the paper?" Matt smiled wide and I saw a glimpse of what he must have been like before Angela drained him. His eyes twinkled and he posed like a rock star.

"Cheese, dude-ette!" he said as the camera clicked. There was a bright flash of light and a whiff of smoke. When my vision cleared Matt was nowhere to be seen. Riss swayed for a moment but steadied herself.

"That was well done, Nathan." She said to me with a smile.

"Now there's one more, right?" I asked. Riss nodded, slowly, "One more, yes." She sighed heavily. Suddenly she looked drawn, and so very sad.

"Riss, what's wrong, honey?" I asked, the endearment slipping out before I could think about it.

"It's this last one... I wish..." Her voice trailed off and her eyes were moist. I drew in a deep breath, confused.

"I, did you know him?" I led Riss to a chair, but the room was starting to fill with con goers and it wasn't the right time to talk.

"We need to talk, Nathan." Riss took the lead, and we left the room. I followed Riss out of the conference halls and to the elevator. Then we were in Riss's room again, and I wasn't sure how that had happened.

"What's happening to me?" I asked Riss, suddenly feeling afraid. Something loomed overhead, and I didn't want to look.

"You need to think, Nathan, I can't do this to you, not like the others." Riss looked miserable, and a tear slid down her cheek. She was achingly beautiful in her pain. I reached out to comfort her, but my hands slid into her. I pulled back, sharply.

"Wha..." I stumbled and fell onto the floor. I couldn't see my legs, and my body faded into mists below my waist. I think I may have screamed, but then there was Riss, in front of me, her face filling my vision.

"Stay with me, Nathan. Think; try to remember," she urged. I closed my eyes, breathing in her scent. Vanilla and a trace of something more pungent, almost smoky. Unbidden images sprang to mind. I was at the concierge desk, like usual. Just waiting for my shift to end.

I was walking with an old lady down the halls of the hotel, carrying her bags, and listening to her complaining about her son-in-law.

I was in the elevator when it suddenly stopped. The lights flickered, and I felt a strange sensation. A girl was there with me—Angela—that's where I remembered her from, and she was only partially there. She kissed me, held me and whispered words of nothing in my ears. I felt weaker, and then she was gone. The elevator moved along. I finished my shift, feeling so weary. For the next few days, I was tired, I couldn't eat, and nothing felt good anymore. I was sitting in the break room when I collapsed. My co-workers gathered around me, and I watched as the paramedics tried to revive me. And then there was nothing...

* * * * *

"Oh, god, how many more?" I heard a voice sob, "I can't do this anymore!" The voice rose to a shriek at the end.

"He's the last one, I promise." Another voice, softer, and familiar. I couldn't quite place it, but I felt comforted by it.

I felt warmth on my skin, like I was sitting in sunlight. I couldn't see anything, but I soon realized that my eyes were shut. I opened them. Light, golden light surrounded me, and I couldn't make out anything else. I blinked, and slowly my eyes adjusted. I was inside a circle set in a concrete floor. The light flowed up from the circle, which was made of some kind of metal.

The light dimmed, and I could see more details. The room I was in felt large, and the air was redolent with the scents of hot metal, burning wood, coal and other smokiness that I couldn't identify. Looming out of the shadows was a huge machine. The machine went from the floor to the ceiling, maybe nine feet overhead. It was made of metal and wood and stone. Pistons churned, and tubes of glowing liquid were set in rows along the sides of the machine. At the front of the machine was what looked to be a control panel covered in buttons, knobs and levers. In front of the panel stood a figure, a woman. A woman I knew, but couldn't remember.

I floated, yes, floated inside the circle. It was warm there, almost cozy, but something felt off.

"You promise?" The sobbing voice, I looked for it. There, next to me, in another circle, floated a girl. She seemed familiar, too.

"I promise," said the woman at the machine, "Just give back what you took, and then we'll go from there."

The girl floating next to me reached out toward me. In her hands I saw a ball of glowing and sparking energy. It drifted away from here, toward me. Part of me thought I should be afraid, but I wasn't. If anything, the closer the ball got, it felt right. Soon it touched my chest, and I watched it sink into me. As it did, memories came rushing back. My back arched, and I felt a scream rip from my throat. It burned, and yet, it still felt right.

Soon, the pain ebbed and I panted, my feet now on the ground. I felt more here, more real than I had before. The girl floating next to me, Angela, I remembered, looked far worse. She was almost completely transparent, and seemed a wisp in the breeze. She looked at me, whispered, "I'm so sorry." I nodded at her; I didn't feel anything toward her, even though that other voice inside me insisted I be angry.

"It's ok," I told her. Angela smiled and flickered. I heard a noise and turned to see the woman at the machine, Riss, my Riss I thought, pull a large lever. The machine roared to life, a loud swooshing noise filled the room, and the lights flickered madly. The smell of ozone filled the room, blocking all other scents. Riss's hair stood on end, as little bolts of lightning swirled across her body. The bolts leapt across the room and slammed into Angela, but she didn't scream. She simply faded in and out between jolts until she was completely gone. The machine settled back into an expectant hum. Riss stepped away from it and came toward me.

"Why didn't you tell me?" I asked. "I deserved to know that I'm dead."

"You do now, and would you have believed me then?" she replied. She was right. That ugly voice deep down commanded me to yell, to scream insults and cry my pain, but, honestly, it wasn't there. I told the voice to quiet down, and it did, reluctantly.

"I think I'm supposed to be mad at you, but I don't feel much of anything right now," I said.

"It's the circle; it's dampening your energy, keeping things in check. When...ghosts... realize their state, they can be volatile," Riss explained. She placed a hand against the soft light coming up from the circle, like resting it against a glass. I put my hand over the same place on my side.

"Yes, I can tell. Part of me, inside, wants to be very mad. I don't want that," I said, then, "What now?"

"That's up to you. I can send you along, to whatever fate lies beyond for you..." She paused.

"Or..." I said, "Can I stay? Like Lisa?"

Riss drew in a shuddering breath, "Yes." She said, "You can. It won't be easy, but you can."

I smiled at her, and whatever the ugly voice tried to tell me I ignored because another part of me spoke with more conviction.

"Then I'd like to stay… with you. If you'll have me." I leaned my face next to the circle's light.

"I'd like that," Riss whispered. "Of all the men in the world, why did I have to fall for one of the dead ones?"

Sara Camarata, couldn't wait to learn how to read. Once she did she devoured pretty much any book given to her. Then one day she decided it would be great fun to start making her own stories. Eventually she decided it would be even more fun to share those stories. Sara lives in Bellbrook, OH with her husband, two children and two large furry beasts who claim to be cats.

Lilah

by Robert Lowell Russell

Three elders, three being customary for the Windborn, stood silently at Jonathon's door. The youngest was as old as his father, the eldest, much older, was bent and frail, and the woman was somewhere between.

The eldest held out the knife, and Jonathon's hands shook as he took the ancient blade. Behind him, his wife's face was ash. His son clung to her, pressed against the swell of her belly.

Jonathon said, "Please... You can't ask me to do this. You can't."

But they could. "Do you have what you need?" asked the youngest.

Yes." Jonathon stepped from his home, and his wife shut the door behind.

* * * * *

They trained at the base of the mountain, and each day Jonathon said, "You've made a mistake."

"All the chosen say this. We've watched you. There's no mistake," said the youngest.

"I can't do this. I don't know how."

"You'll learn," insisted the woman.

"But, it isn't in me."

They said nothing.

* * * * *

As months passed, a letter came for him with pictures of his wife and son, and also of an infant girl. His wife wished him well and asked of his return. The letter was pleasant, empty. The old woman brought him a second one, a sealed note, and in it his wife spoke of private things. Jonathon kept the pictures pressed against his skin.

When at last the signs came, they brought him to the forest's edge. "The Mother cannot know what's been done," instructed the eldest.

"All that we've built dies if she remembers," said the youngest.

Jonathon asked, "Is there no other way?"

"What would you risk?" asked the old woman.

Jonathon touched his shirt where the pictures lay. "Why must I wait? It seems cruel."

"Enough," said the youngest, "You will know the time."

The old woman held out her open hand, "You cannot bring them with you."

Jonathon gave her the pictures and walked into the forest.

* * * * *

A young woman stood at the edge of a small lake, barefoot on the pebbled shore. Wind blew ripples across the water. Tall, green trees around the lake bent and swayed. In the distance a blue gray peak soared above, shrouded with clouds.

The woman wore a white dress, and the breeze and bluster revealed she wore nothing else. She moved black hair from her face, gazing at the surface of the dark water as if it were glass from a mirror.

He stood behind her, watching her. She had not heard him come through the forest. "Hello."

She turned, studied him, and then smiled. "Who are you?" When she spoke, it was like bird song.

He stepped forward, stopping beside her. "I'm Jonathon. It's beautiful here."

"Yes, it is... Do you know me, Jonathon?"

"Of course, you're Lilah."

She brightened. "I'd forgotten. Where did you come from?"

He gestured behind him. "Through the woods. I'm a little lost."

"Where are your people?"

"I'm alone."

"I'm sorry." She touched his hand. "I have people..." She turned her head, as if listening for a distant sound. "Somewhere."

He touched his shirt and felt his heart pound. "I'm hungry, are you?"

She seemed surprised. "Yes, I'm starving."

"Maybe there are blackberries."

She pointed behind him, the way he'd come. "Yes, there."

He laughed. "I didn't see them before; I must have walked right past. Would you like to pick some?"

She nodded, and he let the breath hiss from his mouth.

They ate blackberries until their stomachs were bursting, and their chins were dripping purple. And they laughed as they cleaned themselves in the cold water, splashing each other. For a moment, they stopped and glared at each other, and then, grinning, they flailed their arms, turning the water around them to froth, screaming and shrieking before falling to the ground, soaking wet and giggling.

He shivered in the breeze. "I'll build a fire."

She helped him gather wood and grass, and, after long minutes of swearing and banging stones, he got a spark to fall. As the sun fell, they sat on each side of the fire, staring at the stars.

He said, "I wonder if there are fish."

She glanced at the water when a loud splash answered in the distance.

She woke the next morning to his shout as he sent a fish flying from the water. He said, "Give me a minute, and I'll have breakfast for us both."

She laughed as he flopped though the water, dangling his hands below the surface until, at last, another fish lay gasping next to the first. He cut them open with a sharp rock and set them on the embers.

She disappeared into the woods, then returned with a dozen red apples gathered in her dress; the white fabric bunched well above her thighs. She blushed at his stare, and she set the apples on the ground, letting her dress fall back. She smiled at him.

They ate, enjoying the flaky white flesh of the fish and the sharp sweet of the apples. He said, "I was cold last night, even with the fire. I think I should build a shelter."

"Isn't there anywhere to go? Isn't there anyone else?"

"Only the two of us."

"But there were more, I remember." She walked toward the forest, and wind gusted through the trees, the sky darkening.

He looked around, clenching and unclenching his hands. He took a breath. "There were more once. I will go with you to see what remains if you wish." He moved to join her; then, he stopped. "But it's far. We should gather food for the journey."

"Will that take long?"

"No, not long. Then we'll go together."

She hesitated before heading back to camp, the wind returning to a gentle breeze. "But what happened?" she asked. "What became of the world?"

"All things grow old. All things die."

She nodded, pained. "There are no more children?"

He shook his head and turned from her.

She asked, "What's wrong?" Then she put her hand to her mouth. "You had children."

He was not to mention his children, but he faced her, his hand where their pictures would have been; a tear wound its way down his cheek. She came and held him to her, pressing his head against her breast.

* * * * *

He spent days building a home from sticks, logs, and branches. It was small, and they were forced to lie close to each other at night, his skin touching hers. During the day they gathered fish, fruit, and other food to dry in the smoke of the fire.

One day, he told her they must make something to hold water. Before leaving to gather firewood, he remarked, "If only we had some animal skins." Later, emerging from the forest, he saw the three deer that lay on the shore, necks broken; he stood still for a moment mindlessly dropping wood from his arms, piece by piece, from his surprise.

"Are they enough?" she asked.

He nodded, trembling as he recovered the wood.

One afternoon he brought her wildflowers. She held them to her chest, breathing deeply. He placed a single, red flower in her hair, brushing her face with his hand. She shivered, and he stepped forward and kissed her. She stood, pressing her fingers to her lips.

"I'm sorry," he said, backing away, "I shouldn't have..."

She rushed to him and knocked him to the ground. She climbed on top, returning the kiss. A blast of wind whipped her hair as thunder from a sudden storm boomed around them.

He pulled her dress from her shoulders, and she tore his shirt, digging her fingers into his chest. He winced as she kissed him. She sat up, just long enough to tear his pants, then fell back onto him. She arched her back, and lightning blew a tree to splinters behind her. Hard rain pounded them. Rivulets ran from her breasts to her hips as she moved against him. He coughed and sputtered as rain flooded his mouth.

They spent many days after, enjoying the freshness that followed the storm. She touched him often: his hair, his skin, and his hands. But even as they lay together, she'd ask of the world and want to know when they would leave to see it. "Soon," he would promise, and she'd frown, the air falling still.

One evening, as dusk turned to night, he wrapped his arms around her, holding her close. She kissed his neck, and he let his hands run down her back to rest on her hips. They went to lie together by the fire, so close that they saw the flames shining in the other's eyes.

"I love you."

Her eyes glittered. "And I love you."

The fire flared, blazing white, while the shadows danced.

* * * * *

Jonathon sat alone on the shore, bathed by dawn's light, throwing stones into the blackness. He saw the water ripple toward him, and felt it also rippling away.

They had gone swimming the day before, making love in the water. Lilah had told him that she would leave in the morning and asked him if he would come.

"Of course," he replied.

"Are you hurt because I want to leave?"

"No." But he had quickly dropped his hand from his shirt.

* * * * *

She lay behind him now, smiling and still, in the shelter. She could be sleeping if not for the knife jutting from her chin.

After a time, he went to her and removed the blade. There was far less blood than he thought there'd be. As the sun rose higher, he cleaned the blood from her; then, he wove the red flowers she liked into her hair. He pulled a wall from the shelter and made a litter. He held her to him before he set her in it. She was so light, as if gravity had given up its hold on her. Five miles lay between the lake and the edge of the forest, but he felt he'd walked for days, pulling her behind him, before he came to the clearing. A long, heavy, high walled truck lay idle near the road. The men and women who came from it took her, resting her body in the back. They did not look at him.

He rode with her as the truck bounced and slid along the rough road falling from the mountain. Halfway down, he saw the first of the Windborn standards, fixed upright in the earth.

Jonathon's people buried their dead, but the Windborn returned theirs skyward in great pyres. The flags that marked their passing were adorned with trinkets and bright colored cloth that danced and popped in the breeze as Windborn souls dove low—or so they'd believed. Thousands upon thousands of flags lay at the base of the mountain, and Jonathon knew they went for miles.

As Jonathon's people crossed the sea, fleeing lands of dead gods and ash, the Windborn had welcomed them but cautioned them to take care with the Mother. The clans did not listen, laughing at Windborn superstitions.

The Windborn did not resist as they died. And they repeated their warning to take care with the Mother. Even so, the clans did not heed the advice, laughing at Windborn threats.

When the elders, the last three of the Windborn, gave the clans the knife, they begged them to take care with the Mother yet again. And still the clans did not listen, laughing as the elders screamed.

* * * * *

Lilah lifted her head from his chest and asked, "What should we do today?"

"We could swim."

She smiled, striding to the beach, letting her dress fall to the ground. She looked back at him then dove into the water.

"Is it cold?" he asked, and she shook her head. The chill of the water shocked his skin as he dove in. He shrieked, and she laughed. "Liar," he sputtered through chattering teeth.

She swam to him with slow, looping strokes. She wrapped her arms and legs around him. Her touch seared him. "Is that better?"

He nodded.

She dropped her hand below the water. "And that? Is that better?"

He gasped, nodding again.

"And this?" Pain tore through him, and he fell away from her, blood pouring from the knife in his chest.

Jonathon jolted awake and rubbed his ribs. He picked himself up from where he'd fallen in the truck, then staggered back to his seat and looked over the side.

They now traveled down a rough road torn through a sea of stones; there, the carved stones bore the names of the dead, the clan's dead. Windborn souls returned to the air; the clan's souls rejoined the rock.

He looked down at her body. She still smiled. He leaned close to clear her hair from her face, and, as he did, his hand brushed her lips. They were still warm.

When the Mother had come for the clans, they did not know her, and they laughed at her pain. Only a scattered few had survived her rage. The clans were ready to listen after, but none were left to teach them.

They rebuilt, learning what they could; as time passed, the clans changed and prospered. Jonathon's people had not killed for so long now they sometimes forgot they ever did. But each day the sun rose above the Mother's mountain to fall on the plains of stones and standards.

A large garden lay beyond the stones; the truck stopped at its edge. Men and women came and took Lilah's body from the back. They carried her through fields and flowers as Jonathon walked behind. A statue of the Mother stood at the center, surrounded by a shallow pool that reflected the sky.

A pile of wood had been prepared for them. They set her down and wound white silk around her while Jonathon watched. When they'd nearly finished, Jonathon said, "Wait."

He kneeled to kiss her, tears spattering against the silk. He stood, and they covered her face. One touched her shoulder as they placed her on the pyre.

A man asked Jonathon, "What did you name her?"

"Lilah."

The man said, "A good name," and he lit the blaze.

"You've done well," said the youngest.

The elders stood behind him. Jonathon asked, "Have I?"

"We are safe," said the youngest, "Until the winds bring her back. Then another will be chosen."

The eldest held out his hand, and Jonathon gave him the knife. The old man said, "You were not chosen because you could kill her. She bends the world to her, even when she slumbers, and now she dreams of new love."

Jonathon looked to the old woman. "I want them back."

Holding his pictures in her hand, she said, "You can't return."

He snatched the pictures from her and ran to the truck. Soon, they were driven away from the garden; he did not look back as the Mother burned.

He rode for a sleepless day and night. As dawn broke, he could smell his sprawling city before he could see it. They entered the gates and crawled through crowded streets. And when he could stand it no more, he asked them to leave him.

As he walked through the city, he imagined that people shied from him when he brushed past, like they knew what he'd done.

At last near his home, he walked past his neighbor's houses. They'd seen the elders at his door and knew what it meant. They called their children in as he moved by.

When he entered his home, his wife looked up, startled. She held his daughter to her breast.

"Dad!" His son ran to embrace him. His wife smiled and brought his daughter, placing her in his arms.

* * * * *

"I love you."

Lilah smiled and touched his face. "I love you too, Jonathon." She ripped the knife across his throat.

He bolted up, his heart pounding. His wife slept, teetering along the edge of their bed, far from him.

After the children had gone to sleep, she'd kissed him, taking his hand and placing it on her breast. He'd felt her tremble as she did. He'd told her that he was tired, that they'd have plenty of time.

He went to his son's room and put his hand on him as he slept. Then he went to his daughter's crib and listened to her breathe—a soft rustling in and out—as he stood over her. He returned to his bedroom and dressed in silence, tucking his pictures in his shirt.

When he shut the door to his home behind him, two waited for him outside: the old woman and the younger man.

"Where is the eldest?" Jonathon asked.

"His tasks are finished. I am the eldest now," the old woman replied.

"But, there are always three."

"Yes."

The man said, "You will always dream of the Mother."

Jonathon held his hand to his neck. "Does she forgive you?"

"She doesn't even remember there's anything to forgive." He placed his hand on Jonathon's arm. "The dreams will change for you. In time."

"When?"

The man shook his head. He said, "Lilah was a good name. I named her Alanah."

"Lauren," said the old woman. She closed her eyes and sighed, smiling.

"Do you have what you need?" the man asked.

Jonathon nodded and took out his pictures. And a sudden wind ripped them from his hand.

Robert Lowell Russell, a native Texan, lives with his family in southeastern Ohio. He is a former librarian and current stay at home parent. He holds a MLS from Kent State and worked toward a Ph.D. in history at the University of Georgia (until he decided that it was more fun to invent worlds than write about what actually happened). He is working on his first novel, Dragon Rising.

Learn more at http://robertlowellrussell.blogspot.com/

VN: Subject 121
by James O. Barnes

"Welcome back. Today in our studio we have Dr. Michael Anderson of the American Genetic Research Institute. Dr. Anderson, before the commercial break our last caller accused your agency—A.G.R.I.—of secretly conducting genetic experiments on humans for the government. How do you respond?"

Dr. Anderson, calm and collected as always, leaned forward. Pushing the *seek* button on the console of the car stereo of his late model Volkswagen, he grumbled. "How many times can a station run the same tired old shows?"

The radio advanced through the stations as he mashed the button several more times. The same thing was on every station.

"...Starvation has spread...Asia and parts of South America..."

Dr. Anderson finally settled on a local station and put both hands on the steering wheel to turn into the Institute's run down parking garage. Pulling into his assigned spot on the top floor, he sat back and finished listening to the news before turning the car off.

"The ecological disaster which struck the United States only two years ago now threatens parts of Greater Europe, South America, and Asia. Scientists remain at a loss. The search continues for a way to stop the world-wide famine that threatens all of humanity."

Turning the car off, Dr. Anderson's world became mercifully quiet. He ran his thick fingers through what little hair he had left. Silently, he wondered when it had all started to leave his head and collect within his nostrils, eyebrows, and ears. Taking a deep breath, he readied himself to get out of the car.

Had anyone been watching, it would have been a comical site to watch as Dr. Anderson pried himself out of the 'bug'. Now able to stand at his full height, Dr. Anderson enjoyed the quiet as he made his way through the garage. He couldn't help but notice all the vacant parking spaces. Most people didn't come to work these days until late afternoon, when things started to cool off a bit.

Wimps.

Dr. Anderson reached the secure entrance to the containment unit and fumbled for his ID card. He slid it across the card reader, keyed in the appropriate sequence of numbers, and placed his hand on the palm pad. The door hissed open revealing a stark-white interior. Before entering, he looked up through one of the many holes in the parking structure's roof and noted the position of the sun.

With the money the government puts into this place, you'd think AGRI could afford to have a parking garage that didn't look like Swiss cheese.

He stepped through the entryway and continued down the hall to the observation station. "Then again, who would A.G.R.I. pay to fix it?"

* * * * *

In the beginning, Dr. Anderson hadn't agreed with Project VN. The idea had first been pitched to him by a young and barely-out-of-diapers, as he saw him, unknown geneticist. It sounded like too much science fiction for him to even take seriously. That was then, and, at the time, the Institute was not paying him to agree. A.G.R.I. was paying him to do his job, to fix the mistake his own years of research had led to. It would at least give him the time he needed to work on the real solution of how to reverse the damage his experiment had done to the Earth's vegetation.

Dr. Anderson's crowning achievement of science was now destined to end the existence of humanity on the planet. The field of genetically altered wheat he had been working with had not been as quarantined and sterile as he had thought or was led to believe. It was within the same stadium sized research facility he now worked on his current project.

It was human error as well as arrogance that did in the first project. An overworked maintenance employee pulling a double shift had left the filter screen off a ventilation hatch after cleaning it. A nearby colony of bees found their way inside to the crop. After the bees left the crop and then cross pollinated with other plants, the poisonous mutation spread like wildfire changing the genetic structure of every species of plant life it came into contact with, as it had been designed to do.

Instead of increasing plant production, it altered the genetic structure of every plant. Within one cycle, food crops were unfit for human consumption, but not to animals. It wasn't long before feed animals became saturated with it in their systems. The processed meats of feed animals began to cause the same ill effects as did the vegetation.

The poison did not kill you though. It just made you violently ill, inducing vomiting and severe dehydration. Millions of people around the world were literally starving to death in the presence of ever growing mounds of food.

You could still grow crops and raise cattle, but who would want to if everything you ate poisoned you. Food in storage, fresh water supplies, and waste recycling would only support life for so long. Time was running out, even with rationing. Within another year, only about ten percent of the population of the United States would be left, and not for much longer after that.

It had only taken three weeks to track the disaster back to Dr. Anderson. By all rights, and according to martial law in place in the United States, his life should have been forfeited by now. However, based on his previous reputation and years of experience, he was finally somehow able to convince the governing council of generals that he would be able to remedy the problem. Making the leap from the genetic manipulation of plants to that of humans was a stretch for his career, but this new young scientist believed he had a solution.

After six months of political wrangling and nearly a year of experimentation, he and his team were finally on to something. Dr. Anderson was even able to convince himself that he may have been looking at the problem the wrong way. Maybe the solution wasn't in altering the world's vegetation to what it once was. Instead, maybe the answer did lie in changing human physiology to adapt to a new way of life, a new source of food. He hated not being able to do it without help though.

* * * * *

The klaxon sounded, sending its blaring spikes into Subwundoone's unprotected ears again and again. It had been more than five cycles since he last slept, maybe more. It was hard to tell in the place of half-light that was his home. Sub opened his eyes and stared at the great cavernous ceiling high above him. Slowly turning his head from side to side, he observed the actions of those crowded around him—the other *subs*. He knew there was something different about them now.

We don't look so different.

The klaxon wailed a second time. Like puppets, the *subs* were compelled by the sound of the klaxon. Reaching into the pouches they carried about their necks, each removed a pill the shape of a tiny round ball. It was as if they had no choice of their own as they dropped the pill into their mouths. All of A.G.R.I.'s *subs* had been conditioned to do it, conditioning that Sub had somehow broken.

Mindless shells, Sub thought. *Is that what I was like?*

Sub had learned early not to jump when he heard the klaxon; it gave away position. It seemed to him that he was unique. He had found no other able to fight the compelling urge to take the pills.

The Scanners will come soon.

Sub looked around. There were only so many places he could hide. The Scanners would eventually find him, and he knew it. It was only a matter of time. Slowly, Sub sat up, and he knew that soon the chase would begin again.

He stretched his head out past the overhang of rocks he had been hiding under. Surveying the area around him, he could see nothing but more overhangs above and rubble below.

There's nowhere else to hide. Today's the day.

Hanging his head, Sub stared at his hands. He had to find a way out of this cavern that was his prison, or he would have to fight again. Kill again. Besides, he was so damn hungry, and this place held nothing for him. Nothing he ate seemed to satisfy his hunger.

Don't think about it, Sub scolded himself.

Searching the cavern walls in the half-light, he kept an eye out for the shafts of light that sometimes seemed to come from the rocks themselves high above. The lights appeared at different times throughout each cycle. The only pattern he was able to figure out was that the lights always began on the same side. Over time, the lights would show up in different spots along the cavern's ceiling and seemed to make a straight line during the first half of the cycle to the opposite wall of the cavern. Sub had learned to use the movement of the lights to anticipate when the next klaxon would sound. He also discovered he could use them to anticipate the flights of the Scanner teams on patrol. There was another light though, one that never moved. It was always there, always watching.

* * * * *

"Larry! Isn't it about time to turn that thing off?" Dr. Anderson yelled as he passed through the double doors of the observation station.

"Hey, Dr. Mike." Larry, not looking up from the heated MRE he was eating, was 30 years Dr. Anderson's junior and loved his work. He also had all his hair. Larry held his fork in his mouth and reached to push a button on the console in front of him. The klaxon went silent.

"So, how's the weather, Dr. Mike?"

Dr. Anderson found Larry's sense of humor in poor taste. Maybe it was Larry's way of dealing with the horror of what had come upon the United States in recent years. Who could blame him? Now with the famine spreading around the world, Dr. Anderson couldn't blame anybody for trying to lighten the mood a little bit. He'd probably joke about it himself if he hadn't been responsible for it.

"Have you found Subject one-two-one yet?" Dr. Anderson was all business. It was all he had left.

"Right to the point, huh?" Larry handed over his report. "Not quite yet, but we think we've got him cornered down in sector six. It's the only place left he could hide." Larry ran his fingers through his hair.

"Isn't that what you said about sector three yesterday?" Dr. Anderson tossed the report onto the only section of the console he could find that was not so cluttered that it would get lost.

"I know, but that was yesterday. I'd swear the damn thing's as smart as we are. There was pride in Larry's voice. It was the pride of a father unable to admit that his son had surpassed his every expectation. Larry had been the one to crack the genetic code-cohesion problem. Without it, Sub would not be alive today and able to escape. It was also the reason why he had been able to escape in the first place. Many unique qualities had been built into Sub's genetic code. Larry stood and walked to the observation window and finished his thought. "Could be he's smarter than we are."

Dr. Anderson studied Larry's reflection in the observation window. "Let's have it, Larry. What's on that mind of yours?

Ever since Subject one-two-one deactivated the tracking implant and escaped monitoring, you've been different."

"I don't know. It's almost like he's sentient, like he's able to think on his own instead of just running on instinct. I can't help but feel that what we are doing here is wrong."

"Wrong? Larry, it was your design."

"I know, but still…"

"Larry, look," Dr. Anderson said in his best, warm fatherly voice, "you may have created Subject one-two-one, but he is not your child. Hell, he's barely human. Subject one-two-zero was the same way. Besides, the information we learn from them may help us save the world. In case you've forgotten, humanity is on the verge of extinction."

"I know," Larry replied, still not feeling any better. He shook his head and rubbed his eyes. "Let's get back to work."

Larry turned back to the window and looked out into the cavern below; it was not really a cavern at all, but instead a retrofitted and outdated football stadium. Larry froze not quite believing what was happening.

"Uh, Mike?"

* * * * *

Sub had learned at least one thing since becoming conscious of his existence. He was not inside an actual cavern. Something was different about this place. He couldn't quite figure it out, but this place was definitely wrong. It didn't smell right.

There it is. Sub found the light that didn't move. *It still doesn't move. If I could only get up high enough, I might be able to see where it comes from. It may be a way out.*

He shifted his gaze to where the next shaft of light should be. It wasn't there, and he leaned forward for a closer look.

It should be there by now. The Scanners will be coming. I

am so hungry. The air above Sub flashed, and he was temporarily blinded.

Scanners! They found him. He shaded his eyes blocking the spotlights of the hover-cycles. He searched high and beyond the oncoming Scanners, seeking the light above. He had to get to the light because there was no place left to hide. Maybe the hole it shines through would be big enough for him to squeeze through, but he wouldn't know that unless he tried.

There were two Scanners on top of him now. Sub recognized the one in the rear; he was called Alpha. He could almost feel again the pain that had left the scars, and he felt fear as he remembered Alpha. On their hover-cycles, the Scanners were in front of him and just beyond his reach, blocking his path. Staring at each other in the dim light, the decision to run or stay and fight was made for Sub, and he tensed, readying himself.

With no available exit, he launched himself at the hover-cycle directly in front of him. Knocking the Scanner riding it off, Sub jumped onto the single seat, grabbing what appeared to be the control arm; he had seen the Scanners operate them many times from a distance. He held on tightly and pulled the arm straight back. The thrusting force was nearly enough to cause him to lose balance, but he buried the control arm deep into his gut and kept control.

Sub had his mind set on one goal now and one goal only. He no longer cared if the Scanners caught him. At least he would have tried. He wouldn't end up like the rest of those mindless drones that were now falling farther below as he rose higher.

Maybe the hunger will stop at least.

Alpha spun his hover-cycle around following Subject one-two-one's retreat. He wasn't looking forward to reporting this turn of events to Larry. The last time he had to report Sub's escape, Larry had nearly torn him a new one. Alpha didn't want a repeat of that.

Sub angled the hover-cycle higher and soon realized a problem. Hover-cycles were not designed to go that high or fast for sustained periods of time. Still, it brought him closer to the light he so desperately sought high above. As he drew nearer his destination, he was confused by what he saw. There was something unnatural about the source of the light. It was nothing like he had ever seen before. The sides were smooth like the surface of the small pools of water scattered about the cavern floor now far below. The sides came away at sharp angles from each other. There appeared to be an opening in the surface of one of the sides.

This is where the light comes from?

Sub looked through the opening as he closed in on it. He could just make out the outline of two figures standing in the opening. The two men inside somehow looked strangely familiar. It was this thought that drove him onward and to do something that, otherwise, he never would have. Alpha, being more experienced on the hover-cycles, was quickly closing the distance between them.

"You're mine. I'm not losing you a second time." Alpha was nearly on top of Sub. The engine of his hover-cycle started to make the same whining sound he could hear coming from the one Sub had taken. Neither would hold out much longer at this height and speed. Alpha looked down to check the console based in the middle of the steering column. Then he heard it. The whining noise rapidly grew louder and seemed as if it were getting closer. He looked up, but Alpha already knew it was too late.

Dr. Anderson looked over Larry's shoulder and out the observation deck window. It became apparent to both of them just how desperate Sub was to escape.

"He's not going to do what I think he is, is he? He'll kill himself. It has to be at least thirty feet." The fear in Larry's voice was matched only by the pride he felt in his creation to adapt and survive.

"You created the damn thing; you tell me. I'm getting the hell out of here." Dr. Anderson turned to open the containment door. He stopped when he heard the sound that only naked flesh makes as it hits a smooth flat immovable surface.

The damned fool jumped for it, he thought to himself.

Dr. Anderson hit the release on the door, and then stood to one side, turning around as he did so to see the observation window. Glass showered the observation deck, and Dr. Anderson dropped to the floor covering his head protectively with his arms.

* * * * *

Alpha watched helplessly as the hover-cycle in front of him crashed into him at full throttle. The resulting collision caused an explosion. Alpha would not be making any more reports to anyone.

Larry moved closer to the window and saw Sub grasp at the window's seal for some sort of handhold. It was the last thing Larry saw.

As Sub hit the window with the full force of his body, he was stunned to find that he was stopped. If he had any idea what safety glass was, he probably would not have jumped. But here he was, and he had to do something fast because he was beginning to slip. He scrambled frantically for anything to hold onto. There was nothing. Then he heard the explosion and reflexively ducked his head out of the way. The pieces of the hover-cycle flew past Sub and into the hard pool that had stopped him. The glass was not designed to withstand such an explosion and gave way to the debris from the hover-cycle. It was all Sub needed to be able to save himself.

Reaching over the jagged edges of the thick glass still stuck in the frame of the window, he pulled himself up and into the observation station. Rolling through the opening and onto his back on the console just inside, he felt the shattered glass bite into his skin. He kept moving as he slid off the console. Sub fell to his hands and knees and came face to face with the body of the man that had been looking at him through the window only seconds before. The man now lay lifeless on the floor.

Blown backward out of his chair from the blast, Larry lay face up with a twenty inch long, four inch wide piece of the window protruding from his chest. His lifeless eyes were still open and staring at Sub. He seemed to be smiling at him. Sub sniffed at the blood running from the man's wound, and saliva filled his mouth. His jaws clenched and relaxed. He felt his own flesh grow warm as he inhaled deeply, sensing the base iron in the blood. He could almost taste the blood in the air. It made him uncomfortable, while, at the same time, it made his senses come alive like he had never known.

Not enough time. Having no time to investigate these new sensations, he reluctantly pulled himself away.

Must escape.

The klaxon began to blare again, and he came fully back to his goal. His head felt like it was about to split open as he looked around the room. There was an opening at the other end, and Sub could see the form of another man hunched over. He ran straight for it trying to leave the sound of the klaxon behind him.

Dr. Anderson called after him, but he couldn't be heard over the noise of the escape alarm. The explosion had set off the automatic safety protocols. If he didn't get to Sub before the Scanners did, they would kill him on sight. He couldn't let years of research go down the drain like that. Dr. Anderson followed Sub; it wasn't hard, as Sub wasn't exactly trying to hide his tracks. He was operating under that part of the brain that controlled survival instincts, and he had a definite advantage: for that part of his genetic code, he had been given an extra dose.

When he finally caught up with Sub, he had made it all the way to the exit that opens into the parking garage. Dr. Anderson only had an instant to reflect on the fact that this was exactly the same path he had taken just twenty minutes earlier as he came in for work. The door was the first step in the safety protocols. It was twelve inches thick with a magnetic locking system with its own emergency backup power supply. He watched as Subject-one-two-one, not even out of breath, continued to beat on the door.

Even he can't get through that. When the dark liquid began to flow from Sub's hands, Dr. Anderson called to him.

"Wait, let me help you." Dr. Anderson didn't know what else to say, but it was enough to get his attention.

Now what do I do? Dr. Anderson took a deep breath and slowly approached Sub. He couldn't believe what he was about to do. No subject had ever made it this far. This was new ground, possibly even a breakthrough. Dr. Anderson wanted to see what would happen next. *How would Sub react to the outside world, to the light of day?*

The sound of running footsteps from a side corridor grew

louder. Dr. Anderson quickly drew out his security pass card and slid it through. He quickly keyed in the exit authorization code, slapped his hand onto the palm pad and waited. It seemed like forever before the sound of the locking mechanism gave way. When it did, Dr. Anderson was nearly knocked down as Sub threw the twelve inch thick door open and ran out into the parking garage. The Scanners were already there.

Sub stopped shortly after making it through the door. He couldn't see. The light was blinding. He had never seen true sunlight before. It filtered in from outside the parking structure illuminating the area around the entrance, and it was a sensation of warmth he had never felt before. He lifted his face to the sun. As Sub's eyes began to adjust to real light, he lowered his head. Now he could see the Scanners, and they blocked him on three sides. The door and the man who had opened it stood behind him.

The Scanners held position as Dr. Anderson approached. He held his hands out in front of him with his palms down. He gave them a lowering motion, and the Scanners hesitantly lowered their weapons, slightly pointing them at the pitted parking garage floor.

Standing in the middle of his captors, Sub bathed in the sunlight. It began to feel warmer, almost hot. He slowly turned around to face Dr. Anderson. His skin began to feel as if it were on fire. He took a step and found he couldn't support his own weight anymore, and Dr. Anderson caught him before he hit the ground.

Sub opened his eyes and looked into those of his captor.

"Why?" Sub's voice cracked. "Why does it burn? Why does the light hurt some much? What am I?"

Looking down at a face already becoming dark and

stretched by the sun, Dr. Anderson smiled and spoke in soothing tones. "Everything will be all right. I'll take care of everything."

Sub grunted as he felt a pinch in the back of his neck. Darkness began to cloud his vision, and the sound of the klaxon faded away.

Peace.

"Get him back inside before he bursts into flames. That's one flaw the techs are going to have to work out." Dr. Anderson turned to the Scanner standing closest to him and tossed the now empty syringe.

"Do me a favor. Dispose of that."

James O. Barnes, is the author of Thief King, a historical fantasy novel, and numerous short stories. Growing up in the Ohio River Valley region, James learned to dream and tell stories along the banks of the Ohio River. He continues to teach, dream, and tell stories as he has for most of my life. These skills have seen him through a background in education and a Master degree in Ancient and Classical History. Currently, James is working on Imposter, his second Book of Orenck. www.jamesobarnes.com

Seconds of Eternity
by Terry W. Ervin, II

"Major Parson, vital signs indicate that you are losing consciousness." The artificial intelligence voice snapped Mac 'Race' Parson back from near dozing.

"Just daydreaming, Allison." Mac checked the data log and scanned his Starfury IV interceptor's search monitors. "Imagining that I was in my leather recliner, relaxing after catching a string of crappies outside my cabin." He tapped several screens, updating them. "You remember. My tiny corner of paradise in the northern Appalachians."

Mac already knew Allison's reply, mouthing the words as they came through his helmet. "Major Parson, your statement does not match the physiological data stream." He'd selected the AI's voice, feminine and a bit scratchy, but most of the program parameters weren't of his choice. Allison, always business.

He peered through his fighter's canopy at the scattered array of asteroids hanging above him. Most resembled the one his fighter clung to: potato-shaped and twice the size of the Behemoth class freighter that'd deposited the carrier pod in this sector. And while each asteroid rotated on some random axis, all slowly spiraled toward the same gravitational doom.

Rotating into alignment with Mac's line of sight, on a sister-chunk of iron silicate eighty-two kilometers away, Mac's wingman sat in his own Starfury. To Mac's unaided vision, Bronco Bob's asteroid was a barely perceptible shadow, owing to the not so distant red giant. Far more impressive was the star's gaseous tendril unerringly pointing to where it's mass was being siphoned off: the quadrant's dominant astronomical phenomenon—an all devouring black hole.

"If it was indeed paradise, Major Parson," inquired Allison, "why did you voluntarily re-enlist?"

Mac pondered Allison's question. Not why he abandoned retirement. The Truhl-ghat invasion made that a no-brainer. No, to Mac, defending humanity in his Starfury far surpassed any retirement paradise.

Mankind had discovered clues of a space-faring alien existence thirty years ago: interstellar robotic probes and satellites that self-destructed whenever approached. News of that broke when Mac was a raw recruit. By the time he'd graduated from combat flight training, a peace treaty had been 'negotiated' with the Ghats.

Every man and woman with a gram of military training just knew, deep to their heart's core, the treaty wasn't worth the breath the politicians expended selling it to the civilian population.

The pilots in Mac's original squadron poked fun at his

white hair, suggesting it had prematurely gone from blonde to white because he stressed over political promises everyone knew would be broken. "Maybe they honestly intended to remain vigilant," Mac muttered to himself, almost forgetting the AI's previous question.

Allison interrupted Mac's oft repeated grumbling. "Inquiry—"

Mac cut her off. "Sorry, Allison. Access records of previous conversations. Key phrases: 'Failure to maintain robust fleet defense' and 'forced retirement due to precipitous decline in military expenditures.'"

Mac didn't mind that his interceptor's AI program knew his views. A month after the Truhl-ghats seared through the undermanned and poorly equipped outer defenses, they annihilated the rim colonies. Before another week passed, every diplomat and politician who'd diverted resources from humanity's defenses over the years, even in the face of the Ghat's increasingly bold treaty infractions, was gone. More than a few committed suicide once the scope of their misjudgment emerged. Or so it was reported.

Through his canopy, Mac spotted a nearby glint, and clenched his fists. It was one of the scattered thousands of shattered hull fragments, remnants from the previous battle in this sector where mankind had failed to hold the line against the invaders. "Easier and more expedient to accept lies than risk confrontation." He took a deep breath and checked his monitors again. It didn't matter anymore, anyway. The war was already lost.

Before Allison could interject another inquiry, Mac tapped his com-screen. "Let's check in with Bronco Bob and see what he's got to say before rotating beyond line of sight. "How you doing, Bronco. Report."

Allison took care of aligning and encoding the split-second laser burst packet. Radio broadcast, even minimal strength and narrowly focused, produced risk of reflected noise, offering a chance of detection, minuscule as it was.

"All clear and quiet, Race," Bronco replied. "How do you maintain vigilance for such long stretches?"

Mac recalled his first deep space rotation, and how nervous he'd been. And the stakes weren't nearly as high. "Sing *Ninety-Nine Bottles of Beer on the Wall*," he suggested.

"Really? That works for you?"

"Nope," Mac chuckled. "You're doing just fine. Nothing from our friends on *Evanescent Static*?" Having the electronic warfare shuttle hiding on an asteroid about four-hundred kilometers beyond Bronco's interceptor made Mac a little more confident in their mission.

"Negative on that, Race."

Mac expected that reply. Odds were the EW craft would pick up subspace disturbance indicating a Ghat vessel dropping out of hyperspace ten or fifteen seconds before Mac's Starfury IV would.

"Been thinking on what you said, Race," Bronco interjected quickly. "'Bout those New Vegas odds before the government blacked them out."

Mac understood Bronco's anxiety. The odds makers had posted humanity having a one in eighty-six chance of maintaining active military resistance through the New Year and his wingman, less than two months from earning his bronze flight cluster, was just coming to realize that humanity was facing its twilight. "Not now, even on a secure com."

"Acknowledged."

Mac checked his instruments. About twenty seconds before rotating out of LOS. He'd be guilty of adding to already poor com protocol, but he felt it better not to end his transmission on a disciplinary note. Nobody, not even the techs on *Evanescent Static* would intercept. And Commander Roeth back on the hidden carrier pod would understand keeping a green pilot relaxed, should someone decide to query the AI com-logs. "Only three hours, twelve minutes before we're recalled. No answer yet?"

"About your call name's origin. No clue, Race."

"No guesses?"

"No new ones."

"I won't even consider it cheating if you consult, Betsy."

"AI support ain't cheating?"

"Not this time." Mac checked his panel. "LOS rotation interference in six seconds. Radio silence protocol Delta-XJ4."

"Delta-XJ4, acknowledged," replied Bronco. "Next window, two hours twenty-one minutes, eighteen seconds. Out."

"Inquiry, Major Parson."

"I know, Allison. Remember I asked you to update and recalculate the odds of humanity's survival?"

"Affirmative. But you asked me to withhold the results. You indicated it would be depressing."

"That I did. But I'd like to hear it now, anyway."

"Based on available trends and data," said Allison, "by the new year, two hundred and twelve days from today, there is a zero point two-one-nine percent likelihood of military forces successfully maintaining an active defense around Earth."

"That's why we're here, Allison. Safeguarding the plan to shake up the odds."

"Would you like me to inform you of the offensive's chances for success?"

"No, Allison. I know it's a Hail Mary."

"Inquiry, Major Parson. Which definition of 'Hail Mary' should be applied to your last statement?"

"Either one works, Allison."

"Even if successful, Major Parson, the strike is unlikely to favorably alter the long term prospects for Earth's defense."

"I know," said Mac, once again enacting a routine check of his Starfury's monitors. "But maybe the Ghats will learn that some games end with no winners."

"Inquiry, Major Parson."

"Enough for now, Allison." Mac tapped a screen to his left, selecting coffee, two-hundred milliliters black and hot. "Let's wait in silence for a while. Intel suggests an enemy scout ship won't show for at least another three hours at the earliest."

Mac sipped some of the hot caffeinated bean juice—vitamin fortified as always—through his helmet's nutrition tube. He knew Allison's analysis lacked several bits of data, leaving her assessment of Earth's defense overly optimistic. The veteran pilot let out a long sigh and took another drink.

* * * * *

Mac monitored two Starfury interceptors maneuvering under minimum power, taking up position on asteroids about seventy kilometers beyond the electronic warfare shuttle. They were his and Bronco Bob's relief patrol. An hour of layover while detectable signs of thruster energy dissipated, then back to the carrier pod for a little downtime before his next patrol.

"Twenty minutes to LOS with Lieutenant McKinney's Starfury IV interceptor."

"Thanks, Allison," Mac said, calling up the standard visual and anatomy files on the Truhl-ghats for the third time. Based on his military experience and security clearance, Mac found employment as a security analyst at a communications research division during his retirement. That led to recruitment by a military think tank focused on interstellar defense issues.

Who could be afraid of a fifteen kilogram alien? A question often thrown about by naysayers. Until the war started. Best described as a scaley yellow centauroid cross between a centipede and a chipmunk, Ghats were damn ugly. Even if their saliva was venomous, physically they weren't intimidating. But, with instinctive tactical skills and advanced technology, their military prowess was another question. Both on the ground and in the vacuum of space.

One vital bit of data that Allison lacked: Pieced together from disparate information obtained through intercepted communications by stealth probes and deciphered two months prior to Mac's reactivation, and later through brutal yet methodical interrogation of captured Ghats, humanity learned the mystery of the enemy's reproduction.

Humanity only encountered or captured Ghat males. The females of the alien race, believed to resemble bone-crested slugs, emerged like cicadas at the apogee of their homeworld's orbit—once every seven revolutions, or every thirty-eight human years. In addition, the reproductive cycle was reportedly near impossible for the enemy to reproduce on planets and moons they'd colonized.

A weakness.

Mac didn't have the whole picture, only parts gleaned during his military and civilian careers, through private and professional contacts, and deductive reasoning supplemented by intuition.

The second data bit Allison lacked: Implementation of Project Reforger. Many suspected the government's investment in secret colonies, hidden caches to secure humanity's survival, or to avoid extinction depending on one's semantic preference. Very few knew of Reforger's actual existence, let alone its official name. Even fewer knew of its implementation. Mac did, or strongly suspected. His niece, a gifted quantum physicist, had taken a mid-semester vacation. In a whirlwind she'd visited friends and relatives, some she rarely even acknowledged. Gave away her cat. And sent her most favorite uncle a goodbye e-vid that'd been edited to disguise halts in speech and face-reddening tears. It wasn't openly a goodbye communication, but when Lydia Lynn abandoned her university's tenure track position for an 'off world' position—Mac recognized the signs of a black project—he knew.

Then orders came down to reorganize the scattered elements of humanity's once proud interstellar fleet. Quietly, core colony defenses were left to patrol gunboats and def-sats, assuring them the same doom, but a handful of months sooner.

Initially Mac chafed at being passed over for fleet carrier duty. Part of the Final Strike Fleet, part of operation Ragnarok. Any person with rudimentary logistical and tactical knowledge recognized it as a one way assignment. One hovering somewhere between heroic and suicidal, patriotic and foolhardy. But the need to secure a logistical path as far as possible toward the enemy's homeworld was vital. Besides, if the Final Strike Fleet had seen combat before passing through, there *might* be room for him and his Starfury. Otherwise, once the fleet passed through, one of sixty cryotubes housed on the c-pod had his name on it.

Mac's control panel flashed a warning yellow. "Spatial distortion forming," Allison announced. "Eighteen hundred kilometers, six o'clock high," she added, using old-style orientation Mac preferred.

Mac confirmed the coordinates. "Almost show time." With his gloved hand he touched his chest where beneath his flight suit a silver cross hung. A gift from his grandfather, the one he'd worn while a combat pilot.

"Passive sensors detect a Truhl-ghat battle frigate emerging from hyperspace."

"Well, that's not good," Mac said before taking a deep breath to steady his adrenalin rush. A battle frigate was twice as large and carried sixty percent more firepower than a scout ship that *normally* patrolled and maintained tripwire satellites.

Allison reported, "Active scanners and electronic signaling detected."

"Probably trying to locate and interface with their tripwire sat."

"Search pattern focus concurs with your assessment, Major Parson."

"Well, the dummy sat we replaced theirs with won't do much against a battle frigate's armor when it detonates, unless they park right next to it. Which they won't."

"Accurate assessment, Major Parson. Detecting launch of a shuttle."

"Maintenance shuttle. Things are going to get interesting real fast. Hope Bronco Bob's ready."

"I am confident he is, Major Parson."

"Me too, Allison. You know, the last battle in this sector didn't turn out too well for our side." Mac licked his teeth and added silently, "And things aren't looking too good this time either."

"Have faith, Major Parson. You are a skilled veteran interceptor pilot. Our side has the advantage of surprise."

"Maybe so, Allison. We'll fire-up and close when that fake sat detonates. May draw their attention for a few seconds. Or," Mac added, his monitors registering the frigate's expanded intensive scan of the sector, starting with the asteroid field. "They might just pick us out among these floating rocks despite the debris."

Only fifteen seconds passed before Allison announced, "The shuttle has halted five hundred twenty kilometers from the satellite."

"They smell a rat." Mac watched the readouts. "They haven't recalled the shuttle."

"Correct. Enemy battle frigate accelerating in our direction."

"Fire up the second *Evanescent Static* opens up on them, or our c-pod launches the rest of the squadron."

"Counterfeit satellite destroyed by shuttle's class 4 energy beam."

"Damn," muttered Mac. "They've upgraded their maintenance shuttles. Things keep getting better and better."

"The shuttle was on the outer edge of effective blast radius, Major Parson."

"We're gonna do more than rattle a few teeth before this is over, Allison. Get ready."

"I always am, Major Parson."

"I know. Just habit."

"I know. Just part of my programming."

Mac rolled his shoulders in an attempt to keep loose. "Hope Bronco's ready."

"I am sure—" Allison began before switching topics as the Starfury's passive sensors lit up. "Electro Magnetic Pulse detected, Major Parson."

"That's *Evanescent Static*," said Mac, recognizing the

readings of a focused EMP beam. He flipped the switch, releasing the grapple anchoring his Starfury to the asteroid. "Activate sensors, bring power and thrust engines to 100%." He tapped three screens, bringing full communication and tactical tracking online.

"Bronco, form up on me."

"Acknowledged, Race. Ready for launch."

"Allison, launch and vector for interception. Then give me the stick and throttle."

Despite the gravity-dampening plates, Mac braced himself against the intense g-forces as his interceptor rocketed away from the asteroid and came about, the distant enemy frigate centering on his main tactical screen.

"We've got to be fast, Bronco. *Static*'s just shot her wad."

Mac's wingman slid into position. "Not tellin' me nothin' I don't already know. Got your four o'clock low."

Mac began jinking his Starfury using throttle and thruster bursts. "No sense being an easy target. Allison, feel free to add your own complexity to our approach pattern."

"Implementing supplemental Tactical Evasive Approach Program S-X12, Major Parson. Lieutenant McKinney is employing T.E.A. Program X142."

Mac recognized the AI's hint. But he felt an added human touch would be more difficult for enemy targeting computers to guess, despite the reams of data asserting otherwise. He examined the current tactical information now displayed on his helmet screen.

The Ghat battle frigate resembled two thick horseshoes welded together at right angles along the apex of their arches. Beautiful compared to the boxy shuttle it'd launched. Or even compared to Mac's Starfury, which more than a few design engineers described as an outward clone of the late 20th century F-105 Thunderchief, but on steroids.

"Beautiful, but deadly as a rabid wolverine," Mac grumbled.

"Starfuries Three, Four, Seven and Eight," crackled the voice of Major Lidov over Mac's com-system. "Continue on approach vector. Target and destroy enemy message rockets, top priority. Prepare for simultaneous launch of anti-ship missiles."

"Starfuries Four and Three, acknowledged," Mac replied to *Evanescent Static's* commander. Until the carrier pod revealed its presence through launching interceptors or opening fire, Lidov was in charge.

The battle frigate was still closing, but angling to present her starboard side gunports to the approaching interceptors.

"Bronco, arm AS missiles," Mac ordered his wingman in Starfury Four.

"Already done."

"Arm self-defense rockets too."

"All four armed and ready, Race."

Allison said, "All weapon systems armed and energized, Major Parson."

Out of procedural habit, Mac verified Allison's statement, including activation of his Starfury's L4 Railgun. Slower and less energy efficient than newer models, still, it remained Mac's preferred weapon system.

"Damn," muttered Mac, as low energy beams that mimicked light bursts began streaking from the enemy frigate, reaching out toward Mac and the nearby interceptors. Mac knew if one of those beams touched his Starfury, the imbedded feedback signal would return accurate targeting data to its source.

"Did you see that, Race?"

Mac didn't but his tactical readout relayed what had happened, noting *Evanescent Static*'s destruction through a single red blip where the EW shuttle's plot had been. Flashing screen text confirmation followed. *'Evanescent Static* eliminated by class 2 energy beam.'

"Enemy disrupting all com-frequencies," said Allison. "Switching to Line-of-Sight laser com."

The destruction of the EW shuttle and resorting to laser communications made a coordinated attack far more difficult. It also left Mac the senior pilot engaging the enemy.

He ordered, "Furies Four, Seven and Eight, continue on interception vector." Increased light emanations from the frigate's port thrust engines—the terminus ends of each horseshoe housed one primary and one secondary thrust engine—verified what readouts showed. She was increasing speed and turning back toward Mac and his remaining flight of four.

Energy weapons again began reaching out toward Mac's interceptor. Fewer but more than enough. Just as he was about to order launch of primary AS missiles, a class 2 beam seared through Starfury Seven, destroying it in an explosive instant. At the same time Mac detected an aft-ejected rocket racing away from the conflict. Compounding the rising combat complexity, the frigate's dorsal thrust engines vibrated and flared out.

Particle beam from the pod carrier, thought Mac. Readouts indicated it was launching the rest of the squadron as well.

"Bout time," said Bronco over his LOS com.

"Allison, what can you tell me about that rocket?"

"Spatial distortion pattern building around the rocket indicates it is—"

"A message rocket. Bad news," said Mack, realizing if it

entered hyperspace, the fleet and probably all of humanity was screwed. Or at least screwed sooner than otherwise would be. "Furies Four and Eight, use railguns to take out that rocket."

Commander Roeth confirmed Mac's fear, but countermanded his order. "Starfury Three, Four and Eight, break off engagement with battle frigate. Starfury Three, primary objective is to engage and destroy the enemy's deep-space shuttle."

Mac had forgotten about the shuttle. The carrier pod's sensors, along with the backup EW shuttle it probably launched, were vastly superior to his Starfury's. Both he and Allison had mistaken it for a maintenance shuttle.

Mac scanned his tactical screen. Good call by Roeth; the enemy shuttle was heading toward the black hole and his flight was closest. "Allison, plot intercept course. Furies Four and Eight, target enemy frigate and launch primary AS missile, then form up on me." It normally took a wave of missiles to overwhelm enemy defensive fire, but any distraction would benefit Commander Roeth's efforts. And one might leak through.

"Allison?"

"Targeted."

"Launch on enemy frigate then bring about maximum thrust."

The 3.5 meter missile dropped from the left wing, fired its rocket engines, and accelerated toward its objective, 20 megatons of thermonuclear blast to be delivered. Two more missiles, utilizing similar evasive approach measures, raced to close as well.

Despite the grav-dampening plates, Mac braced himself for the g-forces caused by the sharp turn and acceleration. He grunted, "How's it look?"

"The deep-space shuttle's acceleration curve is lesser than that of a Starfury IV, but it has the advantage of eighteen seconds at maximum acceleration."

"Must have suffered no damage from the satellite's explosion." And Mac knew an enemy deep-space shuttle's top-end maximum speed surpassed even the newest model Starfury. "Can we catch her?"

"Negative."

Mac checked the distance and made a snap decision. "Starfuries Four and Eight, charge railguns and engage enemy shuttle."

Bronco and Splitter must've done the math as well, as both simultaneously replied, "Acknowledged."

The railguns would draw too much energy, draining the dampening plates and requiring the Starfuries to cut acceleration. And they were already near maximum effective range.

Railguns activated, Starfuries Four and Eight each began shooting cylindrical tungsten-superalloy bullets at 1.8 second intervals. A single eight-centimeter long, five-millimeter diameter bullet carried enough kinetic impact to cripple or destroy an enemy shuttle.

Mac said a quick prayer, knowing the odds of success.

"How long until she's out of range?"

"Nine point seven seconds."

Already he was leaving his wingman and Splitter well behind.

"Detecting seventeen point two percent reduction in acceleration," Allison stated.

"You did it, Bronco!"

"Actually, Race, I think it was Splitter."

"Nah, fifty-fifty," said Splitter.

"Doesn't matter, pilots. Great shooting! Now turn around and help take out that frigate. I'll take it from here."

Even as they followed orders, Bronco asked, "You sure, Race?"

"Sure as your shootin', wingman. We've each got work to do."

As if to emphasize that point, the enemy shuttle sent an energy beam flash that came within ten meters of Bronco's interceptor.

Mac immediately shoved from his mind, concern for Bronco and the desperate battle going on behind him. He had one objective: Destroy the shuttle, thereby ensuring that it didn't launch a message rocket to warn the enemy.

Light flashes reached out toward the trio of fighters, two of which had vectored off.

"Allison, isn't that shuttle's energy beam front-mounted?"

"It is. The long range shuttle cut thrust engines and pivoted one-hundred eighty degrees."

"Then, we're gaining."

"That is correct, Major Parson."

A light flash shot past less than three meters off Mac's starboard wing.

"Okay," said Mac, "I think we've gained our eighteen seconds back. Initiate protocol R31 intermittent laser transmission back to the C-pod, both tactical and cockpit. Then energize our railgun."

"By energizing—"

"I know," said Mac, bracing himself. "But if he wants to duel..."

The gravitational effects, even under reduced acceleration, compressed Mac against his seat.

"Enemy shuttle pivoting and reengaging thrust engines."

Mac worked with the computer-assisted targeting solution, trying to lock on. The kinetic energy of one solid hit would settle the issue. He depressed the stick-mounted trigger and held it there. Ventrally mounted and spanning the fuselage's length, the L4 Railgun launched its first bullet, which missed wide left by thirty meters. The second missed low by over forty.

Respectable, thought Mac, firing over 14,000 meters with both his Starfury and the enemy jinking about with evasive lateral and vertical thrusts.

"You can run, but you can't hide," Mac said, wondering about the phrase's origin as he de-energized the railgun and ordered maximum acceleration. Certainly Allison knew the phrase's origin, but instead of lending that insight, she provided some bad news.

"The enemy shuttle appears to have repaired sixty-four point six percent of the damage to its thrust engines."

"Can we still—"

This time Allison cut Mac off. "Affirmative. Enemy shuttle has altered trajectory."

"Let's do it."

Mac verified the minor shift in his Starfury's flight path through the tactical readout. "All things remaining equal, we should reach optimum railgun range in fourteen minutes, eight seconds. Maximum range to employ defensive rockets in offensive mode in seventeen minutes, sixteen seconds."

"Major Parson, the enemy shuttle is running directly to where the stellar-mass black hole is drawing in stellar matter from the red giant. That is where radiation emissions are the most intense.

This particular black hole was non-rotational. And since

the black hole and its binary partner slowly circled each other like two dancers clasping hands, the red giant's matter was drawn in through a single shaft stretched between them.

Mac briefly considered ordering Allison to temporarily put him under and accelerate beyond what a human could endure while conscious. But, he knew that some Ghat deep-space shuttles were armed with EMP cannons. Knowing human physiology, the enemy might recognize Mac's gambit and risk the EMP's short-range backlash while knocking his Starfury's systems off line, including Allison. Sitting duck. Dead target before he could recover.

"Keep chasing, Allison. We've got to press—destroy'em before they can launch a message rocket." Mac activated an auxiliary screen, called up the gamma and x-ray emission levels, and frowned. "I need some good news, Allison."

The AI program replied, "The enemy battle frigate was lured within eighty kilometers of an asteroid concealing a new model MT300 thermo-nuclear mine. Estimated combat effectiveness now at thirty-seven percent."

"What about the squadron, and Bronco?"

"Seven Starfuries remain combat effective. Starfury Four is among them. However, they have expended all primary and secondary anti-ship missiles. The asteroid sheltering the carrier pod has taken heavy damage."

"Have you been receiving tactical updates?"

"Negative, Major Parson. Data collected and analyzed from aft sensors on passive setting."

The squadron's struggle against horrific odds drove any notion of self-preservation from Mac's mind. "Don't worry, Allison. They'll take her down."

"My concern is for you, Major Parson."

"The radiation? No problem," he said, checking the

diminishing distance between him and the enemy shuttle. "We eliminate our objective, you put me into hibernation, they shove me in a cryo-tube. Years later, doctors unthaw me and repair the damage." Allison knew better than Mac how fanciful the plan was.

"Major Parson, you are indeed a brave and true patriot."

"No premature eulogies, Allison." For something to do, Mac added a few random jinks to Allison's evasive approach program. "It could be worse."

"Inquiry, Major Parson."

"Allison, we could be chasing them directly into that black hole."

"How is that better, Major Parson?"

"AI programs endure radiation far better than they do the crushing gravitational effects of a collapsed star."

* * * * *

With the anti-radiation drug cocktail flowing through his veins, Mac fought to ignore the headache it invariably caused. "How we doing, Allison?"

"Shielding remains ninety-four point eight percent effective."

"Still too much getting through. Aren't Ghats more susceptible to radiation than humans?"

"Affirmative, Major Parson. They are."

"They did upgrade our squadron's shielding prior to this patrol."

"Central Command was aware of increased background radiation in this sector."

"Guess they did more than one thing right," said Mac. "Maybe a good omen. Two minutes until optimum railgun range."

"Radiation bursts will degrade targeting accuracy, Major

Parson."

"Understood. How goes the fight behind us?"

"Aft passive sensor collection no longer effective."

"Were we winning?"

"Four minutes, three seconds ago, enemy battle frigate estimated to be at twenty-one percent combat effectiveness. Starfuries Four, Eleven, Seventeen, Nineteen and Twenty still engaged. Two of two enemy message rockets successfully destroyed."

"We still sending cockpit and tactical reports?"

"Affirmative. Enemy shuttle altering course."

Mac looked over at the radiation sensor. He'd just passed the LCt_{50}, the lethal concentration and time exposure. "Guess they miscalculated. Turning to fight?"

"Negative. They're vectoring toward the gravity well of the stellar-mass black hole."

Mac gritted his teeth while shaking his head. "That's what I was afraid of."

"Altering course to improve angle of interception. L4 Railgun optimum range now in one minute eight seconds."

"They've calculated their shuttle can hold up to the gravitational stresses and escape greater gravitational pull than we can." Mac tapped up the limited specs on Ghat deep-space shuttles. "Can they, Allison?"

"Indeed, they can, Major Parson."

"Well, let's change the equation. Energize railgun."

Mac's Starfury cut thrust to 40%.

Allison warned, "Enemy shuttle ejecting canister." Before Mac could respond, Allison fired a self-defense rocket targeted on the canister.

Mac allowed the AI program to paint the canister with a laser, guiding the rocket to its target. Allison could do that, along with the ten-thousand other tasks she was dealing with, and assist as he focused on engaging with the railgun. No sweat.

Even though he couldn't get a lock, Mac depressed the trigger. Before the second bullet was fired, the rocket and canister met in a fiery display followed by scattered firecracker-like flashes.

"Canister destroyed before deployment of caltrop mines."

Mac sensed, more than by identifying through status displays, something different with his Starfury.

Allison anticipated his query. "Increasing effects of the gravity well, Major Parson."

Mac examined the tactical screen and the trajectory, and noted how the enemy shuttle was tracing an arc along the black hole's influence, slowly spiraling inward. "So, it's a game of chicken. They go in closer, daring us to follow."

"Recommend rerouting energy from the L4 Railgun to the gravity-dampening plates in eighteen point four seconds."

Mac nodded in agreement. He felt the black hole's tug to his left as they continued the chase, pursuing the enemy inward, toward the event horizon.

"Program the secondary AS missile as follows," Mac ordered, still failing to lock on but continuing to fire his railgun.

"Major Parson, at this range—"

Mac knew a single AS missile wouldn't get through enemy defensive fire or counter-measures, and they were still too distant for early detonation to guarantee sufficient damage.

Mac ran the scenario through his head. "We've got to do this quick, before we go in too far. Have it appear to malfunction, flaring out after eight or so seconds, angling 45.23 degrees starboard, 2.1 degree drop. After twenty and some random fraction of a second after that, set it for minimum thrust to escape the black hole, plus two percent. Once clear set on active target acquisition, drift mode. It's not to engage unless the enemy shuttle rises beyond this distance from the event horizon." He paused. "Allison, time dilation, is that a factor now?"

"Affirmative, Major Parson. At this point the time variance remains minor."

"Minor, now but it'll change." And that added too many formulas and variable calculations. "Given the stated parameters, Allison, you do the math. Set proximity fuse detonation at 1150 meters. Do it now."

Less than a second later, the missile dropped from its mount and rocketed erratically away, Allison having added her personal touch to the deception effort.

"Our ace in the hole. Now, discontinue evasive maneuver so I can get a few good shots." Mac felt the collapsed star's tug even more as Allison fired the portside thrusters to stabilize their trajectory.

"Eight seconds until rerouting of energy."

Then, one of Mac's shots clipped the shuttle along its dorsal edge, tearing a small chunk away and sending a fantail of debris into space—which immediately curved in toward the black hole, caught in its grip.

Mac saw, even as Allison announced, "Enemy shuttle pivoting, one-hundred eighty degrees. Enemy shuttle reengaging thrust engines."

Mac grinned, but it was a lopsided grin as he fought gravity to keep his head straight. "They think they can win a true game of chicken?"

"Port thrusters overheating. Rerouting energy from L4 Railgun."

Light flashes began streaking past Mac's Starfury. He didn't bother to ask Allison if he was imagining the light's slight arc as it shot toward him from the enemy shuttle.

The fully energized dampening plates masked most of the gravity well's effects. But without his railgun, Mac knew the enemy'd begin to slice up his interceptor within seconds. "Target and fire self-defense rockets."

The rockets shot away, but at a starboard angle. Mac knew why. Even so, the black hole dragged them off target. "She ain't getting past us, Allison. Ram her if we have to."

"Distance, 8000 meters, Major Parson. Enemy shuttle trajectory shifting. Now thrusting away from the singularity's gravitational pull, perpendicular to the event horizon."

"They're trying to climb out." Mac angled his stick, adjusting to parallel the shuttle's efforts.

"Allison, can they escape?"

"Seventy point three percent chance of success, Major Parson."

Although his Starfury was one-hundred and fifty meters more distant from the event horizon, he'd followed the warning data on the bottom corner of his tactical screen since entering the gravity well. He asked anyway, "Can we escape?"

"Negative, Major Parson. Insufficient fuel reserves. Tracking of your eye movements indicated—"

"No apologies necessary, old friend. I saw it." He took a deep breath. "If the railgun is energized, could you get a shot off?"

"Negative, gravitational forces would distort the parallel rail system if the gravity-dampening plates were de-energized. Already they are functioning at one hundred ten point three percent. Four-thousand five-hundred meters. Closing at one-hundred ninety-four point four meters per second."

"Take over, Allison." Mac checked the tactical. "Do we have the angle?"

"Negative. Emergency thrust engaged. Twenty seconds to potential contact."

Mac checked the metallic hydrogen fuel status. Ninety percent depleted and draining fast. "Do you think the Ghats know the battle out there is over?"

"Intelligence indicates enemy computer systems are on average four-hundred twelve percent more efficient than those of human design. Ten seconds to potential impact."

"Well, we can't let them get away to wander around and find the C-pod. Everyone'll be in cryo."

"I too am confident that Commander Roeth orchestrated the destruction of the enemy battle frigate."

Even as Allison spoke, she began firing thrusters, trying to counter the shuttle's evasive efforts. But a well-timed point defense laser, even though measurably altered by gravity, accurately sliced into the Starfury's starboard thruster, sending her into a spin—aft of the shuttle and into its thrust exhaust.

The intense heat triggered structural warnings. Mac ignored them and activated the grappling hook. Allison flipped the Starfury and fired it—to no avail.

Once beyond the grav plates, the black hole's gravity took hold. Allison detached the hook's cable and righted the Starfury. "Hull integrity down to seventy-three point two percent. Thrust engines three seconds from emergency shutdown. Reducing thrust by twenty percent."

The AI's words fell on deaf ears as Mac watched the Ghat shuttle slowly climb out of the well as his interceptor slowly sank. Being a deep-space shuttle, she had far more fuel reserves to burn.

"Allison. You knew that grappling hook wouldn't work."

"Affirmative, Major Parson."

"Thanks for trying," said Mac, checking the fuel reserves. "Ninety-eight seconds until we're empty."

"Are you still sending reports, Allison?"

"Affirmative, Major Parson. I initiated high-energy radio transmission once I noted the asteroid harboring the carrier pod had been damaged and its known trajectory was altered. In addition, I boosted the signal when distortion of the gravity well commenced."

"So, as things stand, Operation Ragnarok is probably over."

"Estimated time dilation between us and the Strike Fleet, yes it is, Major Parson."

Mac watched the now distant shuttle. "We did all we could, right?"

"Affirmative, Major Parson." The AI paused before adding, "Knowing your religious beliefs, I recommend the time for prayer is nigh."

Mac felt the growing pull of gravity, pressing him against his seat, and his cross against his sternum. He didn't know if the power systems supporting the grav-dampening plates would fail before the fuel tanks ran dry. And he didn't care to ask. It'd become a task to breathe, and speak. "I don't believe I've ever heard you use the term 'nigh' before."

"I have not, Major Parson. But it seemed the appropriate word."

Mac sucked in a breath and smiled. System warnings began shifting from yellow to red. Hull integrity was below 50%.

"No, I said my prayers before launching this patrol." He

could no longer lift his arm from the seat. "Let's answer a friend's puzzle." He paused, straining to continue speaking. "Call up *Turu the Terrible*. We'll enjoy it...as much as we can... together."

The AI shut down the beeps and flashing that warned of imminent systems failures. "Of course. Your favorite, Major Parson. And mine too."

The pilot closed his eyes and listened to the late 20th century cartoon's introduction: Electric guitar with tremolo, trumpets, and drums, accompanied by eerie bird-cries, gunfire, growls and explosions.

Calming relief of pain medication coursed through the pilot's veins. "Th..thaankss."

"Anything for a friend, Mac."

Metallic hydrogen reserves expended, the thrust engines flamed out.

* * * * *

"Lieutenant McKinney," called a feminine voice. It seemed distant, but descended closer. "Robert McKinney. Can you hear me?"

To say that Bob McKinney felt horrible was an understatement. Every bone ached as if caught in a vice. Every muscle burned as if hot coals danced within them. Even his eyes stung, but he forced them open.

He blinked, trying to focus on the speaker whose head hovered over him.

"Your tear ducts have just started working." She squirted yellow fluid from a syringe into his eyes. "Give it a minute. I'm Med Tech Sheryl Parson and you're in recovery from cold sleep."

Parson? Bob tried to sit up, only to fall back, wracked with pain. Still, the recent memories of his flight leader chasing that enemy shuttle into the grips of the black hole—he had to know. Race's Starfury had turned red; Commander Roeth said due to a gravity-induced Doppler effect. Race's signals chronicling the pursuit stretched out as well. An AS missile emerged, set on trip-wire pursuit mode. That was all.

Then the Strike Fleet passed through and everyone entered cryogenic sleep.

Bob forced the words through his exsiccated throat. "Wha…wha appen 't Raysss."

Sheryl thought she understood the question. In part, she was there to discover the fate of her great uncle as well. "Robert," she said, gently holding his shoulders, pressing him to stillness on the bed. "He's not among those in cold sleep, but we'll find out."

* * * * *

The next day Bronco Bob and Sheryl Parson, daughter of Physicist Lydia Lynn Parson, along with Commander Roeth and the two other surviving Starfury pilots, sat in the recovery room. A semi-circle of padded chairs had been arranged around a holographic projector.

None were happy that, during the past thirty-nine years, Earth and all her known colonies had been ravaged by the Truhl-ghats. But the remnants of humanity, reunited with refugees of Project Reforger, had mounted a second surprise attack, a second Operation Ragnarok, just as the Truhl-ghat females once again emerged like thirty-eight year cicadas.

What all were happy about was the signed armistice forced upon the Ghats through the wholesale loss of two generations. They and humanity were once again on equal footing.

The c-pod's AI program had recorded the deep-space shuttle emerging six weeks after all personnel had entered cryogenic hibernation. It also recorded the waiting AS missile acquiring the target and eliminating it.

Over the intervening years, Starfury Three's drawn and weakened signals slowly escaped the black hole's grip. Bronco Bob held Sheryl's hand as they watched the restored archival view into Race's cockpit.

"Answer a friend's puzzle?" Sheryl whispered to Bob, repeating her great uncle's words. "He means you, right?"

"Yeah," Bob whispered back, listening to his flight leader's final moments, bantering with his Starfury's AI program. "He'd bet I couldn't guess his call name's origin." Bob wiped a tear from his eye before it could fully form. "Race."

Later that evening, Bronco Bob would find a note left on his email account, suggesting he search the key words 'Johnny Quest' to answer his puzzle.

But in the recovery room, none in the semi-circle could see the screen playing the cartoon. Yet all listened to the odd 20th century music and saw Mac's grin beneath his visor. Each involuntarily gripping the arms of his or her chair as the cockpit view distorted, then froze upon reaching the event horizon—as Major Harold "Mac" Parson stretched into that stationary second, drawn into eternity.

Terry W. Ervin II, is an English teacher who enjoys writing Science Fiction and Fantasy. He is an editor for MindFlights and a guest contributor to Fiction Factor, an ezine for writers. Terry's short stories have appeared in over a dozen anthologies, magazines and ezines. Gryphonwood Press published Terry's debut fantasy novel FLANK HAWK and the next novel in the First Civilization's Legacy series (BLOOD SWORD), has an expected release date in late Fall 2011.

To contact Terry or learn more about his writing, visit his website at: www.ervin-author.com

VISIT THE LOCONEAL BLOG AT

www.loconeal.com

Breaking News
Forthcoming Releases
Links to Author Sites
Loconeal Events

www.ingramcontent.com/pod-product-compliance
Lightning Source LLC
Chambersburg PA
CBHW020751250626
47155CB00003B/1014